PRAISE FOR BLUE REFLECTIONS

"My favorite character is Henrietta!! I love how mischievous she is! Always getting herself into anything that she can or take whatever she wants! Makes me want my own crab!" –ARC review

"The story of Selia and Damien is just chef kiss. This book had it all and I can't wait for the next one. I have found a new author to add to my favorites. It has a bit of everything that you count want." –Amazon review

"It's so cozy, and Henrietta just steals all the attention. Now, all I can think about is mermaid booty and Scottish men in kilts." –Amazon review

"I love the characters in this book. They are so lifelike and interesting. I love learning about Scottish folklore and watching authors bring it to life. Selia and Damien's romance is heartwarming and sweet." –ARC review

"This book has romance and adventure mixed into a world of folklore with mythological creatures and magic! You easily fall in love with the main characters and want to know more about secondary characters. Being the first book of a series, there is so much more to explore and I cannot wait for book two." –Amazon review

"A quirky romantic fantasy that features selkies, fairies, and lost treasure. Woven within its pages are themes of grief and loss that the two main characters must overcome." –Amazon review

"Blue Reflections a unique and cute love story that involves sea nymphs, different fae creatures, folklore, magic and heartbreak. I'm interested in finding out if Selia can discover her past and how her romance grows. It was a quick read and was definitely something I needed as a cozy book." –Amazon review

"The elements of this book were AMAZING! Tying in the fae, with some mythology and a mystery is the perfect combination. The book leaves you wanting for more with every chapter." –Amazon review

"I enjoyed the myths and magic of the story, the locations that it took place in and the characters in the book!!! I loved Selia, Damien, and Henrietta!!! I really enjoyed the adventure that this book took me on and I'm excited to see what happens next for Selia!" –Goodreads review

"I dove right in and wasn't disappointed. There is love, grief, mystery, and a lot of Scottish folklore which I adore, since my family has Scottish descendants. Amanda you blew me away with this one. I can't wait to see what is next." –Goodreads review

"Casey's prose is whimsical, and her characters are well-developed and relatable. The plot is intricate and engaging, with surprising twists and turns that keep readers on their toes until the very end. Blue Reflections is a must-read for any fan of fairytales and romance." –Goodreads review

Blue Reflections

Book One of the
Ocean Apothecary Series

Written & Illustrated by
Amanda Casey

CONTENTS

For anyone who believes in fairies.
Believing is seeing.

The North
Sea
The Rusty
Selkie
Auntie's
Cottage
London
Louvre
Paris
Damien's Art
Studio
The Celtic
Sea

PROLOGUE
Strands of Moonlight

One dark night, a selkie swam close to land, chasing after the first rays of moonlight as they fell from the sky. Something was threaded in the water that wasn't silver, but red. Blood had spilled into the sea.

She discovered a man sitting by the water, tending to a deep wound on his arm. She knew he would not last the night, so she left the sea, stepping onto land to help him.

Looking at the wound, she knew what the man had been hunting a fae creature that could only be seen in the light of the moon. The fae who lived near the water were both dangerous and beautiful.

These fae were the source of her moon magic.

As his blood spilled into the sea, so did what his heart treasured. To heal his wound, she would need to offer him what the sea had given her—her moonlit reflection. She gathered her salt skin, her cloak of moonlight. Touching her heart, she unraveled three moonlit strands from her salt skin. She closed her eyes and said, "Breath from my body. Memory from my heart. Salt from my soul. With these three strands of moonlight, I wish to make you whole."

The strands of moonlight found the man's wound, mending the flesh and healing him.

Her moon magic soon grew into love between them.

Many moon cycles passed, and the selkie became blind to her own love for the sea. With her salt skin gone, not even the moonlight would reveal her reflection upon the surface of the water. Her magic began to disappear.

One cloudless night, the moon appeared across the sky, and the selkie asked where she should go to mend the emptiness that had filled her heart.

And the moon answered, "Only your reflection can show you what your heart treasures."

Soon after her meeting with the moon, the selkie left the man, chasing once again the strands of moonlight.

PART I
REFLECTIONS

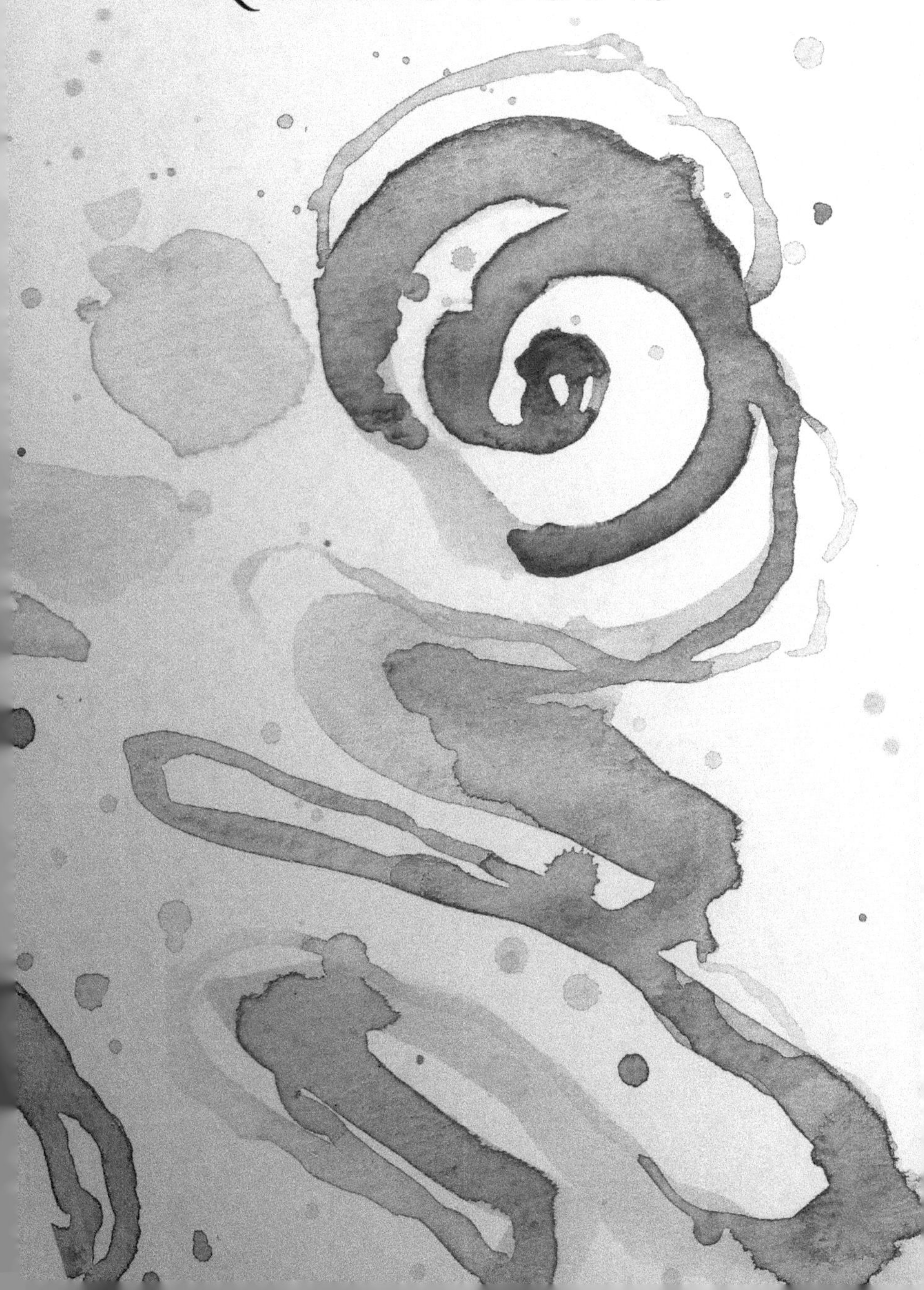

I
BLIND MOON

S elia underlined the words *blind* and *moon*. Both were meanings for her name. She'd written the words next to the moon she'd drawn in her notepad during the morning staff meeting.

Instead of taking notes on the usual museum displays she helped to rotate at the Louvre, she'd tried to sketch an image inspired by a recent visit to the Celtic Sea. The memories of her visit had a crystalline vapor around it, trailing scents of wind mixed with liquid earth and salt—a breath originating from the ocean.

Selia remembered the sound of her own heartbeat syncing with another rhythm she did not own. Together, the pulse in her chest and that sound caught on the wind created a song—a song sang by the sea sorceress Amphitrite.

Golden light drifted through Selia's only office window, illuminating an adorable miniature painting sitting atop her artifact catalog—a gift from a watercolor artist she had developed a severe crush on.

Damien's watercolor painting of the moon helped her form a memory of their first meeting at the Celtic Sea. She would gladly flee from Paris and drift back to the moment they shared together on the beach. Selia was kicking herself. She hadn't gotten his number, just his first and last name. Damien Malloch was as fine as a glass of red wine on a warm June evening.

She set his mini moonscape aside and tugged over another box. She had so much work for the museum to catch up on. Her duties at the Louvre involved handling artifacts—*ancient* ones.

Selia worked her fingers over the dog-eared edges of an empty cardboard box. Dust particles drifted into the golden rays of sunlight. She knew this dust was different from most of the particles that found their way into her life of sorting and organizing artifacts for display. This was the dust of crystals—salt crystals that originated from the sea.

Perhaps the salt crystals were really pixie dust? She'd contemplated that idea, having seen the little fairy drawn next to the address label. Selia assumed the label had been created by a child. The box lay with many others, no origin to call their own. Items lost to a past in which they no longer belonged.

This box was special, as it housed the very first artifact she had memory of receiving—a talisman that only a month ago had whispered the words *blue memories* to her. This was the first in a chain of events that led her to meet Amphitrite. Since that day, the whispering had gone quiet.

Selia picked up the talisman and ran her thumb over the spiral. This spiral was a symbol that, according to Amphitrite, originated from moonlight.

Ching!

Selia set the talisman back into the box and grabbed her phone. Deidra—her dryad, or woodland nymph, friend who lived half-way across the world in California was bugging her again. How Selia had befriended the nosy dryad was by performing an identity search on herself.

Their friendship started a year ago when Selia attempted to create an online dating profile, which lead to an online chat. When Selia couldn't provide the dryad with her date of birth, Deidra asked her what she identified as.

Selia replied with *sea nymph*, which Deidra quickly took advantage of. She learned that Deidra had access to a secret database that allowed her to research the ancestral records of nymphs like her. Deidra wouldn't give any information out about her secret database, other than it dated back to when Gaia first gave birth to her daughters, who were female personifications of nature called nymphs.

The only context Deidra had given Selia about this ancestral record is that it was broken into a thousand little pieces, and that even the most experienced dryad practicing the art of root reading couldn't thread it back together. Deidra had, however, managed to provide Selia with a fake social security number, as well as other things a nymph needed if she was to survive alongside the modern day human scene.

Selia did live up to her name, as it was the only real piece of identity she remembered about herself. She was as blind as the moon over the stormy sea, unable to see her own reflection on the water below. With her lack of identity came mystery of who she was and where she'd come from.

The two nymphs had teamed up, hoping to find the origin of the symbol on the talisman. Selia had come up empty, even with the Louvre's archival databases at her fingertips. Her curiosity had gotten the better of her when she'd gotten sucked into the mythological database that revolved around watery women such as herself.

Mermaids could swim to great depths in the sea to seek out treasure.

Sirens sang hauntingly beautiful songs, luring sailors to a watery grave.

And sea nymphs? According to Amphitrite, they practiced the art of salt trance.

Comparing herself to the watery women found in myth and folklore had done Selia no good to recover her own identity. She'd read something about the seal women found in Scottish and Irish folklore, who had a salt skin. Selkies were if anything, omens of both death and beauty, something Amphitrite's salt trancing lessons embodied.

Deidra was the only soul Selia had shared the salty details of her adventures regarding Amphitrite—who went by Amy for short—at the Celtic Sea. Since sharing certain details, the mystery of Selia's past was not Deidra's interest any longer. The dryad's nosiness dealt with the *current* moment, which Deidra was currently blowing her phone up with inappropriate text messages.

All Deidra seemed to care about was the status of her love life. This time, she'd left a string of emojis that weren't so subtle. Not one, but *ten* bulging blue hearts trailed behind a mermaid with a full moon dancing behind her tail. Each heart she knew was Deidra's non-subtle way of indicating how stale the past decade was regarding her love life.

Selia had mentioned the handsome watercolor artist she'd met, which was a big mistake. A big *bulging* mistake that resulted in another text from Deidra involving ten bulging eggplant emojis strung after a mermaid.

ARTIST BOY DIDN'T HAVE BLUE EYES, RIGHT? I REMEMBER JUST A MONTH AGO U WOULDN'T LOOK AT A MAN WHO HAD BLUE EYES? Deidra asked in her text.

THAT'S RIGHT... Selia texted back.

WHAT CHANGED?

A whole lot. The fact she'd practiced an art with Amy that dealt with the blue memories of another. An art that made her feel her own heartbeat could sync with the fluid rhythm of the ocean. Since her first salt trancing lesson, her sensitivity to the color blue had evaporated. And for the first time in a decade, her life had more meaning and less anxiety.

WELL? WHAT COLOR R THEY? Deidra probed again.

Selia didn't want to type out an answer to Deidra's demanding question. The dryad would find any way she could to get herself rooted in the latest gossip of Selia's dating life, which was currently nonexistent.

Damien's eyes were a *glorious* hazel. Remembering them made her feel warm around the center. Greens and amber swam together, seeming to disagree which of the colors were better.

Selia loved them both.

HOW OLD IS HE? Deidra typed.

LATE 30S, MAYBE 40ISH?

According to Deidra, Selia could be *thousands* of years old. However, nymphs were born with natural beauty provided by Gaia and thus aged well. She insisted that Selia could pass for someone in their twenties or thirties, given whatever circumstance bode best for her.

OHHHHH…DOES HE MAKE YOUR SALT NODES TINGLE WITH DESIRE WHEN U THINK OF HIM?

Like Deidra, Selia had special set of lymph nodes. While Deidra's pollen nodes were on her wrists, Selia's salt nodes sat behind her ears—freckles that gave her senses of both pain and pleasure.

Selia set her phone down. She didn't have time to indulge Deidra's overzealous interest in her love life (or lack thereof). She hoped that Damien's memory wouldn't fade like so many individuals did in her life.

Selia grabbed the journal and a blue gel pen Damien had mailed her and tucked them into her purse. Her finger scraped against the cool glass surface of a bottle. The bottle held a magical substance she had seen dancing in the moonlight along the beaches of the Celtic Sea a month ago.

Selia followed a wave of tourists through the museum and outside to the Napoleon plaza. A bright June day in Paris such as this one was sure to send artists flocking to her city. She loved the City of Lights. A decade here in the hub of worldly artistry, she was practically swimming in the creative energy Paris always seemed to breathe.

She walked into the plaza, relishing in the warm sunlight that swathed her neck and shoulders. It was noon, lunch hour. She was here for one thing only, the timely eruption of the fountain.

She brushed past a tree. Her hair caught the bark from a branch, tangling against it. While she didn't have the wild, unruly locks of mermaid hair, her brunet strands looked a bit wild as the June humidity always made it thicker. She grabbed a handful of the wildness, winding her fingers through the ends, hoping to tame the rebellious mass of it. Finding a place to sit alongside the fountain, set her purse down on the stone ledge, then pulled out the journal Damien had so sweetly mailed to her. She worked her fingers under the journal's cover, opening what could be a fairy tale.

Any second now the water from the fountain would spring to life. She chose this time when the sun was highest in the sky because it reminded her of the lights she'd seen threading through her office window when she stayed late to work at night.

Selia reached into her purse, tugging out the bottle Amy had given her. Another glittery crystal-like substance drifted behind the glass. The substance was hypnotizing, catching light and reflecting it.

Were the lights water, smoke, or something else?

Fwwisssshhhhh!

Right on time, the fountain burst into life.

Thwop!

The surprise, however, had resulted in her dropping the bottle.

"No!" she said, standing up and gathering her things.

Amy's salt extract had already disappeared.

She raced after it, dreading if the water decided to siphon the bottle into the middle of the fountain.

Drat...

She had a couple of options. Make a fool of herself and get in the water, or wait and see if the fountain would spit the bottle back out.

The fountain splashed and bubbled. The bottle drifted out of sight.

Frantic, Selia began to pace alongside the water. It couldn't have gone far, right?

Someone was sitting on the stone edge of the fountain, blocking her from blundering to the spot where she'd seen the bottle disappear. "Excuse me sir, can you please let me through?"

The man blocking her reached into the water and picked up her bottle.

A familiar dimpled smile creased across his face.

Selia's knees buckled.

Their eyes met, and all it took was for him to gaze at her the way he'd done at the Celtic Sea a month before to make her heart thunder.

"Selia?"

She tugged at the fabric on her blouse, suddenly feeling nuclear hot. "Hello, Mr. Malloch. It's so lovely to see you," she said, working very hard to keep her voice lower than it wanted to jump.

Damien chuckled warmly, his dimples appearing—dimples Selia imagined a child would want to poke their finger into. He held out the dripping bottle. "I take it this is yours?"

"It is," she stammered, suddenly out of breath.

The fountain erupted in its final display, sending a spray of colors into the sky.

"Look!" a little girl yelled. "It's a rainbow!"

Water droplets from the fountain rained down, landing on Damien's thick chestnut hair. Damien's gaze leveled with hers, and all Selia could do was focus on the blue lights swirling in the water droplets clinging to his eyelashes.

Damien blinked first, sending the water droplets cascading down his cheek. "What did you see?"

"Nothing," Selia lied, knowing that her imagination had gotten the better of her. It should be illegal for a man to have such gorgeous eyes.

Damien's brow furrowed. "You can see them too, can't you?"

"See what?"

"The reflections on the water, the ones that look like fairies?"

Selia swallowed. Her mouth had gone dry.

Fairies?

She gazed into the eyes of an artist who had more imagination that she believed. Maybe she wasn't losing her mind. Did Damien see the mysterious reflections too?

2

THE COLOR BLUE

Damien shut his easel and stowed it into his leather bag, leaving Selia in a haze of questions as thick as the shimmering mist from the fountain. What was that all about?

Fairies?

Had she heard him right?

His gaze locked with hers—the greens in his hazel eyes looked so much sweeter in the reflective light created by the fountain. "I see them too, have for a long time. Do you mind if we go someplace more private so we can discuss what I think they are?"

Selia had seen the mysterious reflections dancing in her periphery since salt trancing with Amy. But *fairies?*

Why did Damien think the lights were something to do with the fae?

Damien stood up, hoisting his bag full of art supplies onto his shoulder. The strap flattened against the collar of his light blue shirt. His build was stocky and strong, the kind of build that gravity would have a difficult time pulling to the ground. He didn't tower over Selia, but stood near identical with her height.

Damien's musk was a combination of earth and pine wood. His wavy locks of chestnut hair were identical in color to the freckles dusting his nose and cheeks. Lines creased around the corners of his deep-set eyes. He wasn't what humans considered old, however, he wasn't quite young.

The dimple lines framing his mouth told her that he was someone who had smiled and laughed most of his life.

Selia flushed. Suddenly *fairies* didn't seem like such an outlandish thing to discuss, especially if the watercolor artist she had a crush on was asking about them too. How much she loved seeing those adorable dimples of his in person. "As long as you have something artsy to share with me?"

Oh no—she said something she didn't want to say. She was buckling before she'd even gotten the words out...

Damien flashed a smile that made her insides warm. "You're in luck." He held up the bottle she'd dropped. "And in return, you can tell me what magical substance is in this mystery bottle."

Selia swallowed. She'd completely forgotten the bottle, its contents, and the fact that she had been pondering opening it seconds before Damien came sauntering back into her life.

Before she could react, Damien tucked the bottle into his jeans pocket and took off into the crowd.

"Hey, wait!" she stammered, taking off after him. She followed Damien through the courtyard toward the street, struggling to keep up with his pace as he maneuvered through a flock of tourists heading for the museum.

He'd taken Amy's salt extract hostage. She had no choice but to follow him.

The crowd thinned as he reached the end of the street. The mysterious reflections dancing in her periphery weren't really *fairies*, were they?

"How about here?" Damien asked, stopping on the street corner where people were dining outside, enjoying the June sunshine.

Selia surveyed the bistro. There was a patio with rose vines growing up the corner of the street. It was about as private as any tourist destination could get. "Lead the way."

Damien walked to a cast iron table nestled in the back by a climbing rose bush.

Before Selia took a seat, she eyed her bottle of salt extract sticking out of his pocket. "I'll take that back now."

A cocky grin spread across his face. "Only if you tell me what it is."

Selia dug her heels into the ground, flustering. He saved her bottle from what would have been its final resting place in the catacombs under the streets of Paris. But that didn't mean he could steal it.

Selia reached for the bottle, ignoring his attempt to flirt with her.

His thumb moved over the cork stopper.

"Don't!" she cried, throwing her hand out. Heaven forbid Damien spill Amy's salt extract. She wouldn't be able to salt trance without it!

The cork was still in place, and there were no tendrils of smoke issuing from the top.

"I take it that this isn't perfume?"

"No, it's much more potent."

Damien held out the bottle for her to take. Their fingers met as Selia reclaimed the bottle, which she quickly stowed into the safety of her purse.

Damien was gazing into her eyes much longer than what should be normal. Then again, she couldn't remember the last time she'd exchanged glances with a man this good-looking. He broke their gaze first, seeming to sense her nerves. "I expect you to tell me what's in the mystery bottle when I get back. What would you like to drink?"

Selia froze. He *was* flirting with her, right? This man made his move quickly. "Anything that you feel is artsy enough to quench one's thirst with."

He winked at her, setting his art bag onto the table. "I'll be back."

Her eyes dipped to the bottle he'd so gallantly retrieved from the fountain. Explaining to him that she had a bottle of blue kelp—let alone the essence of an *extinct* species would be a challenge. He might assume that she was a witch if she started babbling about salt extracts and sea sorcery so early in their relationship.

Relationship...why on earth was she thinking about that?

Selia peered around the rose vine, spotting two familiar men who worked at the Louvre. Dr. O'Connor and the new male blue-eyed wonder intern visiting from the British Museum.

She walked along the length of the roses, just far enough for her to overhear their conversation. Her boss, Dr. O'Connor, had a cigar drooping from his fingers, while the intern was busy fondling a glass of wine.

"How long has Selia been working for the Louvre?" the intern asked.

"She's been here for at least a decade," Dr. O'Connor replied, bringing his cigar to his lips.

"Has she always worked within the department of Egyptian Antiquities?"

Dr. O'Connor removed the cigar from his lips, exhaling a long drawl into the air, sending his age-spotted jowls aquiver. "That is a great question. I know she's been at the museum for at least a decade. She's introverted. She keeps to herself most of the time. But she gets the job done, as long as she doesn't miss her exhibit meetings."

Selia's ears perked. She inched closer, keeping her back behind the rose bush to eavesdrop on the men discussing her.

"Why the sudden questions about Miss Fontaine?" Her boss asked.

"I know she has knowledge that none of us newbies have—knowledge about artifacts only certain people at the Louvre have access to."

"Well then, maybe I can pull some strings. You've been an intern at the Louvre for a little less than a month now. Egyptian Antiquities is currently a cataloging nightmare, and I could move some staff around to help with the workload."

"Selia is strange. She just now started looking me in the eye. Sometimes I wonder if she is up to something."

"Like what?"

"Don't act like I haven't heard the rumors. How long has she been working alone in the haunted artifact closet?"

Selia froze. Did he know about her salt trancing talisman?

A bird shifted in the bush. Selia jolted, nearly giving her position away. She walked back to their table, hoping that her boss hadn't seen her spying on them.

Damien made his way back over to the table with a bottle of wine in one hand and two glasses in the other. He stopped at their table, his head swiveling until he spotted her.

When his gaze fell on her, Selia's belly felt warm.

She waved at him, wondering what the man who saw fairies in the water wanted to discuss.

He grabbed one of the cast iron chairs and tugged it out. "Have a seat."

Selia flushed as she sat down. She wasn't used to a man wining and dining her at the noon hour.

He grabbed the uncorked wine bottle and poured her a glass. "Be honest—how long have you seen the reflections?"

"You mean, the fairies?"

Damien chuckled. "If you are assuming that's what they are, then yes, the fairies."

Selia watched the red liquid dance at the bottom of the crystal glass. "For about as long as I have known you, Mr. Malloch."

Wine spilled over the rim of her glass. Selia shifted her leg to avoid the burgundy from staining her skirt.

Damien struggled to regain control over the wine bottle. "That's been what, about a *month* now?"

"I believe so. How could I forget?"

Damien sat down across from her, apparently struggling with something she didn't understand. Why did he have more freckles dusting his cheeks now? Was it because he too, was flushing a deep shade of red?

He clasped his hands together on the table. "I could not forget you, that is for certain."

Selia grabbed her wine glass and began tapping her fingers against the bottom. She could get along with this awkward man. Their spontaneous meeting on the beach had obviously made an impression on him.

She noticed a ring on Damien's left hand—a silver ring that coiled two fingers away from his ring finger. Not married, although the ring could have passed as a wedding band. The silver had a Celtic knot pattern engraved on it.

Her heart drifted back to that beautiful moment at the sea—barely anything to separate them other than the balmy breeze drifting in from the water. She remembered how his shirt had clung to the muscles on his broad chest. When thunder settled over the sky, neither of them wanted to run for shelter.

Neither of them wanted to part from one another.

She'd caught an accent on his voice too—one that didn't come from France. There was a song to his voice, as subtle as it was, a soothing silk that wrapped her up. "I'm baffled by your choice of artistic study. Most people come to Paris to paint the Eiffel Tower, not fairies in the fountain outside the Louvre."

He smiled, dimples deepening. "Speaking of fairies, what's in the mystery bottle?"

Selia tried to ignore the fact that her salt nodes were now tingling. "What brings you to the City of Lights?" she asked, taking this conversation back into her control. She wasn't going to give him what he wanted so soon.

"I came to Paris to have you critique some of my artwork. I told you that I would in my letter, did I not?"

Selia shifted her glass of wine away, set her elbows on the table and folded her fingers together. "You also wrote something that has me very perplexed. Why did you address me as a mermaid?"

Damien's face did a funny thing. Not many people knew what she was. While she didn't have a set of shimmering fishy tail fins (that she knew of) or locks of luxurious hair like most watery women, her past was shrouded in mystery. Why she loved her job at the museum so much was because she dealt with a vast collection of artwork of subjects she personally identified with. Nymphs—female personifications of nature—in her case nereids or sea nymphs, were what she'd spent the past decade of her life infatuated with.

Did Damien really believe her to be a *mermaid*?

"The light I saw on you that day. You had an iridescence about you," he said. "A light that inspired me to paint."

"Explain this *light* you saw on me."

Damien clasped his hands together on the table. "It was like an aura—similar to the light caught on a mermaid's tail? Or in the moonlight dancing across the sea?"

Selia's mind drifted to the miniature moonscape he'd gifted her. "Is painting moonscapes your primary job, or is there something else that you do with your artistic talents?"

"Apart from freelance work, I work as an art therapist."

"What does an art therapist do, exactly?" Selia asked, intrigued.

"I help people reflect on their past by having them create art."

"Is asking them if they see fairies part of your creative approach?"

"That's my icebreaker."

Selia squinted at him. Damien was a strange, quirky man—in a good, *odd* sort of way that she was starting to adore.

"I have something I'd like to share with you," He dipped his hand into his bag. "Ouch!" His hand came flying up. He held his arm out in front of him, revealing the source of his pain.

Dangling from his journal was an exceedingly agitated crustacean—a hermit crab who would not allow an opportunity to get into mischief pass her by.

Selia let out a sigh, watching as Henrietta tried to clamp her little claws onto the smudge of blue paint on the corner of Damien's journal. "Really? Of all the places you've chosen to hide?"

Damien held his journal over the table.

Selia pressed her fingers to the bridge of her nose, embarrassment taking hold. The last thing she wanted to tell the man she had the hots for was that she had a problem with *crabs*…"Sorry, I take full responsibility for her inappropriate behavior," Selia said, shaking her finger at Amy's pet.

Damien inched his face closer to Henrietta, keeping her a safe distance from the tip of his nose. "Oh, I remember you. What's this little crab's name?"

"Henrietta…"

Damien gave the little thief a serious look. *"Henrietta* was the crab who kept taking off with my art supplies on the beach!"

Selia laughed. "Henrietta, a thief? No—she merely loves to flirt." Henrietta had in fact been the one to trip Selia, resulting in her toppling down a sand dune and crashing into Damien as he was busy painting along the beach. Had their first meeting been smooth? No. But she was convinced that Henrietta had absolutely been a matchmaker in disguise.

"For one reason or another, she has an obsession with the color you love to paint with," Selia said, relieved that Damien hadn't been scared off yet. What normal woman walked around Paris with a hermit crab for a pet?

"Maybe like me, blue is the only color she can see?"

Selia jolted. "What?"

"Didn't I tell you that in my letter?"

Selia looked from Damien to Henrietta, who *also* obsessed with the color blue. It would make sense why Amy's pet had created so much havoc on the beach a month ago when they'd first met. "No, you didn't tell me that about yourself. Is everything you see a shade of blue, or just things that are blue have color?"

"I see varying hues of black and white—darks and lights and everything in between. I see blue on things that only reflect that color." His gaze fell level with hers. "The only people I know the true color of their eyes, is if they are blue like yours."

Selia flushed. It would also make sense as to why Damien's gaze lingered on hers longer than a normal human should. Blue was the color of her eyes and the only with which he connected. "Do you have any idea why you only see blue?"

"Personally? I think it's because I angered the fae somewhere along the way."

"I'm sorry, *who* have you angered?"

"You know, Pixies? Sprites? Fairies? The wee ones that make everything springs to life when springtime comes? I believe they have something to do with my blue vision. It's the only way I can explain it."

Selia shook her head. Although odd for a grown man to have a discussion about fairies, gnomes and sprites, she couldn't help but think his infatuation with the fae was oddly cute. "I'm sorry, I am not familiar with any of those creatures." She eyed the artist who seemed to allow his imagination to get the better of him. "Have you actually seen a fairy before?"

"I've seen some things that most people would not believe in, that's for sure."

Henrietta began to rummage in Selia's purse. Amy's salt extract came rolling once again out into the open.

Damien glanced at the bottle. "What's this? The mystery bottle has revealed its identity!"

Selia made a double take at the blue bottle. She couldn't believe what she was seeing. The blank tag suddenly had writing across it.

Selkie salt skin?

What was that about?

3

THE SELKIE SALT SKIN

With trembling fingers, Selia grabbed the bottle and shoved it back into her purse. She had to be imagining things. The tag must have gotten wet, creating the illusion that writing had appeared.

Damien's expression became a curious one. "You believe in selkies too, I assume? Women who wear a salt skin gifted to them by the moon?"

"I believe in many strange and unusual things," Selia lied. She knew little to nothing about these watery women known as selkies Damien seemed captivated with.

She grabbed Henrietta and cradled her in her hands. Her little ink-drop eyes swiveled between her and Damien, and down to the bottle she'd flung out of her purse. Deep within that little crab mind of hers, Selia knew she was concocting some sort of mischief to either get into more trouble, or to flee back to the beach from which she came. Those were the two behaviors Selia had observed in the enthused little crab on the beaches of the Celtic Sea.

Amy had warned her that hermit crabs could get into mischief if not given the proper amount of beach time. "Where are your manners? Pinching someone's art supplies is incredibly rude."

With a feisty little pinch, Henrietta jabbed her claw into the air and wiggled her shell, which was also a vibrant shade of blue.

Damien laughed. "Does she understand you?"

"Oh, believe me. We've had this discussion about not stealing other's possessions before." Selia set Henrietta down on the table, where she darted between wine glasses and launched herself back into Selia's purse.

Anxiety knotted in Selia's stomach. Things seemed to be going a little *too* smoothly between her and Mr. Malloch. Between all of the flirtatious body language and eye contact that felt a little too intense, she still didn't know the intentions of this charismatic watercolor artist.

Was Damien one of these mysterious members of Gaia's Order Amy had warned her about?

Selia noticed the corner Henrietta had made an indent with her claw upon. "Your portfolio—may I see it?"

Damien handed the journal to her. "You do the honor."

Selia took Damien's watercolor journal and flipped over the cover. The first page was covered in blue splotches of dry watercolor paint. She continued flipping, finding the subjects of his artistic eye. Most were small pencil sketches, followed by more defined images captured by using a combination of both black inks and blue watercolors. Many of his studies were of marine invertebrates. Ocean creatures covered the first dozen or so pages, until she found the furry faces of dogs and cats. Even a pony stared up at her, their looks full of something sweet and innocent.

"What do you think?" Damien asked.

"You absolutely capture something in their eyes."

Damien smiled. "What do you think about combining inks and watercolor pigments? Is it too...messy?"

"No, the two work quite well together. They bring contrast to the subject's outline while not deterring from the looseness of the medium." She admired how Damien had used the ink subtly, allowing the liquid movement of the watercolors to dictate how the composition formed.

She continued flipping through animal portraits that soon transitioned into landscape studies. The landscapes were full of rocky outcroppings that transitioned between seascapes and shrublands.

"Where is this?" She asked.

"Home."

"This isn't the beach—where are these rocky landscapes from?"

Damien's cheeks dimpled. "Scotland."

"I thought you said in your letter that you lived by the Celtic Sea?"

"I do. I've lived there for quite some time." He set his hand on his chest. "But Scotland will always have my heart."

"I've never seen someone paint a place that was supposed to be green so wildly blue before." Selia continued to flip through the blue Highlands until seascapes replaced tree-dotted hills and rocky outcroppings. She marveled at Damien's monochromatic pallet that was oddly warm. She had never been to Scotland. However, looking at Damien's paintings were a gateway to a distant landscape. She felt herself longing to explore such a beautiful wide-open place.

Moonscapes appeared next as she thumbed through the journal. His brush technique changed. The pigments were much more fluid and ethereal-like as she flipped through the thick watercolor pages. "These are absolutely beautiful..."

Selia's fingers brushed past a symbol at the bottom right of the lunar reflection rippling across the sea.

Her breath caught.

Sitting at the top was a counter-clockwise spiral, with three rippling lines below it that resembled waves.

She blinked a few times, her mind attempting to analyze the symbol. She remembered seeing this symbol on his letter. She also remembered the symbol from a much more personal source. Damien's signature looked like the chunk of limestone Amy had given her context behind—a salt trancing talisman that had whispered a haunting melody to her.

Blue memories...

Selia shivered, remembering the day those words had filled her salt nodes like an aquatic echo. For as long as she'd worked at the museum, the artifact had always been in her possession—one she struggled to put on display as it didn't seem to fit in any of the exhibits.

For one, it was a magical artifact. Amy had shown her how valuable the talismans were when it came time to practicing the art known as salt trance. The source of that magic Amy had not given her a full answer to, other than it had something to do with an extinct species of blue kelp called minca.

Henrietta had been the one to steal her salt trancing talisman and attempt to swap it with one of Damien's blue paint brushes at the Celtic Sea. Had Henrietta's strange behavior been a coincidence? Or was the crab still trying to tell her something?

"Why did you choose to use watercolors as your painting medium?" Selia asked.

"Water has a magical way of making imperfections look beautiful, like—" His eyes dipped to her lips, then leveled with her gaze. "—just beautiful, like I'm sure many of the pieces of art you handle are."

Selia flushed, breaking eye contact with the artist who was still gazing at her too intensely.

Damien's expression became an eager one. "Have you painted before?"

"Oh lord no, I'm afraid I don't have that kind of artistic talent."

Damien chuckled. "Many people don't know they have any creative talent at all, until they try. How long have you worked at the Louvre?"

"About a decade."

"And before that?"

Selia's mind drifted to the talisman that had a striking resemblance to Damien's signature. "I can't recall at the moment..."

Damien's brow furrowed. "What is it that you actually do?"

"My duties revolve around artifact preservation, organization and exhibit display."

"Has there ever been an artifact that you couldn't figure out how to display before?"

The hair on the back of Selia's neck stood on end. *Yes—the one your signature is almost identical to.*

She forced her attention to Damien's signature, which did not make her feel any better. She traced her finger over the rippling waves that danced—like reflected moonlight—below the spiral. "Your signature is beautiful. It looks like strands of rippling moonlight on the surface of the ocean."

Damien cocked his head to the side. "I've never had someone actually describe my signature like the folktale it originated from."

"Oh?"

"Strands of Moonlight is the name of a Scottish folktale."

"Scottish folktales, huh? Who wrote this Strands of Moonlight folktale?"

"I've asked my aunt the same question, and she can never give me a straight answer. Every time she rattles on about some ancient group of Scottish people known as the Sgàthan clan."

"What does skahaaam mean?" Selia asked, the word not rolling off her tongue as smoothly as it did Damien's.

"Sgàthan is the Scottish-Gaelic word for *mirror*. The Sgàthan clan had a very strong belief—that memories and spirits *mirrored* one another—that they were the same thing. They believed that a spirit could reflect upon the memories of other individuals in ways that only moon magic could understand."

"Did you say *moon* magic?"

Damien nodded.

"Your signature is not original then?" she asked, hoping he would give some context to the symbol's history and this *moon magic*.

Damien shook his head. "No. I found the symbol in a collection of folktales I am particularly fond of called *Reflections*. These folktales illustrate stories about the fae. The fae were in fact the source of the moon magic practiced by selkies." His eyes dipped to her purse, where Henrietta was busy once again, attempting to remove the bottle.

Selia's pulse thundered in her chest. *Selkies*?

"When exactly did you begin signing your work with this symbol?" she asked.

"I'd say about ten years ago."

Selia's body went cold. Ten years ago, he'd started signing his work with this symbol that had an uncanny resemblance to the magical artifact back in her office. Ten years ago, Selia stopped remembering her past. Her identity was stolen by an illness the salt trancing talisman had diagnosed her with…

"Can you share one of these selkie folktales with me?" Selia asked

Damien smiled. "Of course. My recent paintings illustrate the imagery in the folktales I was hoping you would offer to critique?"

"Critique?" Selia said, remembering why Damien had come to visit her. She didn't know if she should laugh, or be flattered. All of the folktale talk about selkies had made her disoriented. "My eye is not trained in artistic critique, especially when it comes to watercolor paintings."

"Just a small ounce of feedback goes a long way for an artist. Trust me. I promise not to get offended with anything you have to offer."

"I'd love to see the illustrations from the folktale you called Strands of Moonlight?"

Damien cleared his throat. "All right, Strands of Moonlight it is." He flipped through his journal, stopping somewhere in the middle. "Before I show you the art, do you mind if I share a few notes of what I remember from this folktale?"

The green dancing in Damien's hazel eyes had already captured her attention. "I'm ready whenever you are."

Damien looked back to his journal. "A selkie discovered a man injured by the sea. As his blood spilled into the water, so did what his heart treasured. Knowing he wouldn't survive the night, the selkie unraveled three strands of moonlight from her salt skin, from which she would perform her moon magic."

The hair on the back of Selia's neck stood on end. Someone else had been watching their discussion, spying rather intently through the rose bush.

"Will you excuse me?" Selia asked.

Damien gave her a small nod.

Selia got up, walking over to where she'd spotted movement in the bush. Her boss and intern from the museum weren't there. A chilly breeze ripped through the roses, sending petals dancing into the air.

Someone with cold grey eyes had been watching her.

4

CRIMES AGAINST THE FAE

The pair of grey eyes Selia had seen behind the rose bush vanished. Maybe it had been her imagination playing tricks on her. The sight had startled her, maybe because the eyes didn't seem human.

She walked back to the table, finding that Damien was packing up his art supplies. "Where are you going?"

Damien flung his bag over his shoulder and jerked his head to the side. "Look."

Guests were exiting the Louvre in waves. What was causing such a mass exodus of the museum?

A horrible thought crossed Selia's mind.

"Selia, wait!" Damien called after her.

She took off in a jog, racing through the crowds as people exited the museum.

Security guards—including an arriving swarm of police—were entering the building.

Her boss was maneuvering rather frantically up and down the hall.

"Dr. O'Connor, what is going on?" Selia asked.

He stopped, swiveling on the soles of his shiny leather shoes to face her. The color had drained from his face. "Someone has broken into the Louvre…"

Selia's stomach hollowed. "In the middle of the *day*?" Nobody made it through the front gates. The Louvre had some of the best security in the world.

Selia flashed her badge at one of the security officers as she bustled down the hall to her office. While the guards followed her boss toward the marble sculpture exhibit, she and Damien slipped inside.

Selia stopped once past the threshold.

Damien walked in, stopping at her side.

Golden rays of sunlight branched through her only window, which had been shattered.

Boxes and personal belongings of hers lay everywhere.

"Oh no..." she breathed, her voice barely that of a whisper. She began walking into her space, feeling like a ghost here.

She felt so *violated*. How could someone just come in and destroy the past ten years she'd spent working at the museum?

Her filing cabinets had been ransacked. Her desk was in complete ruin. Any and all of the artifacts she'd been sorting and organizing had been jumbled through.

"What were they looking for?" Damien asked.

That horrible fear lurking in the back of her mind had manifested itself.

Selia knew what these thieves were after.

She began flipping over the stack of manila folders, knocking over the cardboard box where she'd left it.

Damien grabbed the empty box, tilting it up to look at the blue fairy drawn next to the address label.

Selia's heart stopped. "They took it..."

"Took what?"

The salt trancing talisman—it was gone...

Selia thumbed over the tattered paperwork on her desk, finding a bright blue envelope sitting where she'd placed the talisman. A silver coin with an anchor on it sat in the middle.

She removed the coin and picked up the envelope, finding a message written in shiny black ink.

Selia Fontaine has been convicted of a crime against the fae

Selia's stomach turned over.

A crime against the *fae*? This had to be some kind of joke...

She unfolded the envelope and withdrew a handwritten note.

Amy's Ocean Apothecary is under criminal investigation for malpractice of the art of salt trance. Any and all individuals who are discovered practicing the art are convicted of unlawful acts against nature as defined by Gaia's Order.

Please see the natural classification of your crime below:

Name: Selia Fontaine

Offending Daughter of Gaia: Neried (sea nymph)

Ecosystem: Marine

Location of Crime: The Celtic Sea

Potential Contamination: Hydrosphere

Biosphere Contamination Severity: Extreme

Origin of Offense: Amphitrite's Ocean Apothecary

Art of Practiced Corruption: Art of Salt Trance

Fae Status Report: Flora: *Cumatilis minca* (extinct) **Fauna:** (unknown)

We have confiscated the salt trancing talisman. You have one option. Return the bottle of selkie salt skin to the location of the crime, or blue memory blindness will erase more than the past ten years of your life.

Sincerely,

Gaia's Order

Selia's hand was shaking.

Was the Order convicting her of a crime against *fairies*? She'd never seen a fairy in her life!

Minca was a *fae* species? Amy hadn't given her any context to the fae when she first taught her about the art.

Why did they steal the talisman from her? Did the Order know something about the symbol's mysterious origin? Or was this some kind of prank?

"Looks like I'm not the only one curious about what's inside the mystery bottle," Damien said. "The art of salt trance? What are they convicting you of practicing?" He grabbed the letter from her. "Blue memory blindness? What the heck is that?"

The corners of Selia's eyes began to burn. Tears dolloped down her cheeks.

"Hey, it's okay," Damien whispered.

"What am I supposed to do?"

Selia's boss appeared in the doorway. "Miss Fontaine, I suggest that you leave for the day. The Louvre is closed until further investigation of the break-in is made."

Selia nodded, quickly wiping her tears away.

"I will call you personally when I hear what is to come of this investigation." Dr. O'Connor dipped back out of the door.

Damien's brows arched into his hair. "Well?"

"Well, I'm out of a job, and this Order expects me to do what?" She snatched the letter back from him, reading over the threats again. "How am I supposed to defend myself against this kind of nonsense?"

"Where did you get the bottle of selkie salt skin?"

"The Celtic Sea."

"Then it's settled. Why don't you come back to the Celtic Sea with me?"

"Why? What will that do?" She gazed out of her shattered window. It started to rain. Drops of water collided with one another over the remaining shards of broken glass.

The corners of her eyes began to burn again. "Amy gave the bottle to me."

"Who is Amy?"

"Amy was going to help me..." Selia replied, searching once again for the missing talisman—the only item she had known for as long as her memory spanned for.

"What was Amy going to help you with?"

Selia's vision blurred. "Ten years ago is when I stopped remembering my past."

"What do you mean, *remembering* your past?"

"I have an illness that affects my memory. I don't know anything about myself prior to ten years." She looked up at him, his face blurring behind her tears. "I can't remember where I came from or who I am…"

Damien's gaze met hers. "Is this blue memory blindness really a form of amnesia?"

She held her breath, the oxygen in her lungs too painful to expel at once.

Damien's hand came to her face, wiping the tears as she stopped fighting for them not to form. "You don't have to face this alone. Besides, I have something at my art studio I think can help you."

Selia looked away from him, shaking. She didn't know *what* to think. Ten years ago, the talisman came into her possession, filling some strange void in her life. Now that it was gone, what did that mean for her moving forward? Did the talisman have some other purpose Amy had not explained?

What did the Order want to prevent her from remembering?

5

BREATH, MEMORY, & SALT

Selia made a trip to her apartment and packed a duffel bag full of clothing. She didn't know how long she would be gone from Paris, or out of a job for that matter. But running away from her city with a watercolor artist who believed in the fae? There could be worse scenarios, right?

She returned to her office and gave the room one last look before she left for the Celtic Sea. Had practicing the art of salt trance really been a crime against the fae?

She'd never seen a fairy in her life, let alone creatures that resembled them. That was, unless, Henrietta was secretly one of their kin. Maybe the little crab had gone and tattled on her in the night. It wouldn't be the first time that Amy's pet had gotten her into trouble. She had been the one to steal her salt trancing talisman and swap it out with one of Damien's blue paint brushes.

Henrietta's little shell came bobbing through the dismay of her desk. There was a new whimsy about her, even a little anticipation. Her ink-drop eyes turned up, catching light from the broken window reflecting in them. An adventure back to the beach was something Amy's pet was sure to love.

"Don't worry, I wouldn't forget you," Selia said, setting her palm out for Henrietta to scuttle onto.

Selia left for the train station with Damien that afternoon. Damien took their luggage—two small duffel bags—and slung them over his shoulders.

Once on the train, Selia grabbed the railing above her head as she huddled between passengers flocking on board to leave Paris. The train was soon moving, leaving Paris behind. The familiarity of the City of Lights drifted by—a blurring tunnel of white buildings and cobblestone streets. A place where artists flourish and lovers meet.

Her brain was a storm of confusion. Gaia's Order stole her salt trancing talisman. How was it connected to Damien's signature? Did it have something to do with the selkie salt skin from Amy's Ocean Apothecary?

Damien sat down at one of the free booths, saving a spot for her with his easel. He tugged out a journal and some pencils from his bag.

She took the seat next to him, her hair catching in one of the seat cushions. Before she could free the clump that had gotten tangled, Damien's hand was already reaching behind her ear.

His gaze landed on the spot she knew had to be incredibly red and swollen. "Is that a birthmark?"

Selia tugged her hair down. "That is one of my salt nodes," she replied, embarrassment welling up inside of her.

"You have *two* of them?" he said, whipping his head around to try and catch a glimpse of the other.

"I do." Selia tugged her hair down behind her ears, hiding the sure-to-be reddening marks that on a good day could pass as freckles. But with all of the stress, they were hot and bothered.

She eyed the journal resting in his hands—so much magic nestled there between the pages. All he shared with her about the Strands of Moonlight folktale was the beginning of a story about a selkie finding a wounded man and offering him her moon magic.

A spell of some kind was written below the first part of the folktale.

```
Breath from my body.
Memory from my mind.
Salt from my soul.
With these three strands of moonlight, I wish
to make you whole.
```

Selia stared at the word *memory*, which had been crossed out. A heart had been drawn over it instead.

"Why did you cross the word memory out and replace it with a heart?" Selia asked.

"I wrote it wrong. You would think that memories would come from the mind. However, in the folktale, it was written as memories from the *heart*." He tapped his temple. "I always found that a wee bit confusing."

Selia's hair stood up on the back of her neck. She was familiar with these memories that lived in the heart. If there was one thing Amy drilled into her head from her first salt trancing lesson, it was about what separated blue memories from normal memories.

"Blue memories live in the heart, not the mind. The memories forgotten by the minds of men are remembered by the hearts of sea nymphs."

What if the *Reflections* folktales and blue memories had something in common?

"Let's see what I can remember about the folktale. A selkie found a man wounded by the sea. She stepped onto land and unraveled three strands of something from her chest." She shook her head. "What exactly was she unraveling?"

Damien's cheeks dimpled. "Three strands of moonlight form her salt skin."

Selia's hair stood up. "The selkie had a *salt* skin?"

Damien nodded, tapping his finger to the spell he'd written. "These are the words the selkie said to the man before she healed him." He flipped through his journal until he found a blank page. His eyes locked with hers, the greens standing out against the grey blur of the city passing by. "Is the Amy who gave you the bottle of selkie salt skin also a sea nymph?"

Selia thought back to when she first met Amy at the Blue Mermaid Beach Bar and Grill. It was there that she first learned about the art that was getting her into trouble with the Order. "Yes. She prefers to go by the Celtic Sea Sorceress."

Damien's face twisted with thought. "Amy seems like such a modern name for a sea sorceress. Is it short for something else?"

"Nope," Selia lied as Amphitrite's vivid green eyes came flooding into her mind.

"Sounds to me like this sea sorceress has some sea magic of her own. And this blue minca that went extinct. When did it go extinct?"

"I have no idea when. Amy claimed ignorance as well." Another partial fib escaped from her lips. Selia had asked her the same question, and she'd answered with a 'that depends on who you ask,' and promptly dismissed her question.

Damien's brow arched. "Well, it's apparent the Order didn't like that she shared the selkie salt skin with you." He tugged out the note. "It says here that Amy's Ocean Apothecary is under criminal investigation for malpractice of the art of salt trance. I take it that you've practiced this salt trancing art?"

"I have."

"Why did you practice it?"

"To help Amy remember a treasure she lost to the sea."

"What was this treasure you helped Amy to remember?"

Selia spotted Damien's watercolor signature, the spiral making her dizzy. "The artifact the Order stole from my office."

"The salt trancing talisman?"

"Bingo."

Damien traced his pencil around the base of his journal, sketching out his moonlit signature. "There is *something* strange, even magical about this symbol. If Gaia's Order stole the talisman, it must be important."

"So far that symbol has come from *three* different places. My salt trancing talisman, your signature, which you stole out of a collection of Scottish folktales called the *Reflections*?"

Damien's brows furrowed. "Hey, I didn't steal it. I merely *borrowed* it."

"I don't know if stealing anything from the fae is a wise idea," Selia teased.

"The talisman must have some purpose that without it, you aren't able to do something. Why else would they steal it from you?"

"What kind of purpose?" Selia asked.

Damien's eyes dipped to her purse, where Henrietta was coiled around the bottle. "Why do I think it has to do with the selkie salt skin?"

She slumped in her seat. "I'm not so familiar with this selkie folklore the Scots seem so fond of. Can you enlighten me?"

"A selkie's identity *is* the sea. Her cloak, or salt skin, symbolizes her connection with the ocean she calls home." He looked up from his journal. "But after meeting you, I think that cloak is something different entirely, something that is linked with the art of salt trancing."

Ching!

Selia dug her chiming phone out from her purse, finding Deidra's icon of a redwood tree blinking from her text message inbox. "I have to take this—it might be from the Louvre." She excused herself from her seat.

She walked to the back of their train car and tugged out the salt trancing journal Amy had given her, which was damp.

She began quickly fanning the pages as to prevent the water from ruining them.

A message bled across the parchment.

My Dear Selia,

By reciting three simple principles with the aid of a salt extract, a sea nymph can accomplish the following in no particular order:

1) An exceedingly annoying and unnecessary load of harassment from the Order.

2) Oodles of healing knowledge unknown by modern-day medical science.

3) An understanding of your own fertility cycles.

4) Swim within the blue memories of her chosen host.

Selia's eyes drifted between understanding *her own fertility cycles* and *swimming with the blue memories of her chosen host.*

I am sure that by now you have experienced the first item listed. None of these things, however, will matter if the Order steps between me and my current work with the art. That is why I need you to keep the selkie salt skin a secret.

Selia's phone was chiming—no—exploding with texts now. Deidra had messaged her multiple times. She only harassed her like this for one of two reasons. One, it was to probe into the stale corners of Selia's dating life. Or two—it had to do with the recent developments with her root readings, the clairvoyant art that dryads practiced in their spare time.

SALTY SISTA! WHY U AVOIDING ME?

Selia dialed Deidra and placed her phone to her ear. "The Order broke into my office and stole the salt trancing talisman. They convicted me of a crime against the fae!"

"Okay, it sounds like you have a lot on your hands at the moment," Deidra snapped back. "Was there any particular fae they convicted your crime against?"

"Blue minca was mentioned."

"Minca is an extinct species of kelp, correct?"

"According to Amy, yes."

"No wonder the Order is involved. Ever since you told me about meeting Amphitrite, I've been doing a little research on my end about the Order. Have I ever talked to you about Iridescents before?"

"No?"

"Well, an Iridescent is a high-ranking nymph who works for Gaia's Order. They devote their lives to the protection and preservation of the natural arts. In your case, this art Amphitrite taught you about."

"What do they look like?"

"They aren't very tall. They tend to have short hair. Their ears are slender, some have points. Oh, and their eyes are special. They will appear grey, but in the right light, iridescent colors will shimmer across them. I imagine they are similar to an insect's wings."

Selia looked down at Henrietta huddled against the selkie salt skin in her purse. She didn't dare stick her fingers near her, fearing the crab would pinch her like she did Damien. Since the Order had broken into her office and stole her talisman, Amy's pet had become more protective of the bottle of selkie salt skin, refusing to leave it alone.

"Gaia's Order is invested in protecting one of Gaia's kingdoms over any other—the fae kingdom." Deidra said.

Selia nearly dropped her purse. "Since *when* did you have information on this fae kingdom?"

Deidra laughed. "We've talked about the fae kingdom before."

"No we haven't."

"The fae kingdom isn't like what most humans imagine it to be. There are no thrones, hierarchies, or governing forces of power. When I say kingdom, I'm talking about *life* kingdoms. Fae are beings who camouflage themselves next to current-day, and in some cases extinct flora and fauna species."

"Flora and *whata*?"

"Flora and fauna. You know, plants and animals?"

"How do you know if you are dealing with a fae, or just a normal plant or animal?"

"Flora, I'm not so sure. But for fauna, they tend to have a particular obsession with a color or two."

"Do you think a hermit crab could be a flora fae?" Selia asked, thinking immediately of Henrietta's obsession with the color blue.

"Absolutely. Arthropods, or most creatures with an exoskeleton, make up approximately seventy-five percent of all creatures on the planet. I wouldn't be surprised if many of the crab species most people are aware of are in fact fae creatures in disguise. Anyway, I'm a nerd about these things. I could go on and on about the fae kingdom. All you need to know is that Gaia's Order is particularly invested in protecting species of the fae kingdom, which it sounds like blue minca might be a part of."

"Why would the Order come after me for practicing the art of salt trance?"

"Fun fact! The Order apparently tried to change how the art of salt trance was taught long ago. A sea goddess rebelled against the Order by attempting to restore the art to the way her ancestors first taught it."

"Do you have a description of this sea goddess?" Selia asked.

"Does Amy have wild red hair, emerald eyes, and freckles shaped like starfish on her face?"

"She absolutely does."

"Well, we might have discovered our rebellious sea goddess. The records are pretty convoluted. This thread goes back thousands of years and dead-ends in ancient Egypt."

"Where are you getting this information?"

"I told you about my secret database. It can't be a secret if I tell you all of the details now, can it?"

Selia huffed. These *threads* Deidra mentioned were her source to the art woodland nymphs practiced. She ran her fingers past her ears, finding her salt nodes hot and swollen. All of the anxiety from the past day shriveled them into a pair of sad little nubs. She almost dropped her phone as another message bled through the parchment of her journal.

`Don't tell anyone about the selkie salt skin. The Order will be looking for ways to manipulate you, so don't give them any opportunity.`

"I gotta go," Selia said.

"Wait!" Deidra said. "I want more details on the talisman! The Order could be trying to—"

Selia closed her phone and turned it off, turning her attention back to the liquid message that was quickly evaporating.

The fae gifted the art of salt trance to us long ago. You will develop an intuition about the art as you begin to practice with the three principles. Recite the three principles in your mind when you practice with your blue memory host, and the ocean of their heart will open to you.

The three principles are breath, memory, and salt.

Selia's salt nodes began to tingle.

Breath from my body. Memory from my heart. Salt from my soul. With these three strands of moonlight, I wish to make you whole.

Strands of Moonlight was a *fae* folktale. Amy stated the art was a gift from the fae. Did the spell Damien wrote in his watercolor journal have something to do with these salt trancing principles Amy had given her?

Fwump!

"Hey, watch it!" a man stammered.

Selia swiveled as he brushed past her, nearly making her drop her phone.

Selia pressed her back against the train as another man in a black trench coat followed him. *Jerks.* Two men bustled their way through the train car, stopping at the door.

The messages in Amy's journal had vanished.

Selia tucked Amy's journal back into her bag and returned to where Damien was sketching away in his watercolor journal. In the five minutes that she'd stepped away, he'd created a miniature masterpiece.

He held up his journal. "What do you think? Is it minca-ish enough?"

Selia marveled at his graphite study. How fluid his creativity was. The paper was covered in sketches of his liquid imagination. "You are absolutely talented, do you know that?"

Damien chuckled. "I'm not the only artist on this train."

Selia crossed her arms, reciting in her mind what Amy's message said. *Breath, memory, and salt.*

Her stomach knotted. What had she gotten herself into?

6

STORMS

Rain pelted the windows as the train pulled to a screeching halt. The Celtic Sea was nothing like Selia remembered from a month ago. The sky was overcast and the water steel grey. If she didn't know any better, she would have assumed the horizon didn't belong to the Celtic Sea at all.

A north wind blew in, bringing a cold chill that rippled over her skin. Thunder ripped overhead, and Selia's hopes of warming her skin with the evening sun drifted away. For the beginning of summer the air was awfully thin, like the drawn-out breath of someone who'd become ill. There was no use trying to visit the beach in this ghastly weather.

Damien caught them a cab and they both hopped inside as the frigid wind picked up. "To Highland Cove, please."

The driver steered the car onto the road. "The storm was horrendous last night. It ripped right up the cove. They had to shut down the beach twice. Someone must have angered the sea sprites."

Damien's hand tightened on his bag. "My studio is made for this kind of unpredictable summer weather."

A bright blue neon sign of a mermaid tail flickered in the distance—the sign of the Blue Mermaid Beach Bar and Grill. The bar was where she'd first seen Damien painting in an art contest where 'kissing a mermaid' was involved.

"I was going to say we grab a bite to eat there, but it looks like they've already closed up for the evening," Damien said as the cab drove further up the road.

Selia reached into her purse, finding Henrietta's shell huddled against the bottle of selkie salt skin, which seemed to become more valuable the closer they became to the sea. The Order wanted what was inside it, and Amy wanted her to test her salt trancing abilities by practicing with it.

The last item on Amy's list of instructions stuck in her memory the most: **`Swim within the blue memories of her chosen host.`**

As the cab brought them further up the cove, the evidence of a storm appeared along the beach. Debris of driftwood, seashells and algae clumped in the sand. Some of the dune grasses had pieces of trash trapped in them. White caps surged along the water, giving the Celtic Sea a more sinister appearance.

The cab dropped them off, and Selia huddled against Damien's side as they approached a little stucco building. Blue window shutters flapped in the wind, creaking as they found the door.

"Finally home," Damien said, grabbing the door handle and pushing it open.

Selia bustled in after him, eager to get out of the blustery cold. The scent of his home wasn't stuffy, like the space had been recently wind-blown. The temperature was almost colder inside than it was out in the wind.

Damien's shoulders rounded. "Something isn't right."

Selia felt Henrietta shift in her bag, and she wondered if hermit crabs too shuddered when they were cold. A draft caught her around the ankles as a cool breeze moved through the room. Where was the cold air coming from?

She followed him through another threshold, which opened to a much larger room. A couple of wooden chairs were placed haphazardly around a drafting table, which was covered in art supplies.

One, two, no—at least a dozen wooden easels had been turned upside down. Some of their legs were snapped in two, the splintered wood dangling from the hinges.

Selia's breath caught in her chest.

Damien's fists clenched. A grunt escaped from his mouth.

His art studio had been *ransacked...*

What Selia imagined as a beautifully organized space had been turned upside down. Rolls of paper were torn. Boxes full of brushes and tubes of paint were tossed, their contents spilling everywhere.

"I can't believe this..." she whispered, her voice an echo of the horror she felt for him. Deja vu came flooding back to her and the violation she'd felt in her office.

Damien's mouth kept opening and closing with no sound. His color was darker, making his freckles appear redder on his nose. "Who did this?" he breathed, shoulders rounding. "Who are these naft, scabby blokes who come barging into my home!" he bellowed.

He staggered past Selia, grabbing one of the easels and swinging it above his head. Another string of Scottish curses flew out of his mouth as he launched the easel across the room. The easel crippled as it slammed against another that had been broken in two.

Henrietta launched out of Selia's bag at the rage in his voice. Selia hadn't yet seen anger on the man who'd been so calm and collected. She couldn't blame him. So much of his work—possibly years of painting—had been destroyed.

"I'm sorry," Damien breathed, a vein throbbing in his neck. "I'm just so—"

"—you don't have to apologize. It's obvious. The Order wants something from both of us."

"You think the Order did this?"

Selia bent down, grabbing what Henrietta had unearthed from the clutter.

A silver coin came rolling toward her.

Selia grabbed it, her heart leaping. The anchor on it she'd seen before. "See this coin? I found an identical one in my office. It had to be the Order."

Damien's jaw hardened. His shoulders rounded as he shook his head.

Selia pocketed the coin. "They obviously didn't like whatever it was you were planning on showing me."

Henrietta was already knocking through the rubbish, trying on different paint cans for size.

"What was it that you wanted to show me?" Selia asked, nearly tripping over an empty paint can.

"I think I know what Gaia's Order was after," Damien stopped at the edge of the room where his window had been bashed in. "Well, that *was* it," he said, stopping at one of his distorted easels.

Selia eyed the torn watercolor paper. Whatever image had been there had been ripped through. "What had you painted?"

"Reflections on the water," he replied. "Right after I met you. That's when I started seeing them every night. That's what I wanted to show you, before..." his voice dipped again.

Selia shivered. Since she'd left the body of water where she first met Amy, Damien had started seeing the reflective blue lights too. He, however, was smart about them and decided to document what he had seen.

She walked over to the window where the thieves had entered. Heat branched up her spine. How could the Order attack Damien's studio like this? He'd done nothing to deserve this kind of treatment! Her fingers itched for the bottle of selkie salt skin. She wasn't about to return the bottle to the ocean it originated from—she was going to get even with them.

She reached into her purse and tugged out Amy's salt trancing journal. She flipped to the first few pages where she'd seen Amy's messages.

The selkie salt skin works the best if you identify what the heart of your host treasures.

Selia surveyed Damien's studio, treasures of his artwork all around her. The jagged wooden leg of the easel he'd thrown had a sliver of red glinting on it.

"You are bleeding," she said, pointing to his arm.

Damien rolled up the torn fabric on his shirt, exposing his forearm. "Could be worse."

Selia smiled. The perfect opportunity to test out her salt trancing talents had presented itself. "You want to learn more about salt trancing, right?" She tugged a chair that had been tossed over, patting the back. "Screw the Order. I say I teach you what I know about the art before they can intimidate us anymore."

"I like the sound of that." He flopped down on the chair Selia had tugged aside and began rolling up the other sleeve of his shirt.

She sat atop one of the wooden crates in front of him, nerves rippling through her. She didn't think the art had anything to do with healing until Amy's message appeared. *Breath, memory,* and *salt* were the three strands of moonlight the selkie used to heal the wounded man in the folktale.

According to Amy, these three strands were principles used when performing a salt trance. A coincidence? Maybe. There were too many similarities between the folktale and Amy's instructions to not become suspicious.

The veins in Damien's muscular forearms bulged. Blood from his cut began to pool in the wound, turning the sleeve of his shirt red. "Give me your arm. I want to try something."

Damien didn't budge. "What are you trying?"

"The talisman the Order stole from me has me thinking." She glanced over at one of Damien's seascapes that had been torn through. Even ripped to shreds, the moonlight dancing on the water's surface was hauntingly beautiful. "The symbol on the talisman had a striking resemblance to your watercolor signature, which according to you, came from folktales about selkies who could heal by practicing a form of moon magic?"

"Where are you going with this?"

"I'm starting to wonder if the healing moon magic mentioned in the folktale isn't somehow related to the art of salt trance."

"Healing can be tricky. Sometimes, there are wounds that go deeper than the flesh." Damien flexed his arm, making the cut bleed.

Blind Moon...

Selia shivered. Had someone whispered her name? She blinked a few times, focusing on Damien's confused face. She hadn't told Damien about the message she'd seen from Amy about breath, memory, and salt. Before she put her faith into her assumptions, she wanted to try her hand at this art of which Amy had given her so little knowledge.

She wanted something tangible to practice salt trancing with—something she could touch. Right now, that was Damien's worsening cut. "Let's try it. Let's start with something you treasure."

Damien set his elbows on his knees, clasping his hands together. "Define treasure."

Selia set Amy's salt trancing journal down on the ground next to her and glanced around the trashed studio. With all of the chaos surrounding them, she felt oddly connected with the artist sitting so vulnerably in front of her. "How about something you use to create your paintings?"

Damien's eyes locked with hers, intensity lingering behind them. His look made Selia's heart beat a little faster. "Okay. There is *one* brush in particular that I treasure. I could care less about the others."

"Why do you treasure this brush?"

Damien blinked when she asked. "It was a gift from someone I loved."

Selia's stomach did something strange. So he did love someone. Had it been from a family member? Maybe, a girlfriend?

She steadied herself. "Okay, we have your treasure. What quirky details can you give me about this missing brush?"

"I often got splinters from the handle, so I wrapped a little bit of tape around the base. Oh—and it was slightly lopsided from overuse."

Selia's gaze dropped to Amy's salt trancing journal. Another message drifted across the paper like liquid smoke:

A single drop of selkie salt skin is all you need and the entire ocean of his heart is yours to explore…

Hesitation rippled through her body. She had no idea what to expect. She'd not explored anyone else's blue memories before, except for the one Amy shared with her. And that entailed being held hostage on a pirate ship with a Captain who wanted much more than her *mermaid booty.*

Damien's brows lifted. "Well?"

"In order to perform the art, I have to touch you…"

Damien's ears turned pink. "Where do you have to touch me?"

"Hold out your left hand."

"Why the left?"

"Because your left hand is closer to your heart. This is where blue memories live." She set her right hand to her chest.

"What does practicing this art help you accomplish?"

"What does painting in watercolors help you accomplish?"

Damien's dimples appeared again. "I get the feeling that salt trancing isn't comparable to watercolors."

Selia swallowed. She was a fish out of water when it came to practicing this art on her own. The last time she practiced, she had Amy there rooting for her in person. She straightened herself in her seat. "Any other questions before we begin?"

"One last one. Are blue memories different from normal memories?"

"Blue memories reside in the heart, not the mind."

"Why the heart?"

Selia thought back to the one thing she remembered from Amy's first salt trancing lesson, which took place right here at the Celtic Sea. She remembered Amy's eyes when she'd asked her the very same question—a fire flickered from their emerald depths. "The treasures forgotten by men are remembered by the hearts of sea nymphs."

Damien's eyes dipped to her lips, then back up to her. "I guess I'm in for more than only having my fortune read."

Selia blinked, looking away from his gaze. She uncorked the little bottle of selkie salt skin and held it between her fingers. An earthy aroma drifted into the air, making Selia's salt nodes swell. Her belly warmed and her pulse quickened.

What sweet pleasure was this?

Damien propped his left arm on his knee, his palm facing up. "You aren't nervous, are you?"

She looked into his warm eyes, seeing her nerves reflecting back at her. "I have absolutely no idea what to expect."

Damien chuckled. "I guess there is a first time for everything, right?"

Selia let out a nervous laugh. "Let's hope that I don't mess up…"

Splotches of blue watercolor pigment stained the calluses near the base of his fingers. "Close your eyes," she said, and Damien's eyelids fluttered closed. "And no peeking."

She opened one of her eyes just to make sure Damien wasn't playing any games, finding that he was smiling.

"Can I talk?" he asked.

"No. Instead, focus on the first strand of moonlight from the folktale."

"That was breath, right?"

"Right, so take a deep breath."

Damien's shoulders rose as he inhaled.

"You can let it out…"

He exhaled slowly, and his shoulders relaxed.

"Keep doing that…" She had absolutely no idea what she was doing, but he was playing along well enough.

While focusing on Damien's breathing, Selia tipped the bottle forward, dolloping a single drop of salt water into his left palm. "Breath from my body. Memory from my heart. Salt from my soul. With these three strands of moonlight, I wish to make you whole."

Fsshhhhhhh…

An aquatic echo whispered from somewhere deep within her subconscious mind, leaving her wondering if *just winging it* was really the best idea. She set the bottle of selkie salt skin next to the journal on the ground, wondering what her next plan of action should be. There were no new messages from Amy drifting across the parchment.

Selia did what she imagined to be the most appropriate psychic reading technique and set her fingers into the drop of salt water in the center of Damien's palm. She relaxed her wrist. A pulse throbbed through her fingers. Was it his? Was it hers? She didn't quite know. But the rhythmic pulse began to sync with her breathing, and she too, relaxed.

She closed her eyes. A blue flash of light filled her periphery. White spider veins branched out towards the blackness of her eyelids, like a window breaking.

Her pulse was more pronounced as the trance swallowed her consciousness. With each thrash of her heartbeat against her chest, a crystalline blue halo of her surroundings appeared.

She was still in Damien's art studio, but veiled in a crystalline version of it.

Objects in her periphery were large and angular, but she couldn't make them out as they were blurry. The sound of waves crashing in the distance filled her ears. The taste of salt filled her mouth.

Damien, however, was a blur before her. His silhouette was angular, sharp, then smooth. The light around him fragmented, splintering out like branching fingers.

Her left hand tingled. She stretched her fingers as Damien's pulse began to warm her hand. Damien's brush began to manifest before her—but not in a physical sense. She could *feel* the item in this room, and the moment he'd abandoned it.

Heat branched through her fingers. Her pulse quickened as her bloodstream became saturated with Damien's blue memory around this treasured brush.

An ache crept through Selia's body—a kind of ache left by emotion. The item she was searching for had left a residual energy. A cold, prickly sensation of many emotions juxtaposed with one another. She tried to suck in a breath, but her lungs struggled.

What had caused the feeling of complete emptiness? And how was that feeling tied to his missing paintbrush?

Selia opened her eyes, meeting Damien's gaze. Their hands broke apart. With it, so did the pulse they shared. His cut hadn't healed at all. Blood had pooled into his palm, turning the drop of selkie salt skin red.

Damien rolled his shirt down over the wound, splotching up the blood. "Nice try. Maybe this moon magic doesn't work like the folktale said."

"I saw your paint brush!" Excitement rippled through her even though the lingering emptiness tied to the brush still existed in the air.

"Is it normal for this to happen after a salt trancing session?" Damien asked, holding out his palm. A beautiful blue crystal sat at the center.

Selia grabbed the crystal, which was cool to the touch. Was this the source of the brilliant blue lights reflecting in her periphery when she dipped into the trance?

7

SALT TRANCING

Something darted into Selia's periphery more than once now, and it wasn't a fleck of dust.

Why was the crystal in her palm glowing?

She stood up from her chair, focusing on the light pulsing at the crystal's center. The light was undoubtedly trying to tell her something.

"What is it?" Damien asked.

But Selia had already taken off in pursuit of what the light was trying to show her. She understood it was an attempt to guide her to the source of whatever memory was trapped inside of it.

Damien's footsteps echoed behind her as she explored his seaside cottage. The sensations of loss and hurt associated with the brush was unlike anything Selia had experienced. The feelings were thick and suffocating. She found herself wanting to hold her breath.

She still didn't quite understand the purpose of the art, other than it allowed one to experience the blue memories from another individual. If blue memories lived in the heart, did that mean they had a pulse of their own?

Light flashed behind one of the easels that had fallen. Selia walked over to where the light had flickered. She bent down, scratching her finger past a rough spot on the floor, when something smooth brushed past her skin.

She retrieved the brush and handed it to him.

Damien took the brush, holding it in front of his face. "How in the world did you find this?"

"A feeling," she said, still wondering why so much sadness had been tied to a brush he had used to create such beautiful and vivid imagery.

Damien pocketed the brush. "Thank you. I would have been devastated if I lost this."

Selia nodded, knowing that whoever had given him the brush meant a great deal to him.

As the evening wore on, Selia found herself becoming more fatigued. The events from the day drained her. Maybe warming her chilled body in a warm shower would make her feel better.

She retrieved her journal where she'd left it on the ground in Damien's studio. No new watery messages from Amy. Assuming it *was* Amy communicating with her. The author had never identified themselves, other than saying they had a great deal of problems with the fae with which to contend.

She grabbed the bottle of selkie salt skin and dropped the salt crystal inside. It would be safer inside of the bottle and less likely to be stolen by Henrietta.

She took the bottle with her and found her way to the bathroom while Damien got to work cooking in the kitchen. She closed the door and turned on the tap. She removed her damp clothes in a heap at her feet and climbed in.

She moved under the tap, savoring the warmth of the water as it caressed her skin. As the water worked over her scalp and shoulders, the memories of her salt trance with Damien became her focus.

Damien mentioned his paintbrush had been given to him by someone he loved. This someone was from the past. Did he still love them? Who was this person?

The crystal that formed was not transparent. It was murky blue, with hints of brown comparable to mud. Maybe the clarity of blue memory salt crystals depended on the emotions that helped them to form. The crystal oddly enough, reminded her of Damien. Smooth to the touch, slightly warm in places, but mostly cool. And its color was the only color Damien saw the world through.

Salt trancing was odd. It was not the art she expected it to be. The experience was almost *empathic*, stepping into the shoes of another individual, and experiencing the 'treasure trove' of memories they held dear.

In the few seconds she'd spent tapped into Damien's heart, it felt like she had wrapped herself in an aquatic cocoon. Water had an emotion in the trance—its own breath—its own pulse.

The pulse she'd sensed had been weak, like a dying stream. The experience left her feeling vulnerable, even a little drained. Amy had taught her that salt trancing talismans could store blue memories inside of them. It was the salt that gave them this power. Perhaps it was the salt crystals that held onto blue memories, preserving them.

She rinsed herself of any remaining suds, turned off the tap and exited the shower. Dripping, she reached for where she'd seen a towel, brushing her hand against the condensation on the mirror instead.

Water trickled down as her hand shifted against the foggy glass. Selia trailed her fingers over the condensation that dripped past her breasts. She drew what she remembered of Damien's spirit signature, spiraling the center across her heart. His artwork had warmed her in a way she'd not expected. With his strange blue sight, the man who believed in selkies seemed a little softer around the edges.

She dried her skin and dressed into a new pair of fresh clothes, then opened the door to allow the steam from the shower to escape.

Damien was across the hall, standing with his back turned to her in his art studio. He turned, squinting as he faced her. "Did you draw that?"

Selia looked back at the mirror.

The art of salt trance.

The liquid message fogged over and changed once again on the mirror.

"Oh boy," Damien said. "Are you seeing this?"

"Shhhhh!" Selia hissed, as though Damien's voice would shatter the messages condensing on the mirror.

The fae gifted the art of salt trance to us long ago. And with it, we can see a world invisible to most.

A fae treasure holds forgotten secrets about the art.

To locate this treasure, you must find a single strand of moonlight.

As the last of the steam fizzled out of the room, the liquid message vanished.

"I wrote it down," Damien said. "Fae treasure. To find this treasure, you must find a single strand of moonlight."

"Well?"

Selia looked outside. "It's a full moon tonight, isn't it?"

Damien's cheeks dimpled as he closed his journal. "Are you up for a treasure hunt?"

Selia found her seat at the table in the kitchen.

Damien appeared in the doorway. "How long has this sea sorceress been communicating with you through condensation on mirrors?"

Selia looked up at Damien, who was obviously spooked from the message they'd seen. "For a day."

"Have you ever considered that this sea sorceress is working for this Order? How do you know she's not part of them?"

"Stop it," Selia said, defense rising in her voice. "Amy is my *friend*."

Damien dipped out of the room and back to the kitchen.

Selia's stomach was a jumble of nerves. She couldn't answer why Amy had chosen to communicate with her this way, rather than meet in Paris.

Damien appeared with two plates of piping-hot pasta. He stopped at her side and set one down in front of her. The rich red tomato sauce matched blood on his forearm.

"You might want to put bandage on that," Selia said, pointing at the cut.

Damien squinted at his arm. "I forgot all about that."

"You forgot you were *bleeding*?"

"I can't see red." He set his plate down, grabbing a napkin instead.

Selia looked down at her piping plate of pasta. She never imagined that she would take seeing colors for granted.

Damien wrapped the napkin around his arm. He grabbed the fabric with his teeth, tugging it sideways with his other hand, forming a knot. "There. No more blood." He plopped down in his seat across the table. "When did you meet Amy?"

"About a month ago."

"Are you sure it was a month, or longer?"

"What are you saying?"

"You have memory loss, right? Sometimes people experience apparitions or visions of individuals with which they have suppressed memories."

Selia locked eyes with him, heat branching up her spine. "You think I'm crazy, don't you?"

Damien's brow furrowed. "Crazy? No, I..."

"I never agreed to be a patient of yours, Mr. art therapist."

"Selia, that's not what I meant..."

Selia stood to leave, but Damien reached out, touching her arm. "I care about you. I don't want Gaia's Order to take advantage of you."

Selia glared at him, the heat in her body threatening to make her break out in a hormonal sweat. Hormones. Like her hunger, they were wreaking havoc on her judgment. Exaggerated by the fact that she was standing close to an incredibly attractive and sensitive man who just said he *cared about her...*

Damien's eyes pleaded with her. "Please, sit and enjoy dinner with me?"

Selia exhaled away her frustration as she flopped back into her seat. "Okay. But no more questioning my memories, got it? I've had enough confusion for the day."

Damien nodded. "I promise." He grabbed his fork and knife. "Well? Don't be shy. I hope you enjoy my cooking."

Selia grabbed her fork and dug in. The tangy tomato sauce exploded over her taste buds. She reached for her napkin and began to wipe the sauce away from her chin. "Do you cook often?" she stammered, setting her napkin down next to her half-demolished pasta.

"Not unless I'm entertaining, which tends to be centered around my family."

"Do you have a large family?"

"Clan Malloch is large. You should see us for our annual Christmas gathering." His gaze fell level with hers. "Do you keep in touch with your family?"

Selia shoved another forkful of pasta into her mouth, shaking her head from side to side.

Damien's expression became a soft one. "I'm guessing you have no memory of your family then, considering you don't remember past a decade."

Selia chose to ignore his question, focusing instead on the lovely feeling his cooking gave to her stomach. To her gratefulness, Damien took a heaping bite of his pasta and began to eat too.

The napkin on his forearm turned red.

Damien flexed his forearm, making the blood seep through the fabric. "Covering up a wound doesn't necessarily make it heal. It just makes it look better."

"That doesn't look any better," Selia teased. "If you can't see red, what does it look like?"

"Right now, a grey liquid mess." He set his fork down. "That's one of the many reasons I like watercolors. Color doesn't have to be present for you to paint something. You have to train your eye to see in lights and darks. The most captivating images manifest out of contrast between them."

"Like the moon and the sea?" Selia asked.

Damien's cheeks dimpled. "Precisely. Even the best watercolor artist can't cover up their mistakes. The unpredictable nature of water is what makes it so beautiful," he said, his gaze heavy on her again.

Selia shoved her fork back into her pasta, hoping he would stop giving her that heavy look. "Have you ever thought about exhibiting your work?"

"I have, although I don't feel my work is quite to that point yet."

"What's holding you back?"

"Nobody but me. An artist's biggest critic is themselves. I'm no stranger to that."

"When you came to Paris, I thought for sure you were going to ask about displaying your art at the museum."

Damien's eyes grew wide. "Do people do that? I thought the Louvre only displayed artwork for artists who were dead."

Selia shook her head. "The museum does display guest artists from time to time."

"I came to Paris for reasons other than my art," Damien said, smugness spreading into his smile.

They ate in silence, except for the occasional scrape of a fork against a plate.

In between bites, he found her gaze again. "When was your last date?"

"Date, as in coffee?"

Damien shook his head. "No—when is the last time a guy took you out and treated you to a good time?"

Selia shifted in her seat. "Define a good time."

"You know, dinner and dancing? And if he's lucky, a kiss thrown somewhere in there?"

Selia flushed. "I don't know what that's like at all."

"What about love letters?"

She shook her head.

"Not even holding hands?"

She looked into his hazel eyes, loving how they caught the reflection of the storm clouds rolling outside. "No, Damien. This is all new to me..."

The quizzical look of his made Selia's stomach fill with butterflies. Had she told him too much? A man's desire was as malleable as the woman he was pursuing. Flirting was another art that was new to her.

Maybe she could wait a little longer and see where the butterflies would settle.

"Where do you find your inspiration to paint?" Selia asked.

"Magical places. I imagine there aren't many places the fae haven't touched. Oceans, mountains." He looked up from his plate. "And of course, the human heart."

Selia eyed the artist who suddenly turned nostalgic across from her. "How long have you painted here at this studio by yourself?"

"A while."

"How long is a while?"

A lump moved in his throat. "Time blends together after so many years have gone by." His fork scraped his plate as he finished his dinner.

Selia didn't know if he was single or not. He could date a different woman every week, and nobody would know.

She set her fork down, crossing her hands gingerly in front of her. "Living all alone in this lovely beach side abode? I would think that a man would become lonely after a while."

"I have been lonely. In fact, I haven't, well..." he paused, his eyes drifting away again. "I've not had any real company in a long time."

Selia stared at him, wishing he wouldn't be so cryptic.

"Do you believe that blue memories can be forgotten?" he asked.

"I don't know. I've been blind to mine for so long."

"Painting is my way of escaping memories my heart refuses to let go."

"What memories are those?"

Damien shook his head, withdrawing his gaze. "Doesn't matter now. The past is the past. No use in trying to relive it."

"Escaping memories or not, the images here are much different from what you shared with me in your portfolio."

"How so?"

Selia gazed down the hallway, catching a silver strand of moonlight as it illuminated his ransacked studio. "Your paintings are raw with emotion. I *feel* something when I look at them."

"What do you feel?"

"I feel sad, but it's different than any sadness I've known. I feel empty, like I lost something dear to me."

Damien's five o'clock shadow caught the dim light from the kitchen. He had red in his facial hair. The same undertone of red threaded through his chestnut hair. "I guess according to you, these memories would be blue memories then?"

Selia shivered in the huskiness of his voice. "I guess that's up to how you see them."

He grabbed his plate. "You have been absolutely wonderful this evening, miss Selia." He took both of their plates and disappeared back into the kitchen.

At the sound of the kitchen tap, Selia's mind drifted out to the ocean.

What was it that Damien's heart wouldn't allow him to forget?

Damien returned at the table, his eyes glinting bright. "Are you ready to see if Amy's message was right about the moonlight?"

The clouds parted, and the moonlight had begun to show, casting the Celtic Sea in a misty halo.

Selia stepped out onto the beach, her bare toes gripping into the sand. For some strange reason she decided to go barefoot. She craved the texture of seashells, drift wood and sand beneath her feet.

Even with the dampness and the cold wind, the sun had warmed the sand. She had Damien strutting at her side, and she was sure that he would wrap her up in an embrace if she asked him.

He too had gone barefoot, mimicking her. He walked beside her in silence. The kind of quiet that was full of comfort and closeness. She imagined that he would be the kind of man to be able to hold that gait next to her forever, and not a word needed to escape his lips. Their silence was all the communication she needed.

Selia's toes shifted in the sand, dimpling into little mounds as she picked up her pace.

Damien slowed his pace, dropping behind her.

Selia slowed too, wondering what made him drop away from her.

He bumped into her from behind, his bare toes rubbing against her heels.

Selia stopped as his arms wrapped around her front, hands clasping over her navel. She sucked in a breath as he pressed himself against her back. Their bodies felt so natural together. Damien's comforting gravity was something in which she could easily become lost in.

Selia stepped away from his embrace, gathering herself instead in the light of the moon. A man's touch was so foreign and new. She didn't know if it was something she was ready to accept and embrace.

She held her arms out, bathing herself in the moonlight. She closed her eyes and dipped her head back, listening for anything that might help her out of this situation.

Discouragement fell like a stone in her gut. "Well?"

The wind picked up, hushing whatever reply Damien had.

"Is anything happening?" she asked. She felt a little silly out here talking to the darkness, acting like something magical would happen.

"Selia, you—"

She opened her eyes, finding Damien so close, he could have kissed her. The heat from his body wrapped around her, closing the space between them.

"—not even the moon can show how absolutely beautiful you are."

Selia had never been called beautiful by anyone before, at least that she remembered. Was there something invisible drifting out here in the salt-crusted air that had him transfixed? She shook her arms, hoping to persuade him not to look so fiercely into her eyes.

Damien moved behind her again. His hands fell to her torso, crossing over her navel. His belly pressed against her back, pulling her back into his comforting gravity once again.

Selia relaxed into his affection and protective warmth.

Damien's hands dropped, and Selia turned around to face him. Although she could have buried her heels into the sand and stayed like that until the sun rose.

"Cold?" he asked.

"A little."

Selia's heels sank into the sand as his weight combined with hers on the beach.

Damien took her hands into his. "I hope that I'm not being too upfront with you. It's just..." He shifted his feet in the sand. "Ever since I met you, I've had a difficult time reflecting on something."

"*Reflecting?*"

His brows furrowed as he took a firmer grip on her hands. "You've reminded me of what it means to remember in a truly different way." He brushed a lock of her hair out of her eyes. "I can't thank you enough for that."

She blinked, looking away from his gaze that asked for so much more.

Damien's face illuminated as a cloud parted from the moon. The silver light made his features much harder.

Something drifted past his cheek and vanished into her periphery.

Selia jolted. Something bumped against her ankle. A few hermit crabs swarmed at their feet.

Henrietta was there, her blue shell bobbing in front. She was the one leading this moonlit swarm of nocturnal activity down to the sea.

"Look," Selia said, shifting her toes away as a hermit crab attempted to scuttle over her foot.

"Where are they going?"

"Let's find out."

Down the swarm of crabs went, like most nocturnal marine invertebrates should. Whatever they were swarming after, it was hidden in the dark.

Selia's pulse raced as she and Damien followed the dozens, no, *hundreds* of little creatures flocking to the waves. What was making Henrietta behave this way?

"That's strange, why is the tide retreating like that?" Damien asked.

Selia looked to the horizon.

No water, but something else was rushing for her.

Moonlight came crashing toward the beach. Light and sea spray was now tunneling toward them.

She and Damien took off in a run for his cottage. The water caught her at the ankle and crashed over her head.

Selia closed her eyes and sucked in a breath as the wave of moonlight swallowed her.

8

BLUE REFLECTIONS

The crashing sound of waves echoed in Selia's salt nodes. A sound that was both distant and close at the same time. Her toes cramped in the cold frozen sand. The full moon shone on the horizon like a giant lonely orb drifting silently through the night.

The wave of moonlight that had tunneled toward the beach had vanished, evaporating back out to sea.

Selia reached out, searching for Damien's warm hand, touching nothing but cold air. "Damien?"

She spun around. Damien was nowhere. Fear rippled up her spine.

Had the wave of moonlight swallowed him?

She took off in search for any sign of him. If he had walked there, his footsteps had been erased by the sea. The only sound other than water lapping against the sand was the rhythm of her heartbeat.

Her breath puffed out in front of her as she picked up her pace, walking alongside the water. The entire seascape was cloaked in mist that swirled and spiraled out like tendrils of smoke. What made it so eerie is that she couldn't feel a breeze upon her skin. But she could taste the presence of salt.

Light flicked across the water, dancing and waving, reminding her of Damien's moonlit signature.

The light was coming from his studio.

Had the wave of moonlight carried her to an island somewhere out at sea?

There was something strange about the water lapping at her toes, sucking the sand away. The water had a strange film to it—almost like oil. This place, wherever she was, had *no* reflections, other than the threaded strands of silver moonlight. Blue was the only color that she could see reflecting off the water.

It seemed the water had swallowed any other reflections including her own, leaving nothing but blackness. She imagined this was how Damien saw the world—as a dream of endless waves, water and night.

She bent down to touch the water, which shimmered blue and silver.

Had the selkie salt skin come from this beautiful reflective place?

Blue lights appeared, dancing, then sinking.

She submerged her hand, trying to catch one of the lights as it fell through her fingers. She pressed her fingers to her lips, yet there was no bitter bite against her tongue.

The water lacked salt...

She stood up, shaking the silvery water from her fingers. The selkie salt skin couldn't have come from this body of water if it lacked salt, could it? Cold sand bled through her toes as she walked along the beach. She had to find a way to get back across the water to his studio. The further she walked, the more it felt like she was walking in one of Damien's gorgeous watercolor paintings.

Clouds drifted in front of the moon. Stars glittered in the ebony sky. A chilly breeze drifted across the water that seemed so flat, without light to reflect off its surface. What kind of water was this?

Spooked, she kept walking. Her footsteps, however, did not leave a trail behind her. Nobody would ever know that she'd walked here.

The sound of voices echoed off the ebony water. Who did they belong to? Spirits? Memories? She couldn't tell. This place seemed to play with light and shadows as though she was walking through a spell.

Selia slowed to a stop. The outline of an individual stood a few paces before her. The figure was so close, yet they didn't seem to notice her approach.

Should she say something?

The figure turned, and a curling lock of hair unraveled from their face. The ghostly individual had freckles that looked like starfish scattered across her cheeks.

"Amy!" Selia cried, but her friend did not turn to face her. Amy's hair wasn't the rippling red curtain of fire she remembered. The strands were dull and lifeless, drifting out from her shoulders like wisps of dying smoke.

"Amy, can you hear me?" Selia asked as she reached for her friend, but her hand passed through her.

Amy continued staring out at the water. Her eyes were transfixed on something invisible. Amy was not the flamboyant spirit Selia remembered.

Barely a glimmer of light touched her friend's youthful face. Even her freckles were faded. Her eyes were not green. They were colorless orbs of grey light that reflected the ebony water.

The Celtic Sea was a place Amy embodied. She was Amphitrite, goddess of the sea. Amy was full of magic and whimsy and wide-open spaces that brought her spirit to life. Now, Amy was a lost spirit with a look of failure dancing in her eyes.

Fssssbbbbbbbbbbbbb...

Wind whipped across the water's surface, forcing Selia to blink. Tendrils of fog drifted across the seascape.

Another figure appeared on the beach. A hooded figure with a cloak that snatched the freezing wind that threatened to strip the oxygen from Selia's chest.

The hooded figure approached Amy, who turned and looked right through her. "Where is the vault?" the figure asked, their voice raspy.

Amy's colorless eyes drifted from the cloaked figure back to the endless ebony sea. "It's hiding in a place the Order will *never* find."

Amy's voice was hauntingly still. It didn't sound anything like the trill Selia remembered. No sparkle of flirtation rang in her tone. The sound was like listening to someone who was struggling to breathe.

Selia's pulse raced. Why was Amy so weak?

The cloaked figure's hand twitched under the robe. With thin elongated fingers, they tugged out a small blue item.

Selia's heart leapt. Her salt trancing talisman!

The figure withdrew their hood, revealing their face. An Iridescent! This nymph who worked for the Order had short blond hair with hard pointed ends, matching Deidra's description. Her grey eyes shimmered with light hues of different colors one might see on an insect's wings. She had a small pointed nose and high cheek bones, angular and cutting against the dark horizon. Not a blemish existed on her porcelain skin.

There was one imperfection, however—a thin white scar on her upper lip.

The Iridescent held the talisman in her hand, the moonlit symbol at its center giving off its own blue aura. The three rippling lines below the spiral began to glow, casting her face in shimmering blue light. "I might not be able to hear the salt whisper like you can, but I know what you've attempted to have Selia do for you." She took a step toward Amy, the white scar on her upper lip twitching. "Let me guess. If she masters the art, she can rediscover a piece of herself?"

Amy didn't say anything. Even her skin appeared thinner. Places on her face where there should be color glistened little beads of perspiration.

The Iridescent took a step toward Amy, a gleam in her eye. "You believed that Selia would help you pick up where you failed, didn't you?"

Amy's eyes were luminous with liquid—was she crying? "I haven't failed yet, Alexandra."

A smirk appeared on the face of the nymph named Alexandra. "The Order will find the vault before Selia remembers any more. Not even the moonlight will be able to reveal what she has forgotten beneath the North Sea."

Forgotten beneath the *North* Sea?

Amy sneered at Alexandra. "You can't keep Selia in the dark forever."

"That's for the Order to decide. I will do everything in my power to make sure she lives up to her name. A nymph blind to her past will only ensure an end to your manipulative little game."

Amy's face contorted. "She's blind to a world that the Order has forbidden her to remember. You cannot deny a sea nymph the right to practice the art she was born to perfect." Amy's words were stolen by the wind. Her gaze was overpowered by the glowing blue aura pulsing from the talisman in Alexandra's hand.

Alexandra smirked. "That is where you are wrong. The Order can deny any nymph the right to practice any art that you, the great Amphitrite, have failed in your attempts to restore."

Selia's body trembled. Had she heard Alexandra right?

Amy was trying to restore the art?"

Thunder ripped overhead. Rain began to fall from the sky.

Thwop!

"No!" Selia cried, but Alexandra tossed her talisman into the sea, where it was snatched up by a wave.

Neither Alexandra nor Amy made any indication that she had spoken.

Something was concealed beneath the water, a vessel of some kind.

Was it the vault that Alexandra didn't want Selia to find?

Alexandra turned her back to Amy, her cloak catching the wind as it whipped across the sea. "The talisman is mine now. I'll use it to find the vault. All that stands between me and the fae treasure is a single strand of moonlight..."

Selia's heart leapt. *fae treasure*?

Alexandra walked toward the dark water, where she disappeared into the fog.

Selia's stomach hollowed. Amy had vanished too. Not even her footsteps lay in the sand.

The water began to rise toward her, a wave of dancing moonlight.

9
AMY'S MESSAGE

Selia's body tingled all over. Her fingers felt dry and gritty. Sunlight made the veins in her eyelids branch out, splintering like spider webs. The sound of waves crashed along the shore. She opened her eyes into the blaring golden rays of the rising sun.

Had she been out on the beach all night?

Something shifted over her arm, causing her to jolt upright. Henrietta was busy zig-zagging back and forth along the beach. Apparently, the little hermit crab had not left her side.

Next to her arm was a little pile of items she'd collected.

Selia picked up one of the items—a shimmering white pebble. She held it up to the sunlight. The rays filtered through a hole in the center, fragmenting the light into a rainbow.

Selia's stomach hollowed as her memory of what she'd seen manifested before her. Alexandra had thrown her salt trancing talisman into the sea. Lost to the waves, it was very unlikely she would ever see it again. She shuddered, remembering Alexandra's voice rippling over the reflection-less water, her accusation ringing.

Amy, restoring the art?

Selia shook her head. Whatever was inside of this vault, Amy had been fighting with this Alexandra over it.

"The talisman is mine to use now. I'll use it to find the vault. All that stands between me and the fae treasure is a single strand of moonlight..."

As her grogginess lifted and she came to her senses, Selia took in the surrounding sights on the beach. The last time she had salt tranced with Amy, she'd ended up on a beach just like this—dazed and confused—wondering if what she saw was a memory. Or if in fact what she'd seen was real at all.

Selia picked up another one of the pebbles Henrietta had gathered. She reached down and her finger scraped against something hard.

"Selia!"

She squinted into the sunlight, dazed by her name on the wind. The outline of a man raced against the horizon.

Damien tore over to her, dropping to the ground where she lay. He grabbed her around the middle, pulling her into his warmth. "I don't know *what* happened. We were both standing on the beach last night looking at the moon, and next I know it...I woke up in the middle of a sand dune of all places."

Selia reached her arms around his neck. "I'm so glad that you are okay."

Damien's heart pulsed against her chest. Grains of sand stuck to the side of his face. His hair was blown out, rebelling madly against the wind. Damien didn't look like the Damien she knew—he was as white as a ghost. The color had drained from his face, and his eyes were glossy.

He released his grip around her, sitting back onto the sand.

Selia sucked in a breath as the dying green flames in Amy's eyes flashed before her. "I saw something in the moonlight last night."

Damien's brow furrowed. "What do you mean you *saw* something?"

"Amy was there. So was the thief who broke into my office and stole my salt trancing talisman."

Damien's face twisted. "Amy was with someone from Gaia's Order? Why? What did they want with her?"

"Her name is Alexandra. She said specifically to Amy that she's using the talisman she stole from me to track down the vault."

"Vault? What vault?"

Selia's hand shifted in the sand where Henrietta had been piling seashells.

Her fingernail scratched across something hard.

Now she knew what Henrietta was trying to dig out of the sand—something had washed ashore.

Selia and Damien dug into the sand, shoveling sodden handfuls to the side.

"What on earth?" Damien said.

Selia's fingers ached from all the sand-shifting. They had unearthed a chest. Constructed of wood and metal, the chest had been warped by salt water and time. The edges bowed in, giving it a shrunken appearance.

Together, they hoisted the dripping chest out of the sand and walked back to Damien's art studio.

"Whatever is inside of this thing better be worth it," Damien stammered as they jostled up the sand dunes.

With each step they took, it felt like the chest was becoming heavier. Selia's arms gave out, and she dropped the chest in the sand before the front door.

Damien let go of the chest and crossed his arms. He dug his bare feet into the sand. Brows drawing up into his wind-blown hair, his eyes landed on the treasure the sea had brought in. "Where do you think it came from?"

Selia dropped to her knees and wiped the sand away from the barnacle-crusted lid.

Salt-crusted words shone back at her, reading:

Amy's Ocean Apothecary

"Oh, wow..."

"What is it?" Damien asked, kneeling down next to her.

Selia's pulse raced. "Something from Amy…" She fumbled with a seashell-shaped lock on the front.

Henrietta raced up to them both, more whimsy in the crab than Selia had ever seen before. She shimmied up to the lock, dug her claw into the keyhole and with a *click*, it broke open.

Selia grabbed the lid of the chest and forced her weight into it. With a metallic *screeeeeeeeech*! the hinges buckled, and the chest flipped open.

Fwwwwissshhhhooooooo…

Selia's hair blew out as a wind stirred from within the chest, which was surprisingly dry. The entire thing was full of seashells. She reached into the chest, shifting the shells away. A shiny glass bottle glinted beneath them. She continued to sift the shells aside, finding more bottles at the bottom.

"What are they?" Damien asked.

"Salt extracts!" Selia cried. She continued to shift through the bottles, each no larger than her pinky finger. They were slippery with sea water, and gripping them was proving difficult. Three bottles total, each a different color and shape. First came a short purple one with a bulbous body that reminded her a little of a sea urchin. Next came a skinny green one that mimicked the shape of a pipefish snout. Last came a red one, with a spiraling body that could have been the trailing tentacles of a jellyfish. "Take these," she said, jumbling the slippery bottles into Damien's hands. "There is something else down here." Sticking out of a larger seashell was a damp piece of paper. Selia grabbed the paper and unfolded it, finding a string of cursive handwriting at the bottom.

Dear Selia,

By the time you find this message, I will have traveled north. Alexandra has already set out to track down the vault.

"It's a message from Amy!" Selia cried.

"The sea sorceress?" Damien asked, edging closer.

"She's searching for a vault."

Damien's' eyebrow arched. "What's the *vault*?"

Selia's eyes dipped back to Amy's letter.

The fae gifted us the art of salt trance long ago. I've been working to restore the art to its original purpose for centuries. Like you, I am struggling with my memory. I cannot remember why sea nymphs should practice the art, or why it was gifted to us in the first place.

I thought that finding the salt trancing talisman would help me to uncover secrets about the art, but it has done me no good at all. Now it has gotten us both into trouble with the Order.

I have given you three salt extracts from my Ocean Apothecary. I trust you to practice the art of salt trance on your own. It's up to you to use them to locate the vault. Breath, memory, and salt can do magical things if you trust your heart. To understand their magic, I need you to help me locate a fae treasure inside the vault that connects them.

Be warned. Salt extracts are fickle. They are living, breathing things, and you must treat them as such. Some tend to be more seductive

than others. Trust your instincts. Put your
heart before your mind. I know for a fact that
what's inside the vault will help you remember
everything the Order has tried to keep from
you.

Your Celtic Sea Sorceress,
Amy

P.S.
Use the strands of moonlight to help you track
down the fae treasure. The selkie salt skin
will come in handy once you begin to practice.

"Is forgetfulness something that happens to all sea nymphs, or just you two?" Damien asked.

"She doesn't remember the purpose of the art? That can't be good at all," Selia replied. "I knew that Amy's memory wasn't that great, but I didn't know it was as bad as mine." She scanned the sentence again. "Alexandra said, all that stands between her and finding the fae treasure is a single strand of moonlight."

Selia and Damien locked eyes.

Damien's mouth dropped open.

"The three bottles are named after the three strands of moonlight! Breath, memory, and salt!"

"Well, now. You *were* on to something." Damien's eyebrows disappeared into his hair. "That's crazy. I always thought the Strands of Moonlight were just folktales, but a *real* fae treasure?"

Selia's pulse flooded her ears with a rhythm she didn't think her heart was capable of creating.

"Well? It's settled then." Damien said as he stood. He held out his hand. "We're off to Scotland."

"Why Scotland?" Selia asked, taking his hand and standing next to him.

"According to Amy's letter, the strands of moonlight will help you track down this fae treasure. My aunt has the entire *collection* of the folktales that illustrate this moon magic." He propped his hands on his hips. "Well? Are you up to making a visit to my homeland?"

Selia's stomach warmed. She'd never been to Scotland before. One look in Damien's eyes was all it took for her to want to know more about the land where fairy tales were practically born.

PART 2
MOON MAGIC

10

TO SCOTLAND

The sky was swollen with rain and thunder as Selia packed her belongings and left with Damien for the train station late that morning. She was energized by the negative ions drifting in the air. They had a treasure to find, a *fae* treasure that would hopefully uncover secrets about the art of salt trance.

She stopped along the sandy section of the path that would lead back out to the beach. Her purse shifted under her arm quite violently.

"Did you forget something?" Damien asked. He tilted his face toward the sky as the clouds crackled with an ominous roll of thunder.

"I'll be right there," Selia said as she waved Damien along to the train station.

She bent down next to a patch of dune grass to let Henrietta out of her purse. Amy's pet launched herself out onto the sand, where she wiggled her shell and made a few circles. Selia wasn't the only one antsy about getting this treasure hunt started. "All right, back in you go, little one. We have a long journey ahead of us," Selia said, tipping her purse toward Henrietta.

Henrietta dove back in and Selia shouldered her purse. She was a little more convinced now that Henrietta was really a fae creature in disguise. Amy's pet had an intuition about things like most sea creatures, including the weather and the timing of the tides.

Selia spotted Damien as he waved her down. Two train tickets flopped in his hand. She followed him through the station and onto the train platform. Henrietta's vigorous motions in her purse finally stopped. She hoped the little crab would settle down and nap for most of their journey north.

Damien bustled ahead of her to find them seats on the crowded train. Selia's legs were so antsy that sitting would do her not good at all. She gave in and sat next to him, remembering the other treasures sitting in the depths of her purse.

She reached her hand down into her bag and shifted a dozing Henrietta aside. The cool surface of glass brushed past her fingers as she shifted through the treasures. *Four* bottles—the first being the bottle Damien had rescued from the fountain in Paris. The selkie salt skin bottle had a shiny collection of blue memory salt crystal from her first attempt salt trancing with him.

A twinge of anxiety struck Selia's stomach. Whatever was inside the vault was going to help Amy restore the art. Why was she restoring it?

And why did Amy insist that Selia keep the selkie salt skin a secret?

As the train hummed along, Selia tugged out one of the three salt extracts Amy had sent along to her in the treasure chest. None of them were labeled with anything other than a blank piece of parchment that wrapped around each bottle's skinny neck. The sooner she and Damien could find the folktales his aunt had, the sooner she could begin using them to help track down this fae treasure Amy needed.

One of the bottles had started to develop an odor. The second had an oozy substance with the constancy of molasses. Its smell was quite pungent, and she resorted to wrapping it up in a scarf. And the third? She was sure there was nothing inside of it, other than a few crystallized chunks of sea salt.

Selia was not a sea sorceress like Amy. She didn't have an Ocean Apothecary like her either. She felt like a child, who had been given her first dose of cough medicine, and not knowing if it would make her better or more ill.

While she had contemplated how to use the three bottles to help her find this fae treasure, Damien had been busy turning a blank piece of paper from his journal into a work of art. "What are you sketching?" she asked.

"I'm trying to get an idea of what this minca kelp looked like." His pencil drifted in long sweeping motions across the paper. "Apart from being blue, what do you know about it?"

"Very little, actually."

"Do you know how it moved in the water?"

"It looked more like smoke, that's for sure."

"Sea smoke—got it. And where do you think this blue minca lived?"

"I'd think somewhere deep in the ocean. From what Amy told me about the kelp, it liked cold places and didn't need sunlight."

"No?"

"Minca was a lunar species of kelp. It used moonlight to photosynthesize."

Damien continued to sketch. In the amount of time it took for the train to leave the station, he had created a masterpiece.

Selia peeked over Damien's shoulder. He started a list of fae species, which he'd separated into two types: flora and fauna. Minca was listed under flora. Below the fauna were gnomes, pixies, fairies and sprites. At the bottom were selkies, which he had drawn a heart next to. "You have a magical talent. Do you know that?"

"How many species of fae do you think there are?" he asked.

"Enough to make my head hurt. Why, are you journaling about them?"

"That's what us artists do. We use our imaginations when we don't have any proof of what we're illustrating." His eyes drifted up to hers, then back to his journal. "Every once in a while, I return to Scotland to gather some inspiration on the fae. It never hurts to immerse yourself in their invisible world. You never know what you might miss seeing."

"Should I expect to see fairies when we arrive?"

"Auntie has a few choice words for the fae that inhabit her garden."

Selia stifled a laugh. "Your Auntie sounds like a character."

His cheeks dimpled. "Oh boy, you're in for a treat..."

Soon their train arrived at the city of Cherbourg-en-Cotentin. The English Channel was the body of water separating France from England. Selia grabbed her luggage and left the train with Damien. Their next method of transportation came into view.

Docked outside the train was a massive ferry. Seagulls swooped over the line of people waiting to board.

"How long has it been since you've been home to Scotland?" Selia asked as they got in line to board the ferry.

Damien shook his head. "Much too long. You should have heard how excited Auntie was when she heard I was coming home and that I was bringing someone with me who believes in fairies."

Selia's step fell short on the loading ramp and she nearly tripped. "You told her that I believe in *what*?"

Damien wrapped his arm around her waist, catching her before she fell. "In fairies," he replied nonchalantly, as though discussing fairies was a normal thing.

"Wait just a minute. I'll have you know that I've never seen a fairy in my life, nor do I know if such things exist."

"How can you be searching for a fae treasure and not believe in fairies?"

Selia sucked in a sharp breath as she struggled not to yell something argumentative towards him. She unraveled herself from his grip. "You think this is funny, don't you?"

Damien shot her a hurt sort of look. "Are you saying that fairies aren't real?"

"I didn't say that. I just haven't seen one before."

He waggled his finger at her. "But you implied it. Don't say anything like that to my Auntie, or you'll have a garden gnome chasing after you."

Selia smirked. "Do *you* believe in fairies, Mr. Malloch?"

"Many people still do in Scotland."

"You completely ignored my question," she huffed.

Damien tapped his temple. "Being that I only see the color blue, I see the world a little differently than most."

Selia led the way to the back of the boat where there weren't as many people. "I'm going to grab some late lunch. Do you want anything?"

Damien shook his head. "I'll wait until I'm back on land." He patted his belly. "Sometimes I get a bit sea sick."

Selia walked to the concession stand and grabbed a pretzel. While the water wasn't choppy, she didn't want to over eat for fear of becoming sea sick like Damien had mentioned. She retrieved her phone from her purse. Deidra's text messages had gone quiet, for now.

Damien set up shop on one of the benches overlooking the back of the ferry. The massive propellers churned against the water, creating clouds of sea spray. Selia walked over to him, suddenly sheepish. He was twirling the blue paintbrush she'd discovered in his art studio. Who had given him that brush? Maybe she could spy on him and see what other paintings he was hiding from her. She was starting to think his trip to Paris was really an excuse to see her, not gather her critique like he stated.

No, that's what she wanted to think. She wanted to believe that an incredibly attractive artist somewhere in his thirties had come gallivanting into Paris to pursue her. He had intended on showing her his artwork, however, with the Order stealing the talisman, this adventure to Scotland seemed a bit whimsical to say the least.

She tucked her phone back into her purse. "Ouch!" She yelled, tugging her hand back out. Apparently Amy's pet didn't like her sticking her hand anywhere close to the salt extracts, which she'd stuffed her little shell against.

Damien looked up from his journal and waved her over.

Selia walked up to him, stopping at his side. The wind had tousled his thick hair, making the ends spike. "Painting another masterpiece, I see?" she said, although the paper in his journal didn't have a splotch of pigment on it.

He waggled the blue brush in front of her. "Not me, *you* get to paint today."

Selia nearly dropped her pretzel. "Oh, no. I'm not an artist."

Damien chuckled. "What else were we going to do to pass the time? Play with your angry little hermit crab?"

Selia shook her pinky finger, which was still throbbing. She took a seat next to Damien, taking the last bite of her pretzel and swallowing. "I'll give it a try, but no promises."

Damien reached into his bag, tugging out a watercolor palette and set it between them. "I promise the color won't be difficult to choose."

Selia grabbed the metal lid and flipped it open. "Wow, I've never seen so many different kinds of blue!"

Damien handed her a spray bottle. "Go on, give them a good mist."

Selia took the spray bottle, dousing the pigments with water.

Damien reached into his bag again, this time pulling out a handful of brushes. "Here is Angular Atlantic. And this one is Patchy Pacific. Oh, don't forget the Angry Arctic."

"You named your brushes after the oceans?" she asked, handing him back the spray bottle.

"Of course. All seven of them are needed when I work on a seascape. I have a few extras in here too." Damien tucked the spray bottle back into his bag and began rummaging in it again. His knee brushed against hers as he straightened himself. He scooted closer, closing the space between their hips. "Why don't you give the North Sea a try?" he said, holding the brush out in front of her.

Selia didn't want to grab the brush. She wanted to grab a handful of his windblown hair and straighten it. "The North Sea isn't one of the seven seas."

"No, but I can promise you the body of water surrounding my homeland has an imagination of its own."

She held the North Sea brush in front of her, having no idea what to do next. She was more focused on how close they were sitting together, and how Damien's leg was now glued against hers.

He tapped his foot, seeming to wait for her to answer.

Selia stared at the blank piece of paper in his hand, suddenly paralyzed. What on earth should she paint?

"I'm going to teach you a basic splatter technique, okay?" Damien said, grabbing the Angry Arctic brush and holding it parallel to her North Sea brush.

"Right," Selia replied, nerves settling into her gut. What if she made a complete fool of herself?

"Pick your pigment and lather up the bristles."

Selia did so, dipping her brush into the blue pigment at the center of his palette.

"Close your eyes," Damien said.

"Why?"

"You had me close my eyes when you practiced the art of salt trance."

"Okay, but only if you insist," she said, closing her eyes.

Damien's warm hand came to her wrist, helping her to position the brush over the paper. "Now, on the count of three, flick your wrist. Ready?"

Selia nodded.

"One, two…" Damien's voice was dangerously close to her ear. "When I say three, tell the water what you want it to show you."

Selia sucked in a breath and exhaled, flicking the brush forward.

"Three!"

She opened her eyes, finding the splatter had created a beautiful winged creature. "No way did I paint that."

Damien's hand withdrew into his coat pocket.

"You cheated!" Selia said.

Damien's face twisted. "What, me? No, you painted that."

Selia blinked a few times. Her eyes had to be deceiving her. "What is *that*, exactly?"

"Something I've seen since the day I met you. They hover around you like an aura."

"The blue lights you believe are fairies?"

Damien nodded. "I knew the moment I saw the lights fluttering around you I knew that you were not a normal woman." He grabbed the North Sea brush from her and set it back into his bag with the others. He withdrew a sketch pad and a couple of pencils. "While your painting is drying, why don't I warm up with a few sketches?"

"Of what?"

Quicker than a magician could draw a wand he held up the pencil. "Strike a pose."

"Oh, no."

"Don't be shy. I'm going to do a quick sketch of you."

Selia froze. In all the years she'd worked at the Louvre, she'd never had an artist request to sketch her before. What should she do?

"Stand in front of the puddle," he said, pointing at the ground.

Selia got up from her seat and stood in front of the puddle. She held her hands to her side, then her hips, then crossed her arms. She couldn't decide what pose would be best. She glanced down at the puddle, horror-struck. Did she really look that exhausted? Maybe she should have worn eye-liner to make the sleep-deprived bags under her eyes less prominent.

She looked up, finding Damien marveling at her. He angled his pencil. "Perfect. I got you!"

A soda can went rolling past her foot and down the boat. It was the perfect distraction for her to evade his artistic eye.

Selia walked after the soda can, squatting down to pick it up.

"What bloody time is it?" a man grumbled from a few paces down the ferry. He wore a black jacket over a tattered pair of jeans. His fingernails were smudged with something dark.

"Why do I care what time it is?" grumbled a man next to the other. He was dressed just like his buddy. The back of his black jacket had a massive boat anchor on it.

Fishermen, perhaps?

"We're going to get in trouble if we aren't back to the port in time," the first man said.

"I'm not about to shorten my vacation just because Alex wants us there by tomorrow."

Henrietta, however, would have none of this standby and watch attitude Selia had adopted. Her ink-drop eyes inched to the opening of Selia's purse, from which she promptly launched herself.

"No!" Selia said, reaching for the projectile hermit crab in vain. She'd already scurried out of reach. Henrietta's little shell hustled with an alarming pace toward the two giant fishermen.

"Where is Alex, anyway?" the first man grumbled, tossing his bulky hands in the air.

"Hell, if I know," his buddy replied. "I'm tired of playing this game. I'll search for pirate booty any day. But this fishing gig isn't like anything I worked on. It's like she wants us to net for some bloody fairy treasure or something."

Selia's ears perked. "*Fairy treasure?*"

"I don't give a rat's ass about finding it anymore. I'm only going to collect my pay, then I'm heading back to France. The beaches are so much better than the ones we have up this—" He stopped, his eyes dipping down to where Henrietta was brandishing her claws at him. "Blimey, what a stupid little creature you are."

Selia's body froze as he lifted his massive boot over Henrietta's shell.

"Oi, look!" His buddy cried.

The other fisherman slammed down his boot as Henrietta seemed to blow out of the way.

Selia darted over to where the wind had swept her off her little legs. Her shell rolling and rolling.

"Don't you ever do that again!" Selia said, scolding the crab as she tilted her shell into her purse.

The two men walked out of earshot.

Damien walked toward her. "What was that all about?"

Movement caught Selia's eye. A woman was standing alone at the edge of the ferry, overlooking the water. Curls of rebellious red hair coiled behind her as fog cloaked around her body.

Selia's stomach hollowed as she stood up.

Amy...

II
TRAVELING NORTH

A my's apparition vanished.

Selia ran to the edge of the ferry, gripping the cold metal railing in her trembling hands. "Amy..." she whispered, and her own voice was drowned out by the churning rhythm of the ferry's metal propellers as they sliced through the water like a knife would butter.

Damien's hand came to her arm. "What did you say?"

"Amy," she repeated. "I saw her." She turned to face him.

Damien's brows slashed. "You're *sure* you saw her?" He set his hand on her forehead. "Are you feeling okay?"

Selia's fingers trembled. "It's like there is something in the corner of my eye," Selia said, blinking as that brilliant blue light went darting once again through her periphery.

The jostling sound of people's footsteps cluttered in her ears. Damien wrapped his arm around her, but his affection did little to dull that aching sensation that was building behind her eyes.

"What do you think caused this reaction?" Damien asked, his other arm wrapping around her.

"I don't know," she stammered, her hands now cramping with cold. What was happening to her?

Damien gave her a tight squeeze. "Let's get you off this boat."

The ferry's engine came to a grinding metallic halt.

"Docking in Portsmouth!" A man cried.

As passengers began to make their way toward the exit, Selia clung to the railing. It felt like the ground had been ripped out from beneath her feet. She searched over the hull where that wild windswept look of the curly red hair disappeared.

She *had* seen Amy, right?

Selia and Damien grabbed a bus that would take them to the train station. Each pothole the wheels jumbled over felt like torture. Selia closed her eyes, hoping the spontaneous nausea would subside. Bad idea. Closing her eyes made the blue lights darting in and out of her periphery worse.

The bus jolted, shaking her luggage loose from the overhead compartment.

"I'll get it," Damien said, standing up.

While he was busy rearranging their luggage, Selia grabbed his watercolor journal that had fallen from his seat, thumbing to a page with Damien's handwriting on it. Maybe looking over his beautiful paintings would make those blue lights go away.

Sophie, I will always love you.

Selia's stomach took a much deeper dive. Just who was this *Sophie* he had written about? Heart thundering, she flipped the page, finding more of his cursive handwriting on the other side. Before she could read it, Damien was already making his way back to his seat.

"That was fun," Damien said, taking a seat next to her.

Selia handed his journal back to him. "You almost lost this."

"You feeling any better?" Damien asked.

Selia couldn't look him in the eye. Was he writing a love letter to another woman? What if he had a girlfriend on the side?

"All the time on that ferry has made me antsy," she replied, desperately wanting to put some distance between them.

The bus pulled up to the Portsmouth Harbour Railway Stations. Selia got up first, grabbing her bag and bustling off the bus. Of course Damien would have a secret girlfriend. She was probably the one who'd given him that blue paintbrush he'd lost!

She focused on the flock of tourists, hoping the busy crowd would help her stifle her jealousy. With each step she took, the blue lights in her periphery began to subside. Thank goodness she had some sense of reality again. However, the new reality about this *Sophie* still made her stomach uneasy. Why hadn't he mentioned anything about this other woman he still loved?

"Hold up," Damien said, brushing up beside her. He scanned the electric sign displaying train departures. "Looks like we made it for the last train to Arbroath for the day. I'll get us tickets." He walked over to the ticket booth.

Selia stared at the crowd of people, wishing those strange blue lights would stop darting in and out of her periphery. Like shadows, they would blend and shift, making her dizzy. Her salt nodes were both throbbing now, and the pain behind each forceful pulse began to thunder in her head. No, it was real thunder overhead now, she was just confusing her pain for what the weather was preparing to unleash.

Crack!

A ripple of lightning spread its yellow-white fingers through the sky.

Henrietta wiggled her way to the top of Selia's purse, shoving Amy's journal to the top.

A trail of fluid writing appeared on the paper.

`In case hallucinations arise, resort to the purple bottle first.`

Selia almost dropped the journal as another thunderhead boomed above. While Damien was busy purchasing their train tickets, she found her way over to a paper stand and began shifting through her bag.

The purple bottle...*drat*!

What if she'd left it on the ferry?

Frantic, she began to backtrack her way to the boat that was preparing to its return voyage to France. A little shiny flicker caught her eye. She'd dropped the bottle, all right, and it was now dangling above a metal grate that guarded the sewer.

Henrietta, however, was already on hot pursuit of the soon-to-be-history bottle. Scurrying along the slick cobblestones she went, unfazed by any humans hurrying past her. It had rolled down the path and ended up at the feet of the two fishermen, who were no longer arguing.

Selia's hair stood on end as a third body appeared—one much shorter than the two men. The individual wore a long black robe that fell to her ankles. Short blond hair tapered behind her ears, which were slightly pointed.

It was Alexandra.

"Oi, Alex," one of the men said as he rounded his shoulders.

Apparently, the men called her Alex for short.

"What the hell took you two so long?" Alex asked, stepping between them. Both men stepped sideways, allowing her much more space than her small frame needed. "Well, where is it?"

One of the men punched the shoulder of the other, dislodging something from his coat pocket.

Alex bent down, reaching for what had fallen inches away from the purple glass glinting at her feet. "This is all you have?" Alexandra said, grabbing what had fallen—a crumpled pack of cigarettes. "I'm docking your pay," she boasted, turning on her heel and sending the bottle flying.

"Meet me at the pub in Scotland tomorrow morning." Alex walked in the opposite direction of the men, who both walked up the path for the train station.

Selia walked over to where the purple salt extract had almost been destroyed. She picked it up, along with stubborn little Henrietta, who had almost been smashed twice now.

She walked back up to the platform, finding Damien.

"Alexandra is here!"

Damien's eyes widened. "Did she take the train?"

"No," Selia said, wishing she knew where Alex had gone. "But Gaia's Order is also heading to Scotland."

Damien walked up to her. "Was she alone?"

"No," Selia said, shaking her head. "Two other men, I overheard them arguing on the boat about some fairy treasure."

Damien's brow furrowed. "Well then. It appears we have some competition to find this treasure." He grabbed her hand. "Come on. We're not going to let them find it first."

Damien led the charge down to the train platform. The diesel fumes spewing from the locomotive had been doused by the torrential rain shower, and the aroma didn't make her quite as queasy.

They found a lone compartment near the center of the train which they claimed as their own. "Here," he said. He tossed something fluffy and warm at her before closing the compartment door with him on the other side.

The moment the door clicked closed, Selia stripped from her outfit. Her sodden blouse, leggings and even her socks were tossed into a pile on the floor. Shivering, she tugged on a new base-layer of clothes that could also serve as something comfy to sleep in. Right now, she needed something to wick that moisture away from her skin long enough for her to warm up.

She grabbed the fluffy warm garment Damien had tossed onto the seat. Her fingers pressed into the loveliest soft fabric she'd ever felt before. She buried her face into Damien's lovely scent; the familiar earthy musk that seemed to follow him everywhere. Was it his normal aroma? She didn't know, but she felt a set of eyes peeking in through a crack in the door.

Damien moved into their compartment and shut the door behind him, blocking off the noisy chatter of other passengers on board.

Selia's body seized. The purple bottle—where had she put it?

She shoved her hand down into her bag, finding that Henrietta had curled her little body up against all three bottles that Amy had given her. "I'm all right, just a bit rattled." She looked outside the window, watching the town disappear. "How long before we reach Scotland?"

Damien sighed. "About ten hours. I guess the good thing is we can sleep through most of it."

Selia finally surrendered to her aching feet and sat down on the cushion seat.

Damien sat down next to her.

She ran her hand through the sweater he lent her, finding a small metallic item the size of a coin lodged in the fabric. "What's this?"

"Bottle cap I found outside the train station. Seems like a brew I'd like to try."

"The Rusty Selkie?" Selia said, reading off the words on the cap. She reached into her pocket, tugging out the silver coin she'd found in Damien's art studio.

The two looked similar. If there had been an anchor on the bottle cap, it had been scuffed off.

Metal screeched below them as the train began moving. Selia pocketed the bottle cap and the coin.

"I take it you're not hungry?" Damien asked.

"Not in the slightest," she said, her thoughts taking her to the purple bottle Henrietta had risked her life to find. She ran her hand over her stomach, which rumbled in protest. She was hungry, in truth. But after all of the strange things she'd seen and heard over the past twenty-four hours, she needed sleep more than food.

"Let's get some rest. We have a long night ahead of us," Damien said, tugging out a blanket from below their seat and tugging it up over them both.

It wasn't long before Damien was dozing in his seat, leaving Selia alone to fester with her thoughts. Rain pelted the window as the train drifted north.

Henrietta was not ready to bed down for the evening. She jostled once again out of Selia's purse, shifting the bottles she'd been guarding to the opening. Selia's hallucinations had disappeared, for now. She did not know how long it would be before the strange blue lights darted in and out of her periphery once again.

She tucked the journal, bottles and little Henrietta back away into her purse, finding Damien's hand had shifted sideways against her hip. An artist's hands were such a lovely thing. She found herself wanting to thread her fingers through his and drift off into the dream of whatever seascape he was experiencing.

She shook that fantasy out of her mind, grabbing a hold of the blanket instead and tugging it over her. As she began to doze, memories of the day drifted like transparent shadows before her. An ocean storm was heading towards her.

What was Amy really up to? Would she find the vault before Gaia's Order did?

She could have sworn that she saw Amy running beside the train. Her red hair gripped the wind, rebelling against sheets of rain as she disappeared into the storm brewing over the North Sea.

12
AUNTIE BERTHA

Pale morning light branched damp, luminous fingers through their train car window. Selia's consciousness emerged from a deep dream. Pieces of that dream floated in front of her, a mixture of Damien sitting on the beach with his easel and brushes facing the sea. Only it wasn't the sea he was painting—he was painting the nude female figure of the sea goddess, Amphitrite.

"Sophie, I love you," Damien whispered toward the water.

Amy's green eyes flickered with a seductive green flame. Her rebellious red hair uncoiled from her shoulders, dancing in the wind. She held her arms out to her sides and began to chant something Selia couldn't understand. A wall of sea water thundered over Amy, swallowing both her and Damien.

Selia's legs were engulfed by the wave, locking her in the sand. Damien's watercolor brushes drifted past her ankles. She bent down, grabbing the blue brush she remembered finding in her salt trance with him.

Written on the handle were two words: *Blind Moon*

Selia shook the dream from her head. The annoying blue lights were dancing in her periphery once again. Damien wasn't sitting next to her, nor was he in their train compartment.

Damien's watercolor journal sat next to her.

Selia's fingers itched to know. What other lovely words had he written in there about this mysterious woman named Sophie?

She grabbed the journal and opened to the back where she'd seen the message.


```
My dear Sophie,
Blue was your favorite color, and it will
always be mine. I will always love you until
the end of time.
```


Selia's stomach clenched. Was Damien writing poetry for another woman?

The compartment door shifted open. Selia tossed his journal back to his seat.

Damien walked inside the compartment holding two cups of coffee in his hands. "Rough night?"

Selia's face burned with heat. "You could say that."

He walked over to her. "If you're like me, life doesn't begin until the black stuff hits my lips." He held out both hands. "What can I get my lady? Latte, or cappuccino?"

Selia looked past the coffee, locking her gaze with the artist who was lying to her. "What do you think your girlfriend would want?"

Damien's ears turned pink. "Are you my girlfriend now?"

"No, that's not what I said," she flustered, grabbing whatever drink was in Damien's left hand and took a swig.

"I wouldn't be opposed to you being my girlfriend."

Selia nearly spat out her drink. So he wanted to date *two* women at the same time? She tossed her coffee into the trash. "It's cold," she stammered, grabbing her luggage from the overhead compartment.

"Selia, what's going on?"

Selia grabbed her luggage and bustled out of the train compartment. So much for Scotland being the land where fairy tales were born. This was a place where men got to run away with a different girl for the weekend and act like it was normal.

"Hey, what's wrong? Was it the girlfriend comment?" Damien asked as he followed her off the train.

Selia stopped where the platform met the road. "I'm feeling ill from all of the travel. Can we please get going to your aunt's place?"

They caught a cab, which took them from town out into the rolling hills of the Scottish countryside. Groves of heather dotted the greenery, turning the landscape a beautiful mauve.

The little town of Dundee went whizzing by. On her right, there were rocky cliffs with the North Sea beyond. To her left, more hills as the Scottish countryside rolled inland. "Where are we headed?"

"Just north of Arbroath," Damien replied. "My Auntie has a small patch of land not far from the North Sea."

The road curved, and tires ground into dirt as the road transitioned from pavement. Soon, the car came to a stop.

Damien paid the driver and helped Selia out of the car. Her boots hit soggy damp ground. The cab returned to the road, leaving Selia to stand with Damien alone in an awkward silence.

The silence in Scotland was very much alive. The sounds of nature were stirring here, whispering little songs. The spirits of the earth, wind and sky were celebrating something important but invisible to the naked eye.

Damien's demeanor had changed in the few seconds that Selia took to absorb the new space. Since her heels had struck the damp earth of his homeland, she noticed how rounded his shoulders became.

Selia sucked in a deep breath, loving the cool humidity that dominated the atmosphere. While there weren't any trees, the landscape was incredibly full of foliage. What appeared to be a thousand different shades of green surrounded her feet. There were grasses, and beneath them mosses and lichens, that all clumped to the surface of stones and pebbles.

The Scottish countryside was absolutely gorgeous.

"Ready to find the folktales?" Damien asked as he motioned at the stone pathway that led to a grove of bushes. A string of white mushrooms lined the path, increasing the apparent plausibility that gnomes inhabited the field.

"I'm ready whenever you are," Selia replied, sinking her heels further into the ground.

Damien blew out his cheeks, making his already red ears even more prominent. He turned to face her, squaring his hips. "This whole girlfriend thing's got me thinking. Truth is, I haven't dated anyone seriously in a very long time."

"We're dating now?"

Damien's already pink ears turned darker. "Right, well. I figured with all of the discussion about your life—my life, and well—"

"A grown man doesn't live by himself for ten years painting waves alone in a beach shack and not have at least *someone* he's serious with," she spat, crossing her arms in front of her chest. Jealousy did wicked things to one's gut. The dream she'd had of him painting drifted into her mind. Was she jealousy of Amy now? "You don't have any girlfriends on the side, now do you?"

Damien's eyes didn't drift away. They stayed locked with hers. "No."

Selia's mouth twisted. *Sophie,* she wanted him to say. His watercolor journal had another woman's name in it.

Damien reached out, touching one of Selia's hands. "The only girl in my life right now is the one standing in front of me looking like she either wants to kill me, or kiss me." His eyes dropped to her lips. "Which one is right?"

Selia's arms began to relax. How could he so easily unravel her from her jealous knot? She tugged her arms tighter around her center, preventing him from touching her hand. "I feel like you aren't telling me something."

Damien's shoulders rose and fell. "It's just—ah, bugger." He ran his fingers through his thick hair, making it curl out wildly at the ends. "I've been playing it over and over in my head just how I'm going to introduce you to my aunt."

"What's to be nervous about?"

Damien sighed, dropping his hand back to his side. "She will be into our business quicker than a fly on a Highland cow patty in the middle of summer. She'll want to know what *you* and *I* are all about. But more than that, she'll want to know what our business is with the folkales."

Selia smirked. She liked this challenge. She was completely naive to think that this handsome man had lived alone for almost a decade, blissfully single in his art studio painting watercolor portraits of waves until *she'd* come along. "Your aunt can't be that bad."

"Oh, you haven't met her yet." Damien took a step forward, closing the space between them. His hazel eyes met hers, looking greener and sweeter in the overcast daylight. "Well? Girlfriend, or not?"

Selia dropped her hands. "I'll be your girlfriend. But remember, the folktales are what I'm here for first, then you. Got it?"

Damien's cheeks dimpled. "Understood."

Before she could take a step, Damien picked her up and hiked her over his shoulder.

"Hey, put me down!" she yelled, her voice breaking into a laugh.

"I'm carrying my new girlfriend off to the Highlands to have my way with her!" he boasted, then took off in a lumbering sprint through the meadow.

Whatever jealousy she still had in her gut was soon replaced with a fit of laughter. She was suddenly enveloped in his gravity. His strength. His creative spontaneity. These were all things that made Damien so wonderful.

When her gut could take no more, he slowed his pace and stopped. When he did set her down, she found herself not wanting to unravel her arms from his neck and spent an extra moment making an excuse to lean on him. "That was the first time I've had a Scotsman whisk me off to the Highlands," she said, giggling.

"May it not be the last time, my lass," he huffed, his face dimpling in a laugh. "I'll run away with you any day of the week," he said, sporting a wink that made Selia swoon even more.

As Selia followed Damien up the hill, a cottage appeared behind a grove of heather. Tucked back into the landscape layered with bushes and hedges, the adorable building appeared to be something right out of a fairy tale. Auntie's cottage was constructed of stone. Bands of dark green ivy grew up the front, framing two green shuttered windows. A lumpy stone chimney poked out of the thatch roof, where all kinds of little green things grew. Patches of moss and a few vines trailed down from the chimney. Set back here in the hills with nothing but open meadows and the North Sea as a backdrop was, to say the least, enchanting.

Damien led the way up the damp stone pathway and stopped at the front door, which was a vibrant shade of leprechaun green. A couple of garden gnome statues sat out front. One was well-rounded around the belly, instantly reminding Selia of Dr. O'Connor.

Damien turned to face Selia. He opened his mouth to say something, but no words came out. Color had drained from his face, making the freckles dusting the bridge of his nose stand out.

"Why do you look like you've seen a ghost?" Selia asked.

Damien's shoulders rose and fell. He shifted his feet beneath him a few times, then let out an exasperated sigh. "I think I should give you fair warning that my aunt can be a bit of a handful at times."

Selia's heart did a flip. Damien had mentioned that Clan Malloch was a bit strange in their beliefs. Then again, this was Scotland, a place where Celtic myth and folklore regarding the fairy kingdom was practically born.

Knock, knock, knock...

Damien rapped his knuckles against the leprechaun green door. The knotted wood groaned back at them. They waited with no reply, other than the sounds of birds and an occasional insect buzzing by.

Damien huffed. "Hmmmm...that's funny."

Henrietta popped her little ink-drop eyes out from Selia's purse, then dove back into her hiding place.

Damien knocked again, this time pressing his ear to the door. A couple of birds went darting overhead, then disappeared behind the cottage. "Let's go have a gander around back. Maybe she's tending to the garden."

Selia followed Damien around the back of the cottage. A white garden shed with a matching thatch roof came into view.

Thud!

"Did you hear something?" Selia asked, wondering where the muffled noise had come from.

"Just the bugs buzzing past my face," he replied, swatting away a few flies.

The door to the shed was ajar. Selia followed Damien into the building that at one time could have been a barn. The space felt like it could have been inhabited by gnomes. A musty scent of damp soil and something floral filled the air.

Wooden troughs were full of animal feed. Rakes and shovels and pots of every size lay against the far wall. A pitchfork stuck out of a giant yellow pile of straw almost as tall as Damien. Above the clutter of gardening tools was a hay loft with a ladder that led up to the top.

Damien walked up to the ladder. "That's strange. I wonder where she's gone." He propped his hands on his hips and scanned the room. "Still no sign of her. This is highly unusual, even for my aunt."

Selia peeked around the little garden shed. The far wall was lined with shelves displaying terra cotta pots of every shape and color. Some were half-full of soil, while others were empty.

Felllpmeeeeee...

"Did you hear that?" Selia asked, stepping toward the shelves covered in gardening tools.

"What?"

Selia strained her ears. Another muffled sound came from next to a wheelbarrow that had been turned over on its side next to the pile of straw. Garden pots lined the ground. Some of the pots were full of dirt, while others appeared to be full of dead leaves, moss, and mulch. "It sounded like someone was saying *help* me."

The pile of straw shifted.

A boot wiggled next to a pitchfork.

"Damien!" Selia cried.

Damien walked over to the wheelbarrow. "Quick! Grab the other side!"

Selia grabbed the other handle of the wheelbarrow. With most of Damien's effort, they tipped the wheelbarrow over, spilling dirt onto the ground.

Strands of straw and dirt went flying into the air. A pair of gloved hands waggled about, as did the face of a woman who had been nearly buried alive. A grubby little woman came bounding out of the straw. She shook her head, sending a frizzle of straw-tangled hair in every direction like a dog shaking off the rain.

Auntie Bertha had a short stout build. She had wavy reddish-brown hair like Damien, darker, hazel eyes. She had dirt under her fingernails and smudges of soil on her face. She wore a green vest with two chest pockets bulging full of what appeared to be acorns.

Damien patted excess debris off her clothing. "Auntie, why are you burying yourself in the straw?"

Auntie shook her head, sending heaps of straw flying. "The pixies are playing pranks on me!"

Selia smirked as Damien made a severe eye roll.

Damien sighed. "Some things never change."

Auntie wiped her face clean. "It's been ages since I've seen you and Gwen. How come you two don't visit me anymore? The moment you called out of the blue, I nearly dropped my tea kettle." Her dark-brown eyes swiveled in Selia's direction. "And who is this charming young woman you've brought with you?"

Damien set his hand on the small of Selia's back. "Auntie, this is my girlfriend, Selia."

The nerves flooding through Selia's body dissipated. Having the word *girlfriend* roll off Damien's tongue sounded like a robin's spring love song.

Auntie's eyes moved over Selia's face, she felt, much more tediously than any normal person should. She had the same wits about her that her nephew did, but a whole lot more spunk behind her personality.

Her dark eyes swerved back to Damien. "A girlfriend now? Well, let's hope that my cooking doesn't scare her off. You made it home just in time for your favorite dish. Haggis and tripe!"

The corners of Damien's mouth turned down. "Really? I come home for a visit and you make haggis and tripe?"

Auntie tossed her head back, chortling out a laugh that could flatten a hill. "My nephew, you are so gullible! No, I made you neeps and tatties!"

"Neeps and what?" Selia asked.

Auntie turned on the heel of her boot, a whimsical sparkle dancing in her eyes. "Best we get to prepping for dinner. It's only a matter of time before the vixen sprites start playing their pranks in my garden."

Selia and Damien followed Auntie around the grove of her garden, keeping a few paces behind his proud and adventurous aunt.

Damien nudged his aunt. "Well? How have you been?"

"Unbelievably busy, as you can see. I've had years where the weeding is far worse than others. But I have never seen so many a vine growing like they have this summer. To this day, I still blame your uncle for being too friendly with the pixies. All it takes is one pixie in a bad mood and they'll have their fun!"

They trudged through the grassy clearing, rounding hedges and a line of trees. Some of the hedges had wild, spindly vines climbing over them. A few of the garden beds looked like they could have been better tended. But Selia couldn't judge. She'd never had a garden of her own. She had always loved the magical ones in the fairy tales she'd read that both Damien and Auntie seemed to deeply appreciate.

"I'm still mad at your uncle Callum. He never should have shared those fae folktales with you when you were just a wee boy. Do you remember the prank you played on your sister? You told her that it was the blue pixies who would turn her hair blue if she didn't tug the very last weed from the pumpkin patch before harvest?"

Damien hiked his head back and laughed. "Gwen will never forgive me for that." He shot his aunt a serious look. "Speaking of folktales, Selia and I are on a little treasure hunt of our own." He stopped so quickly, Selia almost bumped into him.

Auntie's eyes dipped to Selia's chest. "What's this? Do you collect pixie dust as well?"

Selia clutched the bottle of selkie salt skin. "Actually, I do?"

Damien shrugged up beside her. "Auntie, why don't we offer our guest a nice spot of tea?"

Auntie's eyes landed on Damien. "Heaven forbid Callum share something age-appropriate with you. Why couldn't he just read a normal fairy tale where the fairy wasn't dead-set on killing you?"

Damien rolled his eyes. "I don't know, some would argue about the relationship Peter Pan had with tinker bell. That fairy was awfully jealous of Wendy."

"Are you saying that I am jealous?"

"No, I'm saying that you tend to be a bit over-protective."

Auntie's cheeks reddened. "Find me a folktale that doesn't have at least *one* jealous fairy in it, and I'll listen to you."

"What about the Reflections?" Selia blurted out before she could cup her hand over her mouth.

Auntie nearly dropped her shovel. Her eyes swiveled between her and her nephew. "I'll leave it up to the vixen sprites to answer that."

"Vixen sprites? What are those?" Selia whispered as Auntie took off up the hill toward her cottage.

Damien brushed up beside her. "I swear that every time I come to visit her she's come up with another name for the pests swarming about her garden. Just play along. You're doing great! I can already tell that she's warming up to you."

Selia shook her head. More than once, she'd caught a glimmer of something blue darting in her periphery. Was she losing her mind?

Was she really starting to see fairies?

13
THE COLOR OF LIES

The aroma of something with the familiarity of cinnamon and the robustness of cloves drifted in the air as Selia followed Damien and his aunt into the cottage. The scent was full and hardy. Years of cooking had seeped into the plaster walls and wooden beams supporting the most charming little cottage she'd ever set foot inside.

A pointy-hatted gnome perched upon the windowsill with his bum outstretched to keep a window propped open. The window opened to a garden overflowing with hydrangea bushes and ivy nestled upon them.

Auntie disappeared into a dining area where a wooden table surrounded by four chairs sat by the window.

Damien stopped in the foyer, turning to face Selia. "I'll be right in. Keep her company. The sooner you warm up to her, the quicker she'll let us have a look at the folktales."

"Is she guarding them?" Selia asked, wondering if his aunt would also expect her to do some kind of trick before they could peek at the folktales.

His cheeks dimpled. "I'm off to fetch the biscuits. Don't give her any hints about the fae treasure we're after, all right?" He walked into the room that Selia assumed was the kitchen, leaving her standing in a jumble of confusion. How was she supposed to entertain his aunt?

The sooner they could find this folktale called *Strands of Moonlight*, the quicker she could figure out how to use the three little bottles Amy had given her to track down the vault.

Butterflies filled Selia's stomach the moment she spotted Auntie sitting down at the end of the table. Auntie's hazel eyes landed on her, probing with unspoken questions. "Please, have a seat."

Selia approached Auntie, who kept her gaze on her like a hawk would a mouse it desired for its next meal. She sank down into a chair that felt like it was made for gnomes. The table, too, was smaller than normal. She wondered if she had stumbled into a Hobbit Hole.

She set her purse on the chair beside her, thankful that Henrietta was dozing quietly at the bottom.

Auntie clasped her still-grubby hands together over her round center, giving her the ruffled look of a mother hen. "Miss Selia, how many children do you want?"

Selia's mouth went dry. The question was as loaded as the buttery biscuits that suddenly didn't sound so appetizing. "I haven't quite decided upon that," she stammered, struggling to force the words out of her mouth. She would rather take a deep inhale of the compost outside than have this woman interrogate her about her love life with her nephew.

"*Woof!*"

"Oh!" Selia jumped as something damp brushed past her knee under the table. A shaggy grey head of a dog appeared at her side. It had floppy ears and what appeared to be a beard and mustache of fur sprouted from both sides of its long snout.

"Mr. Kisses, stop begging. Go help Damien fetch the biscuits now," Auntie piped, and the dog moseyed towards the kitchen, disappearing around the wall. "When my Scottish deerhound isn't begging for potato peels, he's digging holes in my garden beds," Auntie huffed.

"He seems like a good dog," Selia replied, although she'd never spent much time with a canine before.

"He's as good as any creature can be. But I do wish that he would keep the more annoying creatures away from my property."

"Damien tells me that you are fond of the fae?" Selia asked, hoping to break the ice with this feisty woman.

"I am. Why do you ask?"

Selia swallowed. "I am attempting to learn more about the the creatures who live in your garden."

One of Auntie's thick eyebrows withdrew into her mossy bangs. "Elementals. Sprites. Familiars. Whatever they are, it suits one best to familiarize themselves with fae habits. If you don't they can quickly become pests."

"Are there any fae other than the vixen sprites that you find annoying?"

"Many of the wee ones are pests. The fairies, the gnomes. Oh, and selkies of course."

Selia's arms rippled with gooseflesh. "Have you seen a selkie before?"

Auntie's eyes narrowed onto her, flickering with an intensity that was sure to leave anyone frozen on the spot. "Putting my nephew under one of your sea spells, have you?"

Selia's stomach did a flip. "What are you talking about?"

"Think I'm a fool now?" Auntie's eyes narrowed onto her. "You aren't human, are you?"

Selia's body seized. Her mouth had gone dry. "Why do you think that?"

Auntie's eyes narrowed. "I think you're so interested in the reflections because you are in fact, a fae. A selkie, perhaps?"

Selia froze as Auntie's dark eyes narrowed onto her.

"I think you buried your salt skin somewhere along these hills, and here you are now trying to find it and dig it up so you can uncover where you come from." She shrugged. "That's how most selkie folktales go, anyway. Her salt skin is her identity. Without it, she stands no chance of returning to her home in the sea or performing her moon magic." She tapped her fingers behind her ears. "Do all of you have gills back here, too?"

Selia tugged her hair down over her salt nodes, both of which were still sore and swollen. She got up from her chair. "Will you excuse me for a moment?"

"As long as you don't go casting any of your watery spells on my kitchen."

Selia left the room and found Damien by the stove. Little puffs of steam issued from a tea kettle. Damien was moving the biscuits from the baking dish to a basket. Mr. Kisses sat on his haunches, tail sweeping across the rug, his black nose turned up towards Damien. He obliged the begging dog by tossing him a few crumbs.

She walked up to him, her hands trembling. "Damien, your Auntie absolutely hates me."

He chuckled. "No, she doesn't."

"She knows that I'm not human."

He rolled his eyes. "Let me guess, because you want to know about the folktales?"

"Exactly!" Selia huffed, tugging her hair down behind her ears. "That, and she saw my salt nodes. She thinks they are *gills*."

"Don't let her intimidate you. As you saw from her garden patrol, she suspects everything that is not human is up to no good."

Mr. Kisses began to whine.

"Damien, where are those biscuits already?" Auntie shouted from the other room.

Damien grabbed the tea kettle and three cups with tea bags dangling inside, while Selia grabbed the basket of biscuits. She followed him back into dining area, tugging up her shirt as high as it would go to help cover her salt nodes.

Selia's heart sank. Three bottles had all been placed in a line on the table. So much for Henrietta doing her job as a guard crab.

Auntie's gaze landed heavily on her, and Selia thought for a moment the woman might be preparing to throw her out. "She's brought three incredibly colorful bottles I'm sure she'll be using to curse someone."

"They're not mine. They were a gift from a friend," Selia protested. Had the old woman really gone through her purse?

"Oh, a gift from another selkie now?" Auntie said, her eyes narrowing onto Selia once again. "I'm sure the two of you have plenty of curses in store for us common folk."

Something of a growl rumbled in Damien's throat. He set the tea kettle and the cups down onto the table with a clatter. "Okay, we need to set some ground rules here." His shoulders squared. His jaw clenched. "Look. Selia is our *guest*. She is welcome here. Selkie, fairy or sprite. Clan Malloch treats their guests with *respect*."

Auntie's cheeks reddened. She shifted in her chair as she clenched her hands tighter across her center.

Mr. Kisses let out a quivering whine.

Damien rounded on the dog. "As for you, *sit*. I've had enough of your whining." Damien tugged out one of the chairs and motioned for Selia to sit back down. "Now, we are going to enjoy biscuits and tea like normal folk, all right?"

Selia sat back down.

Damien sat next to her, snatched a biscuit, and shoved it into his mouth.

Selia grabbed a biscuit and pressed the flaky crust to her mouth, but her taste buds didn't register the flavor. All she could focus on was the purple, green and red bottles Auntie had so stealthily stolen out of her purse. Curses inside of them or not, she still didn't know how to use them. Right now, the gifts from Amy's Ocean Apothecary were starting to make her look suspicious.

Auntie's shoulders began to tremble. Her brows drew up, her mouth dropped open and a wail erupted.

"What's wrong?" Damien asked, dropping his third crumbly biscuit onto his plate.

Auntie brought her face to her hands and started sobbing into them. "Damien, I lied to you." She shook her head. "The folktales are gone."

Selia's stomach hollowed. *Gone*?

Damien set his hand on his quivering aunt's shoulder. "What do you mean they're gone?"

"I've had them for over twenty years now. Every time I passed that room, memories of when Callum was still alive would overcome me. Memories of your father. Memories of you and Gwen when you were young. So many memories just...gone."

"What happen to the folktales?" Damien asked, his voice dipping.

"I had a yard sale a month ago, and well...I mixed in your uncle's boxes somewhere in there. It was an accident. When I realized what I had done..." She began to tremble again.

"You can't have gotten rid of everything he had, could you?" Damien pressed.

"Gwen might have something from when she moved out long ago. But I don't know for sure."

Selia looked over at his blubbering aunt, and something that could have been pity welled up inside of her. The old woman was grieving the loss of her loved ones.

Auntie grabbed a napkin out from under a saltshaker gnome at the center of her table and began to dab her eyes. "Your uncle Callum would be rolling over in his grave if he found out what I had done."

As the afternoon wore on, the shock of not finding the folktales began to settle. With no strands of moonlight to follow, Selia was beginning to wonder if the magic inside of the bottles would expire. Amy warned her that salt extracts were living, breathing things. Their potency was only as good as the sea nymph who looked after them.

She gathered breath, memory, and salt, and tucked them back into her purse, finding Henrietta still dozing away beneath her scarf. She and Damien found the guest room down the hall, which was quite cozy.

Once inside the room, Damien turned to face her. "Hey, sorry about that back there."

"Why are you apologizing? You aren't the one who ravaged my purse. I'm quite disappointed that Henrietta wasn't awake to pinch her."

Damien chuckled. "Would have served her right. My aunt had no business doing what she did. I didn't think she'd break down while we were having tea like that. She gets a bit protective when it comes to discussing anything about the fae." He blew out his cheeks.

"She's lonely. She misses you and loves you. Shame on you for not visiting her more."

Damien ran his hand through his hair. "Yeah, that's something I need to improve on."

"She said your sister might have salvaged some of the folktales?"

"Possibly."

"Could we talk with her?"

"I'll try and call her, but Gwen is on holiday."

Selia sighed. "I have no idea what to do."

Damien's gaze fell level with hers. "Why don't we stay the night and we'll come up with a new plan to find this vault first thing tomorrow morning?"

One small bed sat in the corner of the bedroom. Even though she still had plenty of day left ahead of her, Selia wanted nothing more than to curl up and take a nap. It was just big enough that she could see her and Damien snuggling in it together. "You haven't scared this selkie away yet."

Damien smiled at her, a look of relief bleeding through his expression. "I'm going to go help her clean up in the kitchen, all right? She's still flustered. For now, you should settle in."

Selia nodded.

Damien's hand came to her waist as he leaned toward her ear. His stubbled cheek brushed past hers. "I promise you that you'll soon fall in love with Scotland, my bonnie lass."

"What did you call me?"

"I said you were beautiful."

Selia closed her eyes, savoring the softness of his voice next to her ear. Damien sure knew how to put on the Scottish charm and make her swoon. Why did he have to sound so sexy when he brought out that accent?

He withdrew his hand from her waist and ducked out of the room.

Selia walked into the bathroom, seeing that there weren't any towels by the shower. They were probably stuffed in a cupboard somewhere.

Voices sounded from the kitchen where Damien and his aunt were talking.

"I can't believe you accidentally got rid of the folktales," Damien said.

"How was I to know that you would come looking for them? You and Gwen stopped believing in the folktales long ago. Only when Sophie found them did you start believing in them again."

Selia walked toward the kitchen, hoping that Mr. Kisses wouldn't whine and give her location away. Had she overheard the name *Sophie*?

"Pass me the red one," Auntie said.

"No, that's quite yellow," Damien replied.

"Okay, how about the purple?"

"No, purple won't match with the gnome theme you have going on for your table."

"You remember them like yesterday!"

"I remember which colors they were by the shape of their hats!"

Selia stopped. She *couldn't* have heard what he'd said. Damien told her that he couldn't see any other color other than blue. Why was he discussing other colors with his aunt?

"Ever since you and Sophie found the folktales, I..." Another sob escaped his aunt.

"It's okay. That happened a long time ago," Damien said, his voice soft and comforting.

Selia strained her ears. *What* with this *Sophie* happened a long time ago?

Damien appeared in the hallway, holding a handful of colorful napkins. "What are you looking for?"

Selia froze, jealousy knotting her stomach again. "I just needed a towel."

"Get over here beautiful," He grabbed for her, but Selia evaded his grip. "Hey, what's wrong?"

She shoved past him. *Sophie* had been mentioned, again.

"Where are you going?"

"Out."

"Out where?" He grabbed her arm. "It's supposed to rain this afternoon."

Selia pulled away from him and kept walking down the hall. Somehow walking in the rain sounded *marvelous*.

She found the back door and opened it wide.

Mr. Kisses darted past her and into the garden.

"Selia!" Damien cried.

Selia took off in a run for the meadow. It didn't take long for her to lose him as she bound up the hill. Her legs began to sting as the terrain transitioned from meadow to rocky outcropping. Mosses and lichens found their strongholds between the cracks of stone. It began to drizzle, and with the light rain the smooth stone surface she was walking on soon became as slippery as her thoughts.

She slowed her pace as the hill peaked, offering her a view of the darkness looming on the horizon. The storm was rolling across the North Sea now. The corners of her eyes stung with emotion.

The North Sea appeared so much darker out here in the middle of the rain. The lines of the horizon were less defined. Everything blurred together. The stinging jab of salt in her tears combined with the fresh water falling from the sky in thick heavy sheets. She'd come all this way to Scotland believing that he had something to show her, and now she was at another dead end that led her to this mysterious *Sophie*.

Movement caught Selia's eye. Someone was making their way down to the water. A cloak billowed behind them as it descended down into the meadow and disappeared into the fog rolling across the landscape.

Selia blinked. Maybe it was another hallucination. Right now, she didn't care what she was seeing. She'd been blind to her past for so long that she'd become desperate to remember something.

14

TRUE COLORS

Painful, jabbing spasms shot through Selia's calves as she descended the slippery clover-covered hill toward Auntie's cottage. Drizzle became sheets of rain. Cold crept into her sodden clothes and under her skin, making her muscles ache.

"Selia!"

Damien's voice echoed through the meadow, drowned out by the thunder.

She wanted to break out in a run, but the rain fell in freezing sheets. She wouldn't be able to stay out in the cold for long. Her hands started to turn blue. Her fingers were numb.

Damien's misty silhouette appeared around the garden bed. A rain halo spattered off him as he too became soaking wet. He took off in a run toward her, taking only seconds to reach her side. "Selia," he said, his voice hard.

Selia kept walking toward the cottage while Damien trudged alongside her across the muddy meadow.

He grabbed for her, taking hold of her arm. "Hey, stop this. You are avoiding me. I'm not playing this game anymore." He tugged with more force. His gravity overpowered her, bringing her to a stop.

Selia dug her heels into the sodden ground. She turned to face him, the heat rising in her chest and neck until it felt like she would burst. "The only reason I came with you to Scotland was because I believed you were telling me the truth about the fae folktales."

"What are you talking about?"

Selia threw her arms down at her sides. "Let me tell you something, Mr. Malloch. I might not believe in fairies. I might not know anything about the folktales that your uncle passed down to you. But I can tell you one thing. Colors don't lie. You either see them, or you don't."

Damien backed away from her. His shoulders slouched, and his chest deflated. "I knew you were mad at me, but I had no idea you were this furious."

"Is this whole blue color vision thing a lie? Who is to say that everything else you've told me about the folktales isn't a lie too?"

"Why are you getting so upset about the folktales?"

"Who was it that rediscovered the folktales with you?"

Damien's face contorted with confusion. "I'm not following you."

"Oh, come off it! Your secret girlfriend you've been writing poems to? *Sophie*?"

Damien's brows drew up. "Where did you find a poem about Sophie?"

"In your watercolor journal."

Damien blew out his cheeks. He shifted his feet on the ground, propped his hands on his hips and dropped his head. He stared at his shoes, working grass and gravel between them. His shoulders rounded and he exhaled.

Salt nodes burning with anger, Selia shoved past him.

"Selia, wait..."

Selia slowed herself to a stop when her mind told her to run.

"Sophie isn't with us anymore."

Selia stopped. She turned to face Damien, finding the color had drained form his face. "What do you mean, she isn't with us?"

"Sophie died ten years ago." He jerked his head up, his eyes glassing over. "Sophie was my daughter."

Selia tried to exhale, but her lungs seemed paralyzed.

Damien took a few steps toward her, closing the space between them. He stopped in front of her, sucked in a rattling breath and exhaled. "Maria and I met fifteen years ago. I was a freelance illustrator working for a scientific periodical. She was a marine biologist working on her doctorate at a university in France. We were paired together for a marine life project at the Celtic Sea, and well, it was love at first sight."

Selia staggered, taken aback. "Was Maria your wife?"

Damien nodded. "We became pregnant early on, so we eloped. Sophie was born the next year. Five years of bliss followed. My career as an artist took off, and Maria became published for her research. Then things changed. Sophie became sick. We had come up to Scotland for holiday and stayed here with my aunt. Sophie developed a bad cough. Maria didn't want to wait to take her to town and be seen by a doctor. She had some errands to run in town. I had been painting, and I didn't want to let the paper dry. So Maria took her." Damien's gaze drifted, and his eyes glassed over. "My aunt answered the phone. Maria's car swerved from the road and plummeted into the North Sea, killing them both on impact."

Selia couldn't breathe. Her mouth had gone dry. "I'm sorry...I..."

Damien's face blurred in front of her. He took her hands into his, which bore the same coldness she felt. The whites of his eyes were crimson. "I can't explain why blue became the only color I could see after that day. But I know one thing. Blue burned that memory deep inside of me. Ten years ago, I lost the most important people in my life."

The corners of Selia's eyes stung. "Why didn't you tell me?" she said, realizing how stupid her question was.

Damien gave her hands a squeeze, looking away. "I couldn't paint for the longest time, blaming myself for putting my artwork before my family. Every time I picked up my brush, memories of my family flashed before me. I confined myself for the past decade to my studio, hoping that one day I would be able to paint that memory away. That maybe, color would somehow come back to my life." His eyes lifted, meeting hers. "Then, I met you. You helped me."

"How have I helped you?"

"When you told me that blue memories resided in the heart and not the mind, you made me reflect on that day in a way I never had before." He gave her hands a squeeze. "*You* made me see that memory in a different light. Since meeting you, my artist block has evaporated, and I began to paint again."

The corners of Selia's eyes stung. She'd lived alone with blue memory blindness, allowing herself to become shadowed by her own doubts that washed over her like the waves in his paintings. Never had she experienced the memory of loss. Damien had a burning blue memory of losing two people he loved very much.

That afternoon while Auntie got to work preparing dinner, Selia changed into a set of dry clothes and followed Damien outside to the garden. Auntie had tasked them both with weeding what they could before another storm rolled in. The smell was sweet and green. If green had a smell, it would be of Scotland in the midst of summer.

As Selia made her way down the grassy hill, her misconception of Damien's past blurred before her. Soggy, damp earth shifted under her feet, grounding the whirlwind of emotions she didn't quite know how to process.

Grief was based on memory of a time passed, never the future. Then again, she'd never grieved the loss of anyone. Maybe losing someone made the blue memory grow.

"Ouch!" Selia's ankle buckled under her.

Damien stopped, turning to face her. "What's wrong?"

Selia reached for her ankle. "My foot."

"Have a seat," Damien said, patting his hand on the stone bench next to him.

Selia sat on the bench, careful not to knock the garden gnome from its spot overlooking the flowers. His little crooked hat tipped sideways, shiny with moisture.

Damien knelt in front of her. He grabbed her legging and tugged it up, revealing the swollen lump that was her ankle. "Oh, you did good."

"That's what I get for running off into the Highlands without proper footwear."

He tugged off her boot, then worked down the damp fabric of her sock. "You just need to rest it, and you'll be as good as new. Lucky, no weeding for you!"

"Can you tell me more about these myths around selkies?"

Damien looked up at her. "What do you wish to know?"

"How did she lose her identity once she left the sea? How did she just up and forget everything about her past?"

"Once a selkie steps onto land, she must shed her salt skin. The skin symbolizes her identity with the sea. This is the only way she can disguise herself and blend in with humanity."

"Where does her salt skin go?"

"Legend says that she buries it somewhere she hopes nobody will find it. If they do, they trap her into a life on land. She cannot return to the sea without her salt skin."

"Well, that's sort of counterintuitive. If she forgets where she buries it, what luck does she have of ever finding her identity again?"

"Good point."

Selia stared down at her hands. "Sounds a bit like me."

Damien shrugged. "I wasn't going to say anything, but yes, it does."

"In the folktale, why did the selkie lose her magic when she gifted the three strands of moonlight to the wounded man?"

Damien shook his head. "I always wondered the same thing. To obtain what your heart desires, you have to give it away. It's always been a strange concept, but it sounds good in the stories that are supposed to make you feel better."

"Do you think the man in the folktale realized that by accepting the strands of moonlight, he'd trapped the selkie on land?"

Damien shook his head. "If you trap something, can you ever really have it in the end?"

"I don't think so."

Damien's gaze met hers. "Some could say the same thing for love."

Fwop!

Something tumbled out of the rosemary.

A familiar seashell bobbed between the flowers, then dove out of sight.

"Looks like someone else is digging around in the garden." Damien grabbed what Henrietta had unearthed by the foxglove. "Oh look, she's found a hag stone."

"A *what*?"

Damien staggered to his feet and sat next to her on the bench. "Also known as a fairy stone. My sister and I would collect them all the time when we were kids." He held the stone up to his eye. "Look through the hole, and you can see the fairy world."

"Do you see anything?"

He turned the stone to face her. "Just a beautiful selkie sitting next to me." He held it out for her. "Go on, have a look and tell me what you see."

Selia took the stone and held it up to her eye. Spider webs funneled around the hole, encasing what she hoped weren't a bunch of eggs. "Nope. No fairies." When she removed the stone from her eye, she jumped. Damien's face was so close to hers that she could feel the heat coming from him.

She lowered the stone from her face, holding it in her palm. "The Strands of Moonlight folktale, what do you remember about it the most?"

"The love story. The fact that both a man and a selkie were searching for something neither could offer to one another. Most selkie folktales depict a human man who falls in love with her. But in the end, he cannot give her what she longs for as the sea is her one true love."

Selia handed the little hag stone back to him. "Until, of course, they saw the fairies?" Selia teased.

Damien chuckled. "Hey, I was *trying* to be original."

"By stealing from a Scottish folktale?"

"That's not all I stole. My signature, too, came from those writings."

"Your aunt mentioned that when Sophie discovered the folktales that you started to believe in them again. What did she mean by that?"

Damien's body tensed. He sucked in a breath and exhaled slowly, rolling his shoulders forward. "Sophie found them in the closet one day when we were visiting. I began to read them to her, and she wanted me to paint the characters. She loved the stories about selkies the most, so naturally I began painting seascapes."

Selia's heart ached. These were more than folktales to Damien. He had used them to connect with his daughter's imagination. His moonlit signature had developed from that connection and her loss.

Damien's shoulders rolled back and he straightened himself. "Sophie was incredibly creative. There were days that she had me convinced *I* was the one blind to what really lived out here in the garden."

"If there was something from the folktales your daughter would have wanted you to share with others, what would it be?" Selia asked.

Damien blew out his cheeks. "To love all things invisible, no matter how small or insignificant. To love unconditionally. That's the kind of love my daughter had."

Selia looked down at the stone, unable to make sense of the heaviness settling upon her chest. How could Damien live with this kind of pain for the past ten years of his life?

She touched his hand. "What if the selkie in the folktale didn't desire to return to the sea because she met an artist who captured it for her?"

Damien's eyes locked with hers. A fleck of dust drifting on the air settled on his eyelash, but his gaze didn't break.

Selia's heart thundered in her chest. "What if his moonlit paintings were the only sea she loved?"

Damien's cheeks dimpled. "That would make him very happy, indeed."

15
SPY

The annoying *buzz* of Selia's phone sounded from her pocket. She stood up, careful with putting weight on her leg. Retrieving her phone, she pressed the redwood icon.

Deidra was calling.

"I'm going to stretch my legs out before dinner," Selia said, putting her full weight onto her foot.

"Good, because I need to buy myself some time. I haven't done anything to start weeding this garden," Damien said, winking at her.

Selia walked a few paces from where Damien got to work pulling weeds. He tossed handfuls of prickly-looking plants over his head, muttering something about *blasted little sprites* under his breath.

She pressed the phone to her ear. "Yes?"

"Girl, are you ignoring me?" Deidra said, her voice ringing with annoyance. "I've been trying like crazy to reach you! I had another root reading."

"Sorry, my service has been spotty."

"Where are you?"

"Scotland?"

"Does going to Scotland have something to do with finding a fae treasure?"

"How did you know?"

"I did more research on our sea goddess. Apparently, Amy sealed this fae treasure shut long ago."

"Well, apparently the Order is after the treasure too. I'm in Scotland because I'm trying to help Amy track something down they call a vault. Whatever is inside of this vault will help her restore the art."

"Did you meet someone from the Order?"

"I more or less overheard some things. Do you know of an Iridescent who goes by the name of Alex?"

"No, but I can check. If the Order was trying to stop Amy from restoring the art, that would make sense why Amy sealed the treasure away. Speaking of Scotland, I hear the men up there are something to fancy. Are you with someone? Or is this some random fling thing off to the land of men who adorn their loins with kilts?"

Selia bit her tongue. She had to lie and *quick*. But the fantasy of Damien wearing a kilt flashed before her before she could shut it out. "Amy told me to meet her here," she lied. "What is it about this root reading that you wanted to share with me?"

"I've been absolutely plagued with root readings to the point I think I'm going insane. Have you ever been bombarded by both a hummingbird and a dragonfly migration simultaneously?"

"No?"

"Well, I don't recommend it. You know that sound of a billion creatures desperately trying to get laid? That's my existence right now. Having a bazillion wings humming in your ear like that is enough to make a dryad go crazy!"

"What do you think the forest is trying to tell you?" Selia asked.

"There is one thing in common when it comes to mass migrations like that. It's got to be a gathering of some kind, one of mass proportion."

Selia began to imagine what this gathering of mass proportion as Deidra had put it might look like. Members from the Order were aligning forces, hoping to stop Amy from restoring the art of salt trancing. What lengths would they go to in order to prevent her from accomplishing her goal?

"I don't know what Gaia's Order has in store for you, but if an extinct fae species is involved, you can bet they're going to be snooping around. Keep an eye out for anything suspicious." Deidra said.

"I will," Selia replied.

"Wait a fat second. I get the feeling there is something more to this picture that you're not telling me about. I briefly recall you saying that Amy was going to meet with you in Paris to teach you more about this art. If she's not with you in Scotland, who inspired you to go there?"

Selia swallowed. She still hadn't told her about Damien, or the fact that the handsome watercolor artist had somehow whisked her off to the Scottish Highlands in hopes of helping her practice an art she did not understand. "I've wanted to visit the Highlands for quite some time."

"If I had the choice, I would visit the land of men in kilts, too. Well, I'm off to feed Frankie before he throws another fit that I haven't given him his weekly egg roll. Don't ever adopt a cat who is addicted to leftover Chinese food. Ciao."

Auntie appeared from behind her gardening shed, pushing a wheelbarrow full of lumpy dirt.

"Fresh tatties are ready! Let's get this feast prepped!" Auntie cried, then parked the wheelbarrow by the thinking gnome outside her cottage.

Selia noticed the wheelbarrow, realizing the brown lumps weren't dirt at all. The tatties Auntie mentioned were actually potatoes.

Selia found her way into the spare bedroom where Damien had set her luggage onto the bed, which seemed smaller even if it was meant for two people. Henrietta, however, had already claimed half of the space as her own. While she had napped a good portion of their journey north, a new wave of energy sprung through her.

Since arriving at Auntie's place, she had already explored most of the room, turning over anything she could wedge her claws underneath. One item she'd picked apart was Damien's set of blue watercolor pigments.

Selia walked through the room, finding his blue paintbrushes scattered everywhere. The sight reminded her that hermit crabs would get into all kinds of mischief if not given the proper amount of beach time.

Damien walked into the room, his brows drawing up. "What happened in here?"

"Oh, you know. Just a hermit crab doing her hermit crab things when she thinks nobody is looking."

He chuckled. "She's a *wild* thing, that wee one is."

Damien grabbed his journal that had been flipped over, sending Henrietta darting out, claws extended, from beneath the pages. "Does she *ever* stop moving?"

"Not really."

"If she would just sit still for two seconds." Damien grabbed a pen and began sketching. Henrietta dove in and out of Selia's luggage, where she unraveled one of her under garments.

Selia grabbed her silk panties with haste as Damien continued to work on a quick sketch study of the hyperactive hermit crab.

He propped his journal against the pillow on the bed. "There, what do you think?"

Henrietta went darting across the bed, tapped her little claw against Damien's sketch, then darted away.

"I don't think she approves." Selia said, laughing.

"Hey, I didn't say I was finished yet," he grumbled, picking up his journal. His eyes dipped to where Selia was busy tucking her silk panties deeper into her luggage.

Selia helped Damien gather the plates of food Auntie had prepared and set them out on the dining room table. Damien collected quite a few of the shiny stones from the garden that reminded her of salt trancing talismans. There were lots of them. They glittered in a way, whether it be from the rain or not, that made her think twice about them being little gifts from the fae. Orange, greens, yellows, and even purples danced with each other, giving the stone a brilliant show of colors.

She set the stones in a miniature circle around the gnome salt and pepper shakers, creating a rendition of a stone circle. At the center of the circle, she set the bottle of salt extract Amy had given her and propped herself on a chair. She tucked her knees into her sweater and peered at the little thread of silver smoke dancing between air bubbles as they drifted to the top of the salt water. "Blue reflections," she said out loud.

"Come again?" Damien asked as he set the silverware out for three to dine.

"*All that stands between me and the fae treasure is a single strand of moonlight.*" Alex's words rang in Selia's ears as the reflectionless water came flooding back to her.

The metallic sound of Damien placing silverware brought Selia back to the moment. "Amy told me that blue memories reside in the heart and not the mind when she gave me the selkie salt skin. Then you told me about the Sgàthan clan's belief that memories and spirits reflect one another."

Damien's brows drew up. "What are you getting at?"

"You *reflect* on your memories, do you not?"

"I'd say so. You look back at them and remember them, almost to the point where you could be reliving them again."

A bead of sweat trickled down Selia's ribs. "Well, if you are in my unique situation—blind to your past—you really can't reflect on your memories at all." She looked over at the shimmering stones, wondering if they were trying to tell her something. Flecks of blue light danced on the smooth surface. "What if the color blue was somehow connected to this fae treasure Alex is trying to find?"

Auntie shuffled into the room with. "What on earth is wrong with you two? I make all of this food and you just stand around lollygagging? Dig in and eat!"

It didn't take long before everyone had filled their plates full of those every-kind-of-potato dishes, steamed baby carrots and collard greens. Selia sat down at the far end of the table next to Damien.

Auntie raised her spoon. "Damien, pass the tatties before they get cold."

Selia dipped her spoon into her heaping portion tatties, when something in the window caught her eye.

Her breathing stopped.

A pair of grey eyes were staring back at her through the water-droplets trickling down the window...

Her fork clattered on the table.

"What's the matter?" Damien said, his brows slashing.

Selia blinked. Whatever had appeared behind Auntie had vanished. "There was someone in the window."

Auntie spun around, holding her potato-topped knife in hand. "Is someone spying on us?"

Damien rose from his seat and tore towards the front door. He grabbed a flashlight from a basket on the table and ran outside.

Selia and Auntie walked to the window. The yellow artificial light of Damien's flashlight flickered across the garden as he circled the cottage.

He re-entered through the back door, shaking water droplets out of his now-curling hair that stuck to his forehead. "I didn't see anyone," he huffed, his chest heaving.

Auntie shook her head. "Wouldn't be the first time I've had someone poking about looking for a place to stay. The Highlands are haunted by the wee folk. Sometimes there are spirits wandering about who have been led astray."

Selia swallowed. The sighting had left her uneasy.

"I trust you, Selia. If you say you saw someone, I believe you." Damien said as he shot the happy-go-lucky hound a sour look. "Mr. Kisses didn't even bark."

Auntie shook her head. "That dog is worthless when it comes to guarding anything. Why do you think Gwen retired him from her farm to me? He refused to herd sheep!"

Selia's stomach turned over. Weren't dogs supposed to see spirits? If he hadn't reacted, what did it mean for whoever had just been spying on her through the window?

Something didn't sit right with how the individual had vanished into the mist like that. The water droplets gathered along the windowsill had sparkling blue lights dancing in them.

PART 3
FAE TREASURE

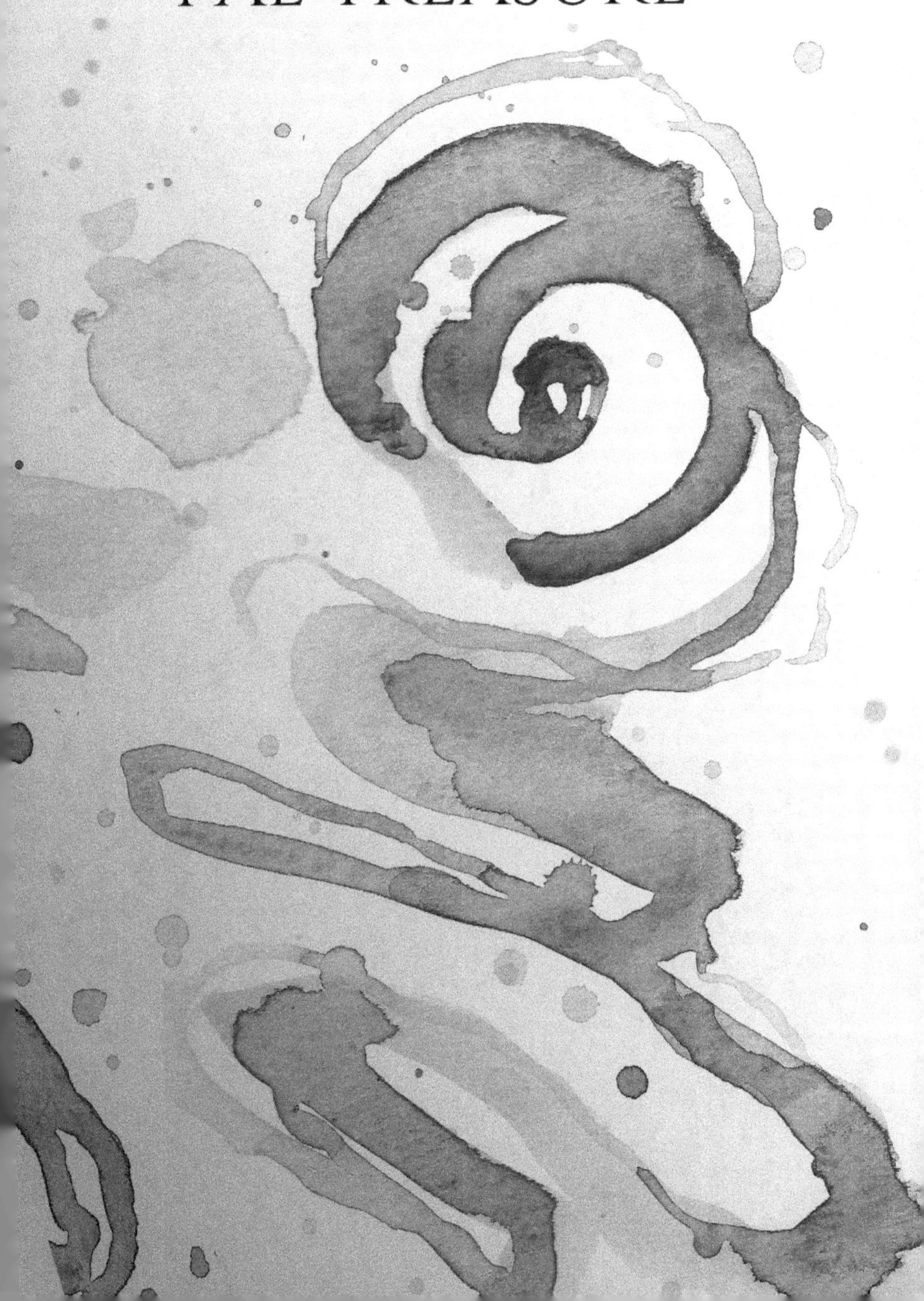

16

REMEMBERING YOU

Rain drops cascaded down the glass windows, erasing whatever color Selia had seen shimmering in the rain water. She and Damien nibbled on Auntie's feast, both too spooked to stomach the generous portions she had provided them. With the folktales gone and little hope of picking up a trail on where to find the vault, she and Damien were at a loss.

After Selia cleaned her plate and excused herself from dinner, she walked past the guest bedroom to a door that was half-way open.

A little seashell went darting across the floor, disappearing into the room with the door that was ajar.

"Oh, no. What did you do?" Selia scolded Henrietta, darting after where the little crab had gone. She pressed her hip against the door as it was heavy to open.

After heaving and huffing against the door, she finally convinced it to open. She peered behind the door, finding a pile of cardboard boxes. The entire room was full of boxes, furniture, and even more boxes. The sight combined with the dusty aroma created the illusion that she was back into her own artifact-cluttered office.

Selia walked to the spot she heard the sound of scurrying exoskeleton legs of a certain crab. Finding Henrietta amid the clutter would be nearly impossible.

"What's going on back here?" Damien's voice sounded behind her.

"Quick, close the door! Don't let her escape!" Selia ordered.

Damien shut the door.

Selia held her hands out in front of her, shifting her feet slowly as to not accidentally smash Henrietta.

Chink!

Something fell out of one of the cardboard boxes.

"Wow, it's a mess in here," Damien said, walking over to a stack of boxes set atop a dresser. "Found your little friend."

Selia walked over to the box, finding a pair of ink-drop eyes sticking out from the corner. What had fallen out of the box were a few of the smooth hag stones just like the ones she and Damien had discovered in the garden. "You are so rude," she scolded, dipping her hand down and swooping Henrietta out of the box.

She grabbed the stones and set them back inside, finding the box had writing on it: **Uncle Callum**

"How long has it been since Auntie lost her husband?" Selia asked as she perched Henrietta up on top of the dresser. High off the ground, where the little thief could serve her time-out.

"Probably a dozen years now?" Damien said, his voice a whisper. He shifted from one box to another in the stack. He was hunched over a musty cardboard box with something written on the side: **Damien's Art Stuff**

"How was it that you got into painting, anyway?"

"My mother fostered my interest in art when I was just a wee lad. She was librarian from Denmark who painted in oils. She actually illustrated children's books, mostly folktales." Damien grabbed the edge of the box, shifting it closer. "She met my father, a farmer from Scotland. He was visiting Denmark to find help in researching the origin for the folktales he and his brother Callum discovered in the barn. When my father shared his love of folktales with her? Well, she was already in love."

Selia's heart warmed. "Then you came along?"

"My parents came back to Scotland, making a home here. I was born out of wedlock. For years, my father refused to marry my mother for fear that he would leave her early."

"Why didn't he want to marry her?"

"He didn't want to break her heart. He'd been diagnosed with heart disease, which he always feared would claim him early."

"What did your mom say?"

Damien chuckled. "She wouldn't take no for an answer. They became married and a few years in, my little sister came along. Not long after Gwen was born was my mother diagnosed with terminal cancer."

Selia's chest ached. "How long did she live for?"

"I was twelve when mom passed, Gwen only seven. Gwen didn't know her mom like I did. Dad was there for a while, but his heart disease claimed him too, only a year later. That's when my Uncle Callum and Auntie took us into their home."

"I'm so sorry," Selia said.

"Don't be. I never truly felt alone. My parents left us a family that loved us and cared for us, as you can see with Auntie." He shifted his hands over the edge of the box. "If there was anything I learned from my parents' story, it was that you should treasure the time spent with your loved ones."

Selia thumbed through a stack of paper, finding a yellow piece of parchment. The splotchy texture reminded her of the archival documents that would often accompany an artifact she was working to put on display. "What is this document about ocean currents and the origins of marine life?"

Damien grabbed the paper, which appeared to be a title page for an academic article. "Looks like you found one of Maria's scientific articles. Maria studied the reproductive cycles of marine life." Damien's cheeks blew out. "She was extraordinary when it came to understanding these things. She understood the ocean like it was a work of art."

A twinge of jealousy knotted in her gut. "You still love her, don't you?"

"Maria was the love of my life. But she was in love with the sea. I often thought that if she ever did leave me, it would be for the ocean." His voice shuddered. "The sea brought us together, and the sea stole her and our daughter away from me."

Selia walked to the window, overcome with an emotion she couldn't understand. The same emptiness she felt when she'd salt tranced with him at his art studio crept over her once again.

She gazed through the rain-spattered glass, the biting cold more comforting than the emotions blurring through her. An ache crept up her spine, branching out to her shoulders. Damien had an entire lifetime of memories stored away in this dusty room.

Selia's haunted artifact closet back at the Louvre was full of items that belonged to people and civilizations she barely knew. The items in this storage room belonged to people he had personal relationships with.

Damien's warm hand came to her arm. "What's wrong?"

She turned to face him. "I can't help but feel like I'm a ghost here."

"I promise, you are not a ghost to me," His eyes dipped away from her. "I never should have lied to you. I've spent ten years trying to run away from the feelings Maria left me with about the sea. I'm beginning to realize that by avoiding those memories, I'm distancing myself from what I loved so much about her."

Selia looked away from him. A knot in the wooden floor between their feet became her new focus. "I'm not asking you to forget anything or anyone. I just need you to remember that I'm—" She choked, forcing herself to look up at his softened face. What was she supposed to say? "—I'm here for you."

His cheeks dimpled. "That means more than you know."

Selia's eyes burned. Was she falling for a man who was still in love with his past? Would she be able to live up to the life Maria had given him?

He took her hand, leading her over to another stack of boxes. **Ocean Maps** was written across it.

Selia's fingers itched for the dog-eared cardboard box flap. "May I?"

"Of course."

Selia reached into the box and pulled out a rolled-up piece of parchment.

"This map is *remarkable*," Selia said, her breath catching. "Did you paint this for Maria?"

"I did. I never thought I'd end up becoming an amateur cartographer. But when you marry a marine biologist? A lot of magical things happen."

That twinge of jealousy in her gut unknotted a little. Maybe it was because he was still holding her hand. She ran her fingers over the map, loving the imperfections the paint left in the parchment. Undecided boundaries. Places where pools of water merged with the next.

"Why is most of this map in color?" Selia asked, noting how vibrant the greens, oranges and yellows were in spots.

"I had been working on this map for a long time—*months*. I was preparing to put the finishing touches on it the day I..." His voice dropped and his shoulders rounded. "This is what I had been painting the day I lost them."

Selia's eyes burned. She scanned over the map, watching as though by magic, blue swept over the remaining half.

"I never finished it. Blue just sort of took over, and I stopped painting completely." He ran his hand over the bottom right of the map where his brushstrokes changed. Lines no longer set boundaries between land and water. The shapes where landmass would be were no longer detailed with browns and greens. Instead, there were long, sweeping asymmetrical shapes that bled and pooled and morphed into one another.

"Why did you create it?"

"Maria had been studying a new species of coral. But something was different about this species. After they would spawn, a bunch of these strange seashells would wash up on the beach. But they would disappear within a day or two, so you had to collect them before they were gone."

"Disappearing seashells?"

"Sophie and I would find these seashells all over the beach. She *loved* them. I promised her that when I brought her to Scotland, I would—" he choked up. "I'm sorry. After that day, my life became promises I never kept. Fairies I knew she would fall in love with were gone. Beautiful places I could never show her had vanished, because I'd been too focused on my own artwork."

Numbness crept through Selia's body.

Damien let go of her hand and reached for a stack of watercolor parchment inside the box, which he began flipping through. Images of stylized seashells meant for a child appeared. "I started these illustrations over a decade ago. I can't believe I just shoved them away like this."

"I can't imagine what you must be experiencing," Selia said, guilt branching its twisted fingers through her. These emotions were so raw and vulnerable. She wondered if a knife would be able to cut through the cloud settling on her shoulders. How was she supposed to comfort him?

A lock of Damien's hair unraveled behind his ear. A thick wave of silver was threaded into the coppery-brown. She'd noticed the grey first as water droplets from the fountain outside the Louvre. Then threads of silver moonlight in his art studio. All of the times she'd seen the subtle detail in him, she hadn't understood it.

Now she could see that silver strand was really *grief*.

Damien ran his hand over the table, scattering the dust. "The folktales must have been right here. I remember this space like it was yesterday."

"How come?"

He swallowed. "Because shortly after I lost Maria and Sophie, I began signing all of my artwork with this."

Selia stared at the moonlit symbol—his signature. The same symbol found on the salt trancing talisman Alexandra stole from her office.

"I *threw* myself into those folktales. There were so many stories, their messages so pure and comforting. I wish I could have shared them with you. I guess some part of me thought that if I painted with the symbol, Maria and Sophie would..." he shook his head. "I've been a fool all of these years, burying myself in this folktale stuff."

"You were grieving. I can only imagine that painting with the symbol was your way of healing." Despite her better judgment, she met his gaze. The loss in his eyes was dizzying, threatening to break her all over again. "I can't know that pain because I've never lost anyone I love."

Damien set his hand atop hers on the table. "For someone who is blind to their own past, you sure have a way of making others feel like you've seen them." He closed his fingers over hers, giving her hand a warm squeeze. "You've given me more over the past few days than anything I've been able to find alone over the past ten years."

Selia squeezed his hand back. "That makes two of us."

Damien closed the box, sealing his paintings away. "Well, I don't know about you, but this day has been absolutely exhausting."

Selia took his cue to leave and turned for the door when his hand reached hers.

"Selia?"

She turned, finding the corners of his mouth upturned into a smile. "Thank you for coming home to Scotland with me and helping me remember parts of my family I've tried to forget."

"Sometimes it's the things we forget in life that help us remember what we love." She grabbed Henrietta, who had already retreated into her shell. She seemed to know that she was in trouble. They left the dusty room, and Selia found herself walking into the guest bedroom.

The sky was overcast and grey again, and the low light in the room told her the sun was also retiring for the day. She set Henrietta onto her nightstand where she could keep an eye on her in case she did decide to dart off for one of her nocturnal adventures.

Damien went to the kitchen, where a discussion with his aunt began. Selia needed the time to be alone and introvert. She grabbed her travel bag and retreated to the restroom. Traveling had made her gritty and in need of time to freshen up.

After she washed her face, brushed her teeth, and changed into a fresh set of clothing meant for sleep, she felt much better than she had preparing for a night on the train. Passing the living room, she found a pile of blankets had been stacked together. Damien was apparently setting up fort out here with the dog, who'd already claimed his half of the sofa.

Her body ached both with emotion and fatigue as she eyed the small, lonely bed in the corner.

"Tired?"

Selia jumped as Damien had snuck up on her. He too had changed out of his travel clothes and was wearing much less clothing than should be appropriate given the chilly evening.

"Aren't you going to freeze in that?" Selia asked, wondering how on earth anyone could wear a t-shirt, sleep shorts, and no socks.

"Nah, I run pretty warm," he said, reaching his arms up in a yawn above his head. His body flexed under the cotton shirt that was a little too tight, something he'd probably worn on purpose.

And had he put on cologne? What was that lovely, masculine scent?

Selia wrapped her arms around herself. "I'm exhausted."

"Me too. Are you cold?"

"I'm chilled is all. The cold is one thing I have yet to fall in love with about Scotland."

Damien's hazel eyes met hers with raw emotion. Loneliness existed there, emptiness Selia too had experienced.

He too gave the lonely bed in the corner a glance, then took a step toward the door. "Right. I'll be setting up out in the living room for the night. I'll see you in the morn—"

"—Damien." Selia said as she walked into the room. She sat down on the bed and patted the blanket. "Sleep next to me?"

His neck flushed into the same hue as the cherry wooden door frame. He shut the door, walked to her side and sat down next to her.

Creeeek!

They both bust out laughing as the bed moaned under their combined weight.

"Promise you'll not go running off again without me?" he asked.

"As long as you promise to warm up this bed."

The two climbed under the sheets, and Selia lay on her side facing out toward the room. She needed to keep an eye on Henrietta in case she did decide to scurry off into the night. Besides, she wasn't ready to stare into the lonely fire in Damien's eyes.

She turned out the light and laid her head upon her pillow.

Damien didn't wait for her to settle into place. He shifted his body up against her and draped his arm around her core. She would have to get used to his bumps and curves and how hard his body felt against hers. Damien had a strength about him, something she first felt when he hiked her over his shoulder and ran toward his Auntie's cottage. That strength was different now as he wrapped his arm around her center and pulled her toward him.

She sucked in a breath as his nose brushed behind her ear. His breathing pulsed against her salt nodes. What kind of pleasure was this?

"Damien?" she asked, her voice rasping as his grip on her center relaxed.

The steady rhythm of his breathing told her he'd drifted off. Now she was alone with all of those wonderful bumps and curves of this artist. She wasn't used to having someone else in her bed. Syncing her breathing with his—did their hearts sync as well?

She closed her eyes, focusing on the rhythm of his breathing, and her mind began to drift. From the salt extracts, to the stones they'd found in the garden, then to the fragments of Damien's ocean maps.

The fragments of his past and who he'd lost, and the timing of it all. Ten years ago, Damien lost hope for his future when the North Sea had taken his family. Ten years ago, blue started to dominate his life. He began signing his artwork with the symbol he'd discovered in a collection of fae folktales.

Ten years ago, Selia had discovered the salt trancing talisman with that same moonlit symbol. The talisman that had first whispered to Selia the haunting words: blue memory blindness...

She forced her thoughts about the talisman out of her mind and Damien's breathing slowly matched the soft rhythm of her own. He hadn't lied about his body heat. Their bed was much warmer now. Damien's warmth was something she was beginning to love.

17

STRANDS OF MOONLIGHT

reath, memory, and salt sat atop the dresser, glinting in the pale
morning sunlight. None of Amy's salt extracts had exploded or set
fire to Auntie's cottage like in Selia's nightmares. She lay in bed, staring
across the room, wishing she didn't have to leave the comfort of her bed.

Damien's arm draped over her center. The cut on his forearm was
still there, however, it had scabbed over. Up to this point, making sense
of the art of salt trance made Selia feel like she was chasing after some
invisible treasure. Damien had given her something tangible, something
that wasn't as abstract as the strands of moonlight in the folktale. Given
time, the body was easily mended. But wounds like grief? Something told
her that even strands of moonlight couldn't mend it.

"Sometimes, there are wounds that go deeper than the flesh..."

She'd not known at the time what Damien meant when he said those
words in his art studio. Now, his words weighed like a heavy stone upon
her chest. She gazed down at Damien's sleeping face, wondering if he
dreamed with the same blue artistic vision. She had come all the way
to Scotland to find the folktales that were meant to shed light on how
to find a fae treasure. She'd set out not knowing if fairies even existed.
In the short amount of time she'd spent traveling with Damien to his

homeland, she'd come to question more about her own beliefs about the healing moon magic practiced by selkies.

She trailed her fingers through his hair, finding that stubborn chestnut curl laced with silver. A strand of moonlight? Maybe.

Grief? Absolutely.

She wondered if Maria would had shown him this kind of affection had the silver been there. As time passed with Maria's absence, the silver found its way deeply embedded in his hair.

Selia's stomach swathed with butterflies. Damien had been married, passionately in love, and had a child. She felt like a shadow here, stepping into the deep void that death had left in Damien's heart. Who was she to lay here next to him and fantasize what it might be like to enjoy the love he once had?

Could they ever experience the same love he once had in his life?

Maybe the strands of moonlight she and Damien had come all the way to Scotland in search of weren't buried in a collection of folktales. Maybe the strands weren't moonlight at all. She worked her fingers through his hair, wondering if perhaps those strands were really something that threaded around Damien's creative heart.

She gazed into his face. There was still something she hadn't tried. She pressed her lips to his forehead instead. She kissed him on a simple spot, a place a family member or a friend would express their endearment towards another. Pressing one's lips to another's face was an act she'd not remembered doing before.

She continued draping kisses over Damien's forehead, loving how soft his skin was on her lips.

Damien's eyes fluttered open. "Morning," he muttered, his voice low with sleep.

"Hi..." Selia giggled, suddenly too flush to continue looking into his lazy gaze. She closed her eyes, held her breath and pressed her lips to his.

A low grunting sound erupted from either him or her, she couldn't tell. Damien's whole body was communicating with her. His chest tensed as his hands moved over the small of her back.

His lips worked over hers tenderly.

What sweet magic was *this*?

She let out a little moan as he worked his lips down her neck. His hands worked down from her torso to her hips.

Selia straddle his center, propping herself on top of him.

Movement beyond the window caught her eye.

She jolted off him.

"What?" Damien stammered, jostling up.

"I saw someone outside the window."

"Don't care," Damien said as he wrestled her back to the bed. His lips returned to her neck, moving down to her chest.

Knock, knock, knock!

Selia jumped.

A misty silhouette of someone wearing a raincoat and hat appeared in the foggy window. "Rise and shine! The vixen sprites are causing all kinds of mischief today!"

"Oh for the love of all that is important," Damien mumbled. "Can't a couple of adults get some privacy around here?"

Auntie retreated from the window.

"We have all day to play hide-and-seek in the sheets," Selia said.

Damien pressed a kiss to her neck. "Why are we waiting?" he breathed against her ear.

Selia leaned into his affection, wishing the day didn't have to begin just yet. She maneuvered her way out from beneath her playful boyfriend and huddled next to him.

She sat up, searching for where his aunt had disappeared to. "What is she doing?" she asked as she gazed outside the rain-spattered window.

Wearing a bright green raincoat, a yellow rain hat and fire engine red rain boots, Auntie was moving from one potted plant to the next with a watering can.

Damien lay flat on his back. He pinched his brow with his fingers and groaned. "How could I forget? Auntie has a strange routine for watering her plants to do-away with the vixen sprites."

"When it's *raining*?" Selia asked, stifling a laugh.

Damien sat up in bed, scowling. "She believes that when it rains, the fairies, gnomes and water sprites have a better chance at chasing the vixen sprites away. What does she do? Jump in and help them."

Selia smiled. "I love how superstitious your family is."

Damien's gaze lingered on her dangerously. There wasn't a want, there was a *need* there now, a look Selia didn't know if she could break.

She grabbed a wild strand of his silky chestnut hair from behind his ear. "Let's help her. I wouldn't mind seeing what these mischievous little vixen sprites are up to."

Damien leaned into her touch, letting out a massive groan. "I never should have told you about her obsession with the fae."

Henrietta scuttled about the windowsill. The crab was already plotting how to escape the cottage and into the garden where Auntie was now bounding from plant to plant, pouring generous amounts of water onto her daises.

Selia opened the window, and Henrietta jumped outside.

Ding-dong!

Selia jumped. She'd never heard the doorbell ring in this cozy little cottage. She unraveled herself from Damien's arms, grabbed her sweater and leapt from the room. Answering the door was the excuse she needed to evade his advances. She'd not expected her kiss to stir a desire she'd not yet seen in him. It was a feeling she didn't know if she was ready for yet.

She looped the sweater over her head and arms, grateful she'd slept in a pair of leggings. Without even peering through the peep hole, she grabbed the door handle and swung the door open, coming face-to-face with a watery set of eyes. "Hello, how can I help you?"

"Well, hello there. Might you tell me where I can meet with Bertha Malloch?"

"She's out in the garden right now," Selia said, noticing the strange attire on this tall, lanky man. He was hardly wearing anything suitable for the rainy weather that Scotland seemed to brew up at a moment's notice.

Damien brushed up behind her, looping his arm through Selia's arm and across her middle. "I'm sorry to say but we are busy. You will need to come back another—"

"—where are my manners," the stranger stammered, giving a little bow. "My name is Alfred Wilson."

Damien attempted to pull her away from the door and shut it. She grabbed the door handle seconds before Damien's gravity won.

Mr. Wilson reached into his tweed coat, and Selia felt Damien tense behind her.

The muffled sound of footsteps erupted behind them.

Auntie came rounding the corner, a scowl across her face. "Oh, no! No! No! No!"

Selia had to jump out of the way to avoid being knocked over as Auntie came barreling towards the front door. She grabbed a chair and propped it up against the handle, barricading it shut. "Do *not* let him in. That old bag of hot wind has blown all the way here from England. He is not allowed anywhere near my property!" She set both of her hands on her hips. "Alfred Wilson is *not* welcome here."

"What is he bugging your for?" Damien asked, tugging Selia closer to him.

Auntie's face quivered. "What else? His lunar compass!"

"What's a lunar compass?" Selia asked, giving in to Damien's affection.

Auntie shook her head. "Blasted if I know. That old beggar's been asking all over the place for that old thing. He has been for a year now. Why anyone would use the moon to try and find something in the dark is beyond me."

Selia felt Damien's hand squeeze against her core. "That doesn't sound suspicious at all."

"Do you think this Wilson fellow was the one slinking around the cottage last night?" Damien asked as he let her go.

Selia shook her head. "No, it wasn't him. Whoever had been looking through the window had grey eyes, not brown eyes like he has." She turned to Auntie, who was now trembling. "Is there anything that you think has set him off recently?"

Auntie clenched her fists. "Ever since he visited the pub up the way, he's been hounding me every-other week, it seems. There have been all kinds of strange folk up that way, including him. For the life of me, I can't get him to go away!"

Selia's leg shifted as wet dog fur brushed past her. Mr. Kisses plopped down on the rug in front of her, his giant pupils dilating. He whined, looking like he expected her to do something.

Selia held out her hand. Mr. Kisses lathered his tongue across her palm, leaving a soggy item.

Auntie threw her hands in the air. "Shoo! She doesn't want your garbage!"

Mr. Kisses bound away, tail wagging as he went.

Auntie shook her head. "The drunkards from the pub are always leaving their litter around. Because of that dog, it always ends up in my garden."

Selia stared down at the slobber-covered bottle cap. Her heart skipped a beat. A starfish with four points decorated the top, something that could easily be mistaken for a compass. She flipped it over, finding an anchor on the underside of the cap. *Rusty Selkie* encircled it.

She'd seen this design before. The design matched the bottle cap she'd found in Damien's sweater on the train. And on the silver coin she'd found in both her office and in his art studio…

"The Rusty Selkie!" She yelled.

"What?"

"The Rusty Selkie is the name of a *pub*! Remember when I overheard Alex telling those two men to meet her at a pub in Scotland? *This* is where they are meeting!" She held up the bottle cap, showing him the words Rusty Selkie written around the top. "I think this fae treasure might be closer than we think."

18

THE RUSTY SELKIE

Images of the elusive fae treasure began to illuminate the dark, confused corners of Selia's imagination. Cool air blowing in from the North Sea helped to clear her senses as she and Damien hiked up a grassy meadow. Whoever had been slinking around Auntie's property had concerns with what they were after.

Selia's gut told her that whoever had been spying through the window with those cold grey eyes was the nymph who had stolen her salt trancing talisman, Alexandra.

They rounded a wall of hedges, hiked another hill, and then a charming little town came into view.

Damien stopped at her side and scrunched his nose. "I smell fish."

Selia peered through the mist, spotting the grungy little building that was absolutely in need of a face-lift. She led their trek the rest of the way down through a meadow toward the building. The sound of waves lapping against the metal hulls of boats filled the air. A pier where boats had been docked sat a little way out, as the building backed up to the North Sea.

Selia stopped at the pub door. The weather-worn building put off more of a pirate than a selkie feel. Sharp coastal winds had weathered the wooden door to the pub. Barnacles covered the wood, their knobby, oblong bodies shiny with condensation. The door handle was a large fish tail that coiled around the bare-breasted body of a woman.

A rusty anchor crusted in barnacles lay not far from the door, which was not fully closed. The distant sound of laughter echoed from within the pub.

"Sounds like someone is having a grand time," Damien said, as he opened the grimy wooden door.

"I wonder if Mr. Wilson is inside," Selia said, walking in ahead of him. Damien set his hand on Selia's lower back as she moved over the threshold. She was beginning to love how physically affectionate he'd become towards her. As they approached the bar, men wearing red and black pirate coats moved between taps, swapping out kegs. Women sauntered between their fellow bar-tending pirates, dressed to kill. Each had a shiny metal brooch of a selkie clipped to her breast.

A giant wooden selkie framed the back of the blue and green lit bar. A shimmering necklace of pearls draped across the bare-breasted woman with a coiling fish tail. The faint smell of seafood wafted in the air, as did some artificial smell that had possibly been used to cover up a more unpleasant fishy scent.

A black chalkboard advertised different evening entertainment options planned for the week.

Men in Kilts Night!
Where your favorite Scot is sure to tilt his kilt your way to have a peek at what's underneath!

Selia scanned the dates. "Darn, I was hoping to see the men in kilts."

Damien chuckled as he wrapped his arm around her waist. "I'll keep that in mind. Where shall we sit?"

"You lead the way, captain," Selia said, playing along as they approached the bar.

A host wearing a large pirate hat and a black coat approached them. "Table for two?"

"Aye," Damien said. "My lady wishes to have the best view of the North Sea."

The host dipped his pirate hat toward a wooden sign to his side. "If you are going to dine in the Captain's Cabin, then you are required to dress appropriately."

The wooden sign read:

`Captain & Mistress Quarters`

`Beware of lobsters pinch'n yer pirate jewels and titties…`

`Dress at your own risk, or you get the privies…`

Selia laughed. "Wait a minute, are you telling me that we get to *dress up*?"

The host chuckled heartily, hiking back his head. "I hope yer both into roleplaying."

Damien handed the host his credit card. "Show us where we play."

The host flashed a set of gold teeth. "Pirate and selkie quarters are this way."

They followed the host to the dressing rooms at the end of the hall. Damien winked at her as he grabbed his door handle with a pirate hook hanging from it and disappeared inside.

Selia opened her door and walked inside. The scent of dusty fabric filled the small room. Hanging on her left and right were dozens of costumes. At the center lay a mirror, which reflected her startled expression.

Hooks were covered in wigs and masks and a bra with octopus tentacles dangling from the center.

Humans sure let their imaginations run wild with what they imagined selkies to look like. Selia had never seen, to her knowledge, any sea creature parts in her anatomy.

She closed the door and shimmied out of her damp trench coat. If Gaia's Order was hanging out in this dress-up pub, they were camouflaging well with the place. A wooden trunk sat in the corner of the room with the label **Selkie Skins** written on it.

She opened the trunk, finding a collection of softer-looking fabrics folded inside. She sifted through the fabrics until something silky smooth grazed her fingers, a blue sequin dress.

She tugged off her clothing then slipped into the silky fabric that hugged her body in all the wrong places. Good gracious. What was she getting herself into?

Her reflection in the mirror caught her attention. Her skin had a lack-luster glow to it. Little patches of discoloration framed her eyes. Patches of her brunette hair were frayed at the ends. Her hips had never been that robust and she tended to bloat after eating too many carbs. Auntie's Scottish cooking was very apparent on her waistline. Her breasts weren't perky like the women in the corsets flirting with their pirate bartenders up front.

Selia gave that blue sequin dress a stiff look in the mirror. She was no selkie. One look at the bra covered in octopus tentacles was enough for her to settle on the dress.

She walked out of the room, spotting Damien giving himself a look in a mirror outside of his dressing room. He was wearing a long black coat that made him look much bulkier.

He turned to face her. His mouth dropped open. "I have no doubt in my mind that I am the scalawag here." he stammered, walking up to her and stopping. His eyes traveled down her front, then back up to meet her.

"Do you like it?"

"Like it? Selia, you look—"

Fwip!

Damien's pants began to fall toward his knees, which he caught in the nick of time. "Hey, how is a pirate supposed to treat his selkie to a date if he can't even keep his trousers on?"

Selia giggled. "Maybe pirates don't wear trousers to begin with?"

Damien did his best to re-fasten his belt. He tipped his hat, sending the peacock feather tickling across Selia's face. "That's pirate captain, to you."

"The pirate captain and his scandalous selkie? What could go wrong?" Selia teased.

Damien took a step toward her. "I can think of a few things." His hand dropped to her waist and his gravity took over.

Selia set her hands on his chest. "Wait."

"What's wrong?"

"We're in public."

"Not back in here, we're not. You're in the *captain's* quarters now." Damien maneuvered her back into the male dressing room, where a whole new chest full of treasures waited inside. A wooden dresser was pushed up against the far wall with a mirror resting on the top.

The captain's quarters had an entirely different treasure trove of items, most of which were made of metal, wood, and a large assortment of leather. There were handcuffs, belts, and other items that could be used for pleasure.

Damien kicked the door closed with his foot.

The look he was giving her now was sure to drown her.

He faced her, reached up toward the slit in her dress, finding her waist.

Selia's butt bumped into the dresser where a skull rattled next to the mirror.

He pressed his face to her ear, his stubble grazing her skin. "Let's give this pub a new meaning for role play."

Selia wrapped her arms around his neck, knocking his hat from his head.

He pressed his body against her, thrusting her onto the dresser. His lips draped across hers, hot with pleasure. He felt so warm and powerful pressed against her.

Selia gathered the fabric of her dress over her leg, bunching it up as Damien's hand slipped underneath. His fingers found her hip, gripping the silk panties Henrietta had attempted to steal from her luggage. His fingers gripped the hem of her panties, tugging the fabric until his fingers were brushing bare skin. How hot his touch was against her quivering inner leg.

His fingers inched across her thigh.

Selia dug her fingers into his back as the spot aching for his touch became hotter.

"Slower, or faster?" he asked, his voice dipping lower as he explored her inner thigh.

Selia's pulse jumped into her throat. How he could make those wide artistic hands of his work their magic.

Knock, knock, knock! "Oi! Appetizers are up!"

But Damien's hand didn't give up.

She grabbed his hand, stopping him from adventuring any further.

He pulled his face away from her neck, setting both of his hands on the dresser. Looking up at her, his brows furrowed. "This selkie is going to make this pirate wait his turn, isn't she?"

Selia's heart trembled. "Always, unless he has some pirate treasure to share with her."

Damien held out his hand, which Selia took, helping her down from the dresser. He set his hands back onto Selia's hips. "You my dear, are the treasure."

Selia closed her eyes as Damien's mouth worked over hers. Tenderly, then passionately.

Knock, knock, knock!

Damien groaned as they broke apart from one another.

Selia smoothed down her dress. She opened the door and rushed over to the dressing room where she'd left her purse and jacket. She tugged it on, flipping up the collar up to conceal the damage Damien had done to her neck. All it took him was a few seconds to turn her into a hot mess.

She grabbed her purse, where Henrietta was still curled up at the base.

Damien stood outside the door, waiting for her. Half of his hair was sticking on end.

Selia gathered his thick locks in her hand, taming it behind his ear, and kissed him on the cheek.

Damien's lips grazed past her ear. "I'm not through with you yet."

Selia shivered in rasp of Damien's voice as he escorted her back to their table. A plate of appetizers sat at the center. An assortment of fried cheeses, breads and some olives were all arranged in the shape of an anchor.

Selia took her seat in the booth, where Damien promptly slid in next to her. He set his arm on the cushion and snuggled up beside her.

"Yes?" She whispered, jolting as Damien's hand brushed across her knee.

"You can't kiss a sleeping man and expect him not to want more of it," he whispered.

Selia flushed. "I didn't think you were awake." She found refuge in the alcoholic beverages at the bottom of the menu. "I'm excited about this. Choose yer level of alcoholic treasure. The rustier, the better!"

The alcohol content was listed alongside the image of an anchor with a mermaid tail coiling around the base. It was the same design on the bottle cap Mr. Kisses had gifted her.

But Damien was obviously preoccupied with something other than alcohol. His hand kept drifting.

A waiter stopped at their table. He whipped out a scroll and a quill. "What will ye be havin' fer drinks today?"

"I'll choose for us both. He'll have the Rusty Anchor," Selia said.

"And you, miss?" the waiter asked.

"I'll have the Ocean Orgasm."

Damien's grip on her leg tightened, and his fingers dipped into her panties again.

The waiter turned and left for the bar.

"Really?"

Selia's leg quivered. "I hope I don't regret my decision..."

Damien tipped his face to her neck again as his hand maneuvered over her lap.

A shadow shifted in Selia's periphery. She turned, spotting a man with a large black trench coat walking down the hall. "Damien, look!"

Damien's hand stopped. "What?"

"There was a man standing there with a long black coat with an anchor on it. The men I saw with Alex in England both had the *same* design on their jackets."

She grabbed her purse and stood up, grabbing Damien's hand. "Let's follow him." She led the way to the back of the pub.

Damien stopped, propping his hands on his hips. "No sign of him. It's almost like he vanished."

Selia's boot heel scraped over a dark stain on the floor, revealing the upper half of a compass. The place where the letter **N** would be expected had been scuffed away, leaving a grimy black residue. A grimy, oil-coated crescent moon appeared.

She tilted the tip of her boot against a rusty ring at the center of the floorboard, making the warped wood groan. A trap door creaked open, revealing the dark cavernous mouth of a tunnel below.

19
TREASURE HUNT

Selia's boots scuffed against a metal ladder wrung as she descended down into the space below the pub. The foul damp air became stronger with each step. The tangy scent of iron filled the claustrophobic space. Salt water had corroded the iron, making it rust.

Henrietta jostled against her purse, seeming to sense the questionable steps Selia took. Anxiety rippled up Selia's spine as a drop of cold metallic-smelling water dripped onto her neck. Was she walking into a trap?

"Ugh, gross." Damien said as he followed her down.

Selia let go of the last ladder wrung, and her ankles nearly buckled as her boots landed with a sodden thud onto the black cobblestone. "There is a bit of a drop," she called up to his two feet dangling overhead.

Damien landed next to her, right into a puddle. "Okay, we've definitely found some kind of nasty crypt down here."

"Who would ever want to work at a pub like this?" Selia said, noting how grimy the small little passageway seemed. Algae-covered kegs of alcohol were stacked against the stone wall, as well as some wooden boxes full of what appeared to be the pizza crusts they almost ordered.

Damien picked a barnacle off his shoulder. "Someone who isn't working for tips. I didn't think this fae treasure hunt would lead us to Davey Jones's Locker."

Selia squinted into the dim light that flickered along the walls, torch-light that held a tint of green. "Why don't we see where this passage leads?"

Damien fanned his face. "Why? So we can tell my Auntie some crazy story about how we got lost somewhere in a sewer?"

Selia brushed up against him. "Where is your sense of adventure? A selkie can't go sailing the high seas without her trusty pirate captain."

Damien's gaze swathed over her. "All right, but only if you guarantee to reward me with some kind of treasure later."

Selia faced the tunnel. Water lapped along the canal, which seemed to lead deep into the rocky cliff the pub was built next to. The walkway was too thin for two people to travel side-by side.

"How far back do you think this place goes?" Damien asked, and his voice was overrun by the water lapping against the stones that lined the canal.

"No idea, but it's definitely getting colder."

Selia continued to lead the way further into the tunnel. She bunched her coat around her center, hoping to fight off the chill creeping up her legs. Wearing a selkie skin dress down here in this frigid crypt was probably not the best idea.

Laughter echoed up the canal, bouncing off the water and out toward the North Sea.

"Sounds like there are people down here," she whispered.

Selia grabbed one of the torches hanging from the wall and shifted the light, illuminating a face on the wall. "Damien!"

"What!"

"Look at this art!"

She held the torch steady against the damp stone glistening in the orange light.

The face of something terrifying was staring back at her. Artwork of a selkie. The selkie's toothless mouth was draped open, from which she had to either be singing, or screaming. Carved into the back of her throat was a waxing crescent moon.

The selkie's eyes were large black holes that had been gouged into the stone roughly, with no effort to give her any pupils. Her hair had been carved like rippling waves that wove in and out from her face, making it appear that she was wearing a hood. Skulls were etched around the selkie's face, as well as some beautiful Celtic knot patterns.

"Whoever made this artwork wasn't a fan of us," Selia said.

Damien grabbed her hand, encouraging her forward. "That's because they hadn't met one like you."

They continued walking down the corridor, where more stone carvings of selkies appeared. Each one seemed to have the same hollow eyes and mouths that gaped open. Perhaps carvings were there to scare trespassers to turn around.

Selia's foot slid on the cobblestone, scraping against algae and something black. Everything was damp down here, including the torches jutting out from the dripping stone walls. Was this a catacomb? Maybe. The space beneath Paris was *full* of them. But this crypt seemed far more ancient than any crypt she'd toured beneath the City of Lights.

A phantom knocking sound ricocheted off the water.

Selia slipped, and Damien caught her before she fell into the canal.

"That was close!" he said, tugging her away from the water.

The stone Selia had slipped on wasn't a stone, but rather, a wooden oar.

She rounded the corner, and the source of that phantom knocking sound came into view. Five wooden boats bobbed in the water, which branched off into five separate canals. Each boat was separated by a wall of stone. From the left, a waxing crescent, then half-moon, followed by full. The right side mirrored that of the moon phases on the left.

"Why are some of them higher than the others?" Damien asked, and Selia noticed too how some boats were bobbing lower than the other two. The chambers below would flood, making the boats jumble their creaking wooden bodies against the stone walls.

The boats had different moon phases etched into the algae-lined stone on the wall behind them, then down at the water level. "I get it. It's a tidal system. The level of the water reflects the phase of the moon." She pointed to the full moon, which the boat in its canal has more water than the others.

Damien walked up to the vessel with the waxing crescent and nudged the side with his foot. "Seems sturdy enough." He squinted into the dark mouth of a black tunnel behind the boat. "What do you say we take this one for a ride?"

Selia smirked. "Let's set sail, captain."

Damien lowered himself into the boat first then helped her down. He took the oar she'd stepped on and shoved it against the wall, sending the little vessel out onto the moving water of the canal. Torchlight thinned and darkness grew.

Selia jolted as something moved past her ankle. She shoved her hand against Damien's side. "Quit it, you're not funny."

"I didn't do anything," Damien huffed.

The torches began to return on the walls, illuminating the source of her ankle brushing. Little creatures with beady black eyes, rounded ears and whiskers scurried about the floor.

"Rats!" Selia screamed, launching herself into the air. "How on earth did they get into the boat?"

"I guess they are the *swimming* kind?" Damien yelled, steadying the boat with his weight as he nearly dropped the oar.

The rats began climbing up the sides of the boat, their tails curling as they adventured through the vessel.

"I want off this boat, now!" Selia said, forcing herself not to scream.

The boat continued to bump and jostle against the stone canal, causing the rats to jump closer to where she and Damien stood.

"Is this canal getting smaller?" she said.

"I hope not."

Some of the stones were dripping murky dark water. Selia held her arms over her head, but the boat shifted violently, coming to an abrupt stop. Roots hung down from the ceiling, their dirty thread-like fingers gripped through her hair as the boat continued to travel deeper into the tunnel.

"Look, an opening!" Damien said.

Selia was the first to launch herself out of the rat-infested boat and onto solid ground. Torches flickered with an ominous green light. Selia focused on the blue centers of the flames. Her salt nodes didn't burn at all when she stared at the blue light dancing on the walls.

She remembered seeing these blue lights on the train and in her dream.

Selia held out her hand to grab one of the torches, and the lights disappeared, casting them both into darkness.

"What the heck?" Damien said.

"This is great," Selia replied, very certain the rats were still scurrying around her ankles. She felt Damien's hand brush across her side.

"Stay close to me," Damien grumbled. His arm linked through hers, and she followed his lead. She had to, or she knew she would fall into the canal below. The water was lapping louder now, and she feared there was a very long trek ahead of them in the pitch-black tunnel.

"Ouch!" Damien stammered, and he jolted to the side.

"What happened?"

"I slammed my shin into something hard," he grumbled.

While Damien bent over to tend to his wound, Selia rounded the corner of the corridor, finding afternoon daylight streaming through an opening. The scent of fresh air taunted her. The canal opened, and the water emptied out into the North Sea.

She walked out into the daylight and peeked her head over the hill where the cryptic passageway they'd explored emptied from. The pub wasn't far from where they now stood at the mouth of the underground passage.

Damien hiked up his pant leg, sporting a massive swollen knot on his shin. "I slammed my leg into one of those," he grumbled, pointing over to a large rock that towered over them both.

Parked in the shadow of that large rock was a group of motorcycles. Further past the rock was a little wooden shack that was in even worse condition than the pub. Most of its shingles were missing, and it appeared the walls had been repaired using a combination of sheet metal and driftwood.

"We must be tucked away in a cove," Damien said as he ran his hand along the rocky shelf that surrounded the area. The sound of crashing waves echoed off the rocks behind them. The tangy scent of rust drifted on the air. Hidden back here in this cove, the little shack was nowhere visible from the Rusty Selkie.

A road drifted into the rocky shelf, answering where the motor bikes had come from. The entire wooden shack was surrounded by corroded metal—a sailor's graveyard. Everything from anchors to chains the size of Selia's hand dangled from the wooden walls warped by time and the salty breath of the North Sea.

"Get back!" Damien said, tugging Selia back behind where the motorbikes were parked.

Selia ducked behind a wooden crate as the rumbling drawl of a tugboat traveled up the rocky cove.

The two men Selia had eavesdropped on while in England appeared. Both looked like they'd seen death. One of them lumbered off the tugboat, while the other lowered a net dripping with seawater and tattered bits of kelp and algae.

It was apparent the two had been fishing the North Sea. What had they been searching for?

"I don't care if Alex likes our treasure or not. After this, I'm done," the beefier of the two said.

Selia's ears perked. *Alex?*

After hoisting the dripping net up onto their shoulders, the two men hauled whatever they caught towards the shack. The smell of alcohol lingered in the air, as did the stench of cheep cigarette smoke. They muttered under their breath something about seaweed, then disappeared into the weather-beaten shack.

20
THE VAULT

Boisterous laughter followed by a sling of curses filled the shack as the two men dipped inside. Selia crouched below a grimy, salt-crusted window as they slipped past her. She peered through the murky glass, spotting the two as they struggled to carry in their net.

"See anything?" Damien whispered as he sank down next to her.

"Barely," Selia whispered back, wishing she could get a better view of the mystery unfolding. Muffled male voices chattered inside.

Blurring shadows moved behind the glass. A beer bottle exploded against the wall inside the shack not far from where Selia peered in.

She ducked as two grimy hands grabbed the window and unlatched it. She huddled next to Damien on the ground, praying that neither of them had been spotted.

Everything had gone eerily quiet.

Damien crouched down to the ground.

"What are you doing?" Selia asked.

Damien grabbed her legs, preventing her from turning around. "Climb on—I'm going to hoist you up."

He dipped his head between her legs, and Selia sat back onto his shoulders. He grabbed a hold of her knees, straightened his legs, and stood up. With their combined height, Selia could peer through another window that gave her a much better view of what was going on inside the shack. The glass was much cleaner and easier to spy through.

Bickering continued between the shady individuals inside the shack. All were wearing dark clothing and were huddled near the far end of the room, standing with their backs turned to where Selia was spying. A spirited Celtic jig danced on the salty air, the melody dulled by the rolling waves behind her.

The shack was full of wooden crates and barrels. Empty beer cans, vodka bottles, as well as some ash trays were jumbled about a table they all huddled around. Beneath the mess was a map of some kind, one that had a couple of knives dug into its center.

"What do you see?" Damien asked from below.

Someone much shorter and thinner than the others was sitting at the far end of the table. They wore a grey cloak with a hood draped over their head.

Selia couldn't make out the face of the smaller figure as their face was concealed behind the shadow of their hood.

A set of grey eyes glinted up at Selia from beneath the hood, eyes Selia remembered. The nymph hidden beneath the cloak had the same eyes that had been spying on her outside of Auntie's cottage. "It's Alexandra!"

Damien struggled beneath her. "How many others are there?"

Selia stifled a laugh. This had to be a joke. Gaia's Order was *one* nymph—an Iridescent named Alexandra—and a bunch of crusty old fishermen dressed in black trench coats?

Sitting at the center of the table were *dozens* of salt trancing talismans. Some were dark and dull, while others glistened like marble.

"Alex, we got your treasure," a man grumbled, and the hooded figure turned.

"I will not believe it until I see it," Alexandra replied.

"I told you she wouldn't believe us," a man grumbled far too close to where Selia was snooping.

Selia finagled herself against the windowsill, praying that she hadn't been spotted by the men now swarming the shack. The clattering sound of metal shook from every direction as they packed into the room. Each carried boxes, bags and an occasional wooden chest.

"We found it floating in a current that near killed half the crew. Rip tide nearly tore our boat in half," one of the men barked, and what that dragging sound was came into view. Scraping across the floor was the item they'd pulled out of the North Sea.

The item was covered in the starfish. Arm after arm folded and shifted as though the creatures were struggling for dear life to stay attached to whatever their suction cups were fastened to.

The net was moving. It fact, it wasn't really a net at all. Was it an octopus? The amount of curling arms the creature had was uncanny. There were no suction cups—just a mass of tiny curling hooks that thrashed out at the men when they ventured too close to the phantom treasure it was guarding.

The net flailed, sending one of the men flying.

Alex brought a blade to the flailing hooks, slicing through them. The net of hooks fell onto the ground, twitching, then still.

Selia's stomach squirmed. Had she killed the poor creature? The musky sent of brine and something tangy with iron filled the air.

With a flick of her wrist, Alex returned her blade to her side. The starfish retreated, seeming to sense they too would be hacked to pieces if they didn't move. The item concealed was now visible.

An oval-shaped vessel sat on the table, glowing softly. Selia had seen this glow before, when she dipped her fingers into the water where Amy and Alex had discussed such an item. Lights had shimmered in the water, disappearing into the reflectionless abyss at her fingertips. A treasure had been there, sitting just beneath the water's surface.

"They have the vault!" she whispered, nearly toppling off the crate.

"You're kidding me," Damien said much louder than he should. He staggered to the left, and Selia knocked her arm against the windowsill.

Alex waved her hand, walking over to another table where a chest lay open. "Balfour? Bring to me this treasure these fools have discovered."

A wooden crate shifted not far from where Selia was spying through the window. A man had been standing there in the dark she assumed was a shadow.

Balfour cupped the vault in his massive hands and walked to the table where Alex had stopped. For a man his size, he moved with surprising grace. His hair was black and wiry. Unruly locks fell to his bulky shoulders. A beard jutted from his chin, thickening along his jaw and neck. Balfour's dark eyes glinted up to where Selia was then darted back to the vault. Did the giant see her? Or was he pretending *not* to have seen her?

In the moment it took for his eyes to flicker up to where she was spying, a hollowing sensation filled her stomach. She could get lost in Balfour's eyes. They didn't seem human. Something about the air around him was different. And the symbol on his back wasn't the anchor the other fishermen all sported.

Balfour's jacket had a blue sea dragon coiling up between his bulky shoulders.

Balfour set the vault down on the table next to the open chest, giving Selia a better look at the fae treasure. The vault was egg-shaped with a colorful sheen that resembled the inside of an oyster shell. It was no bigger than a melon in size. The surface was bumpy in some places and smooth in others. Just looking at the treasure made Selia's salt nodes warm.

Every few seconds light escaped it, blue light that Selia had seen pulsing in her periphery.

Was the fae treasure the source of the blue light she was seeing?

Alex reached into her pocket and withdrew something else. A familiar chunk of limestone appeared in the dim light—Selia's salt trancing talisman!

She held the talisman over the vault and let it go. Like a magnet, the talisman stuck to the vault's side. The pulsing blue light emitting from the vault stopped.

"Hey, that's not the *only* treasure we found," one of the men said, and the others began digging their arms into their pockets.

Everything from leather bags, knives and silver goblets went spilling onto the wooden table. One-by-one, the men revealed stones and gems; all poured out into the open. Everything from pewter goblets to crowns, and even a few golden chains lay about. Mixed in there were the silver coins Selia remembered seeing both in her office and in Damien's art studio.

Alex sifted through the items presented, grabbing one of the trembling talismans that was inching toward the vault. She tilted the talisman over. "The Blind Moon is helping Amphitrite to see again."

Selia's heartbeat jumped into her throat. *Her*? Helping Amy see?

Alex continued to manipulate the talisman in her palm. "Amy has forgotten the purpose for the art. With each day that passes, she loses more of her own memory of why she set out to restore it."

"If this Amphitrit—trit…oh heck. What's Amy forgetting again?" one of the men asked.

The scar on Alex's upper lip twitched. "She's forgotten the fourth salt trancing principle."

Selia nearly toppled over. A *fourth* principle?

Alex stared down at the vault, blue light rippling on her porcelain skin. "Amphitrite sealed the fae treasure away in this vault long ago. What is inside is very much alive, and it's waiting to emerge. Without blue minca, however, that will be difficult."

"Minca is that blue stuff that disappeared from the sea, right?" one of the men asked.

Alex's eyes glinted. "Minca's disappearance has made this treasure even more dangerous."

"What do you want us to do with the vault?" one of the men asked.

Alex grabbed Selia's salt trancing talisman stuck to the vault's side and tucked it into her pocket. She then grabbed the vault and set it into the chest, then snapped the lid shut. "We can't let Amy find it, or she will remember the fourth principle. The vault must be destroyed."

"How do you want us to destroy it?"

Alex unsheathed a knife from her hip. "Use your imagination!" she said, launching the blade across the room.

Selia ducked as it stuck into the wall inches from where Balfour stood. She inched back up to the window, peering through the glass. Two men bustled over to where Alex stood.

"The fae treasure is connected to blue minca kelp!" Selia whispered.

"Minca? Really?" Damien stammered from below.

Selia grabbed a fistful of Damien's thick hair, balancing herself in place.

One of the men brought a metal chain over to the chest and wrapped it around the exterior. He and another man lowered the chest into a net and hoisted it between them on their shoulders, then slipped out of the shack.

Selia slapped her hands on Damien's shoulders. "Let me down!"

Damien crouched to the ground, and Selia slid off his shoulders.

She took off in a jog towards the beach.

"Where are we going?" Damien asked, falling into stride next to her.

"They're trying to destroy the vault!" She grabbed his hand, tugging him along. Her lungs burned with cold as she and Damien struggled to catch up with the fishermen as they approached a pier. Their dark silhouettes danced against the backdrop of sea.

An icy *splash* confirmed Selia's fear. In a matter of seconds, the men had thrown the vault back into the North Sea. The two loaded onto one of the tug boats and floated out onto the frigid waters of the North Sea.

Selia darted towards the pier, her pulse thrashing in her chest. A thousand questions rattled through her mind. How could she figure out what the fourth salt trancing principle was and get the vault open in time?

"Wait up!" Damien said, but Selia's jumble of emotions and thoughts drowned out his voice. Each step she took down the pier brought more fog.

Selia stopped at the spot where the icy splash hit the water. Ripples encircled the spot where the men had thrown Amy's treasure back into the sea.

Damien stopped at her side, panting out little puffs of condensation. "Great."

Blue light pulsed through Selia's periphery.

Something inside of the vault was calling out to her, the pulsing lights returning to her sight again.

Another *splash* sounded from the water.

Freezing drops of ocean water sprayed against her clothes. Damien was no longer standing next to her on the pier.

"Damien!" Selia cried as his body disappeared into the ebony water.

21

MOON MESSAGES

Damien disappeared into the freezing water, leaving Selia helpless on the dock.

A head and arm flailed a few meters from her.

Selia raced for him, the toe of her boot catching on a soggy wooden board as she nearly fell in. "Damien!" she cried, catching herself before she tumbled into the water.

Damien was bobbing in the water below, a huge smile spreading across his colorless face. "I got it!"

She reached down, grabbing a freezing, sodden fist-full of his pirate coat and tugged him up onto the pier.

Damien staggered to his hands and knees, choking out a mouth-full of salt water.

She slapped him. "What were you thinking? You are going to get hypothermia!"

Damien coughed. "I wasn't about to let those blokes get away with drowning this—whatever it is..." He cradled the vault in his arms. Ice crystals formed in his facial hair. His lips were turning blue.

Selia grabbed his freezing hand and tugged him off the pier. "We need to get you home to warm up."

Selia was met by an excited Mr. Kisses as she barged into Auntie's cottage. Her chill finally broke the moment she saw the hearth crackling with fire.

Auntie appeared in the doorway of the kitchen, a wooden spoon in her hand. "Where have the two of you been?" she boasted, squinting at Damien. "And why on earth are you soaking wet?"

Damien placed his sopping wet pirate coat over vault and set it in front of the fireplace. "T-t-thhheee b-b-b-e-each."

Auntie shot Selia a curious look. "You didn't attempt to drown my nephew now, did you?"

"No!" Selia said. "This was all him." Selia shivered just by looking at Damien's soaking-wet clothes and pale skin. "For heaven's sakes, go warm up!"

Damien gave a ghostly nod, then headed toward the bathroom, leaving Selia with the large oval-shaped vault sticking out from Damien's sopping wet pirate coat.

Auntie continued to glare at her, anger glinting in her eyes. "What on earth have you done to my nephew?"

"I haven't done anything."

"Lies!"

Selia grabbed the vault concealed in Damien's pirate coat and left Auntie standing by the fire. A loud thundering rhythm pulsed through her salt nodes with such force she felt her head might explode. But the rhythm wasn't coming from the vault she was holding.

Blue light flashed in her periphery, leaving a trail of an image behind it—an image of the blue bottle that had Damien's blue memory salt crystal inside.

She walked to the guest bedroom, finding the bottle of selkie salt skin sitting there with the other three atop the dresser. It sat apart from the others, but it was the only bottle releasing a kind of blue aura around it.

She set the vault atop the dresser next to the bottle of selkie salt skin. Were the crystals inside trying to tell her something? Or perhaps, was whatever inside the vault trying to communicate with the crystals of Damien's?

She grabbed the bottle of selkie salt skin, focusing on the rhythm it was producing for her. The rhythm was a pulse that didn't belong to her.

It was a heartbeat, Damien's heartbeat. She could feel it.

Memories that drifted behind that blue aura began to manifest before her. Memories of his art studio. Selia closed her eyes, allowing his blue memories to flow through her. Memories of him painting by moonlight.

His signature marked every one of his moonlit paintings, the blue pigment bleeding through the paper.

A tendril of water vapor drifted in front of her. Damien's art studio evaporated, and her office at the Louvre appeared. Sitting on her desk was a cardboard box. A small blue fairy had been drawn on the address label.

Her office vanished, leaving Selia to stare at the bottle of selkie salt skin in her palm. She set the bottle back onto the dresser next to the vault.

Damien appeared in the doorway. He'd changed into a fresh set of warm clothes. His hair was damp and curling, but the color had returned to his face.

"Are you better?" Selia asked.

Damien walked over to where she stood. He wrapped his arms around her, pinning her against the dresser. He pressed his face to her neck, which was still cold. "Much better." He ran his hands down her lower back and pulled her into an embrace.

Anger and gratitude flooded Selia's body. He'd been an idiot and a hero at the same time. "I'm pretty sure your Auntie thinks I'm trying to murder you now."

"Let her think that." His eyes dipped down to her lips, then back up to meet her gaze.

"Your lips are still blue," she whispered.

He pressed his lips to hers, which were still cold. He pressed his tongue against hers, working his mouth over hers. "Not cold anymore, I hope."

Alex's words from the shack rang through her ears.

The Blind Moon is helping Amphitrite to see again.

Selia locked her gaze with Damien. "I know how Amy tried to restore the art. I overheard Alex discussing it with the others. There is a fourth principle."

Damien's brows drew up. "Well, what is it?"

Selia shook her head. "I don't know. Amy has forgotten what this fourth principle is. Whatever is inside the vault will help Amy remember it." She looked down at the vault. "I know why Alex stole the talisman from my office now. Alex believes that Amy gave me the talisman to me to help her find the vault. But she's wrong."

"How is Alex wrong?"

"Alex thinks Amy gave the talisman to me."

"Didn't she?"

"No! Amy did *not* give me the talisman. In fact, she was surprised that I even had it. But Alex obviously believed that Amy gave it to me. I don't know how it ended up at the Louvre, but it is the first item I remember having memories of at the museum."

Damien's eyes drifted to the vault, then back to her. "Well? Why don't we try and get this fae treasure cracked open?"

She grabbed breath, memory, and salt, along with the selkie salt skin bottle and walked toward the door. "Grab the vault and follow me." She led the way back to the room where Damien's ocean maps had been. The symbols on them had an uncanny resemblance to the tools she now had at her fingertips.

She stopped at the table where the cardboard box lay open with Damien's watercolor map sticking out of the top.

Damien set the vault beside the box on the table. "What's your plan?"

"Amy told me I needed to use the strands of moonlight to find the vault. Maybe they are key to opening it too." She looked from the bottle of selkie salt skin back to the vault. "I'm starting to think that the strands of moonlight have something to do with what you've been illustrating for the past ten years."

Damien's eyes searched hers. "What have I been illustrating?"

"Think about the symbol in your signature, the same symbol I had on my salt trancing talisman. Alex stole the talisman so she could locate the vault. Why didn't we consider that maybe the symbol is a clue about what this fourth salt trancing principle is that Amy forgot?"

Damien's expression became a curious one. "You might be onto something here."

Selia grabbed Damien's map from the box and unraveled it onto the table. She then scooted the vault above the map. It would be her compass to show him what she needed it to illustrate next.

"We might not have the folktales, but we have the symbol you stole from them. The *same* symbol on my salt trancing talisman. The Order obviously didn't want me to find something you were painting in your art studio. But this map you started ten years ago, the one they *didn't* destroy—it still has something moonlight does not reflect."

"What's that?"

"It still has *color*." Selia remembered how Alex held the talisman up to the vault, and it had stuck to its side like a magnet. Seeing the vault up close, it *too* had the similar symbol; only the spiral was much larger, encompassing the entire egg-shaped surface.

She set the vault on Damien's moonlit signature at the bottom of his map. Once centered, she set up breath, memory, and salt next to Damien's map, setting the selkie salt skin in front of them.

A blue light pulsed from the vault to the bottle of selkie salt skin.

"Where is that light coming from?" Damien asked.

"The vault," she whispered, watching as the light threaded down to the three bottles. The light filtered through each of the bottles like a prism, combining again as it found the bottle of selkie salt skin.

Something was reacting to the symbol and the salt crystals glowing behind it. Were the crystals trying to show them something?

The light danced and flickered, reacting like the blue lights she'd seen darting in and out of her periphery. The lights centered on the bottom of the map where Damien's watercolor pigments transitioned to blue.

His mouth dropped open.

A moon appeared, glowing softly across the water.

The moon morphed, phasing from waxing, to full, to waning crescent before settling once again.

The moonlight threading across Damien's painting formed a message.

Say the name of the fourth principle and the vault will open. Only the Blind Moon can remember its origin.

The moon disappeared and the bottle of selkie salt skin went dark again.

Damien's brows drew up. "Who is the Blind Moon?"

"*I'm* the Blind Moon. My name, Selia, means blind moon." Selia's mouth had gone dry. "Amy needs *me* to remember the fourth principle she's forgotten."

"Well? Your guess is good as mine, Blind Moon. You know, it has a nice ring to it. Do you have any ideas on what the fourth principle might be?"

Her eyes dipped to the bottle of breath, where a tendril of smoke was coiling. "Look! Another message!" She grabbed bottle, squinting at the writing that appeared on the glass. "With breath, I make the intentions of my heart clear."

"What does this one say?" Damien asked, grabbing the bottle of memory.

Selia grabbed the green bottle of memory. "With memory, I remember what my heart holds dear." She set the memory bottle down and grabbed the red bottle of salt and read the last message. "With salt, I surrender to what my heart treasures."

"Well? Which one do you think you should try first?"

Selia eyed all three bottles. Breath still had a tendril of smoke coiling behind the glass. She grabbed breath and closed her eyes, imagining what Amy would have done. She had a way with words and had quite the magical tongue. She pressed her lips to the bottle and whispered. "I wish to know the name of the fourth salt trancing principle."

The bottle went ice-cold in her hand.

"Um, Selia?"

Selia opened her eyes, finding the liquid inside of the bottle had started to issue a silvery thread of smoke.

The cork stopper went flying, narrowly missing Selia's eye. The silvery thread of smoke erupted into the room, thrashing into the air.

"What did you do?" Damien said, throwing his hands atop his head.

"I don't know!"

The silver thread coiled in the air, rippling like a serpent. The air became warm and cold, warm and cold, until the thread of what appeared to be water vapor began to smoke.

Damien grabbed a handful of Selia's clothing. "Should I try and smother it?"

"I don't see why not!"

Damien tossed the clothes at the bottle. The silver thread evaporated, leaving a billowing plume of condensation overhead.

Selia grabbed the bottle and wrestled the cork stopper back on.

"Is everything all right?" Auntie called from outside the door.

"Everything is fine!" Damien said, turning to Selia. "Why don't we save these magic tricks for when we know what we're dealing with?"

"Right," Selia replied. She grabbed the bottle of breath and shoved it into a drawer in nightstand.

The door flung open. Auntie poked her head in. She looked from the bed, to her luggage, to Selia's bra—which was now dangling from the closet door handle. "You have post waiting for you."

"Where from?" Selia asked, checking her hand to make sure she still had all her fingers.

"It's from Paris. That's all I know," Auntie huffed, her eyes landing heavily on her.

"All right, where is the post?"

"Oh no, you'll have to go to town to retrieve it. I don't get post all the way out here and I like it that way. It keeps the crackpots away," Auntie said, shaking her head as she left the room. Selia knew she was referring to Mr. Wilson.

Ching!

Selia dug her phone out of her purse. Deidra was texting her. She left the room and called her woodland nymph friend. "We got the vault! And whatever is inside of it is related to minca."

"No way!" Deidra said. "I was looking for a status update on this vault. Do you have any idea how it's related to minca?"

"Not yet, but I learned how Amy is trying to restore the art. There is a fourth salt trancing principle."

"*Principles*? You didn't tell me about these principles. What are the other ones and what do they do?"

"I'm still learning what they do. But if you recite them, you can learn a lot about the hearts of those around you."

"Oh, boy. You've been practicing salt trancing, haven't you?"

A ripple of heat ran up Selia's spine. She was no rebel like Amy, but she was definitely having fun with this art the Order was determined in forbidding her to practice. "The principles are breath, memory, and salt. The fourth one, however, is what the Order has been trying to stop Amy from playing with."

"Well, what is it?"

"Amy can't remember what it is, but whatever is inside the vault is linked to it. All I need to do is figure out what the fourth principle is, and the vault will open!"

"Wow, seriously? Dang, girl. You need to crack that egg open now! How the heck did you steal the vault from the Order?"

"Alex's men threw it into the North Sea, then Damien—"

"Wait a second," Deidra interrupted. "*Damien*, the guy you met at the Celtic Sea a month ago?"

Selia's cheeks burned. "Yes, *that* Damien."

"Hot damn, girl. I *knew* there had to be a guy involved! Have you bumped uglies yet?"

"No!" Selia said, turning very hot. She'd barely kissed the man. They were still very far off from the sleeping together part.

"Who cares about this vault? I want to know all of the dirty details between you and this Damien guy you're shacking up with!"

"Deidra..."

"I can't imagine it should be that hard to get the vault open, right? Well, things might get hard. It depends on how much chemistry you two have going on."

"I will let you know when I get the vault open," Selia said, ending the call.

Henrietta had unraveled a piece of string from one of Damien's wool sweaters and shoved it up against the bottle of selkie salt skin. Selia took the string and looped it around the bottle then tied it around her neck. Somehow, keeping his blue memories close to her heart made them seem safe.

22
RAIN

The car ride to town was exactly the kind of distraction Selia needed to begin guessing what the elusive fourth principle could be. Her mind was cluttered with the events she'd seen at the Rusty Selkie. It was apparent the Order didn't want her to know something about salt trancing that Amy was busy manipulating.

Damien opened the passenger side door of the lime green car in the drive, which gave a loud rusty *screech*! Selia squeezed inside, with barely enough room to extend her legs. The aroma of something damp, moldy, and artificial dominated the air. A tiny fairy charm dangled from the rearview mirror.

Damien climbed into the driver's seat. "I haven't driven this ghastly old thing since twenty years ago. All the ladies used to tease me."

Selia laughed. "I'll be sure to tease you as well."

Damien turned the key, and the little car struggled to turn on. Fumes exploded into the air, and Selia quickly rolled down the window as the dash began to smoke.

"That's how the Pixiemobile got her name. She spreads a cloud of fairy dust every time you take her for a fling." Damien patted the dash, and the fairy dust cloud of fumes settled.

The Pixiemobile gave a violent little shimmy, and they were off for town. Selia grabbed Damien's watercolor journal, where he'd written a list of descriptions of what he assumed the fourth principle might be.

The phrases Blind Beauty, Moonlit Reflections, and Blue Serenity were written on the paper. "Your list has a theme to it,"

"They're all descriptions of you, love."

"I hardly doubt that I'm a...what does this say?"

Damien peered over at his list. "Oh, that's heart of the sea."

Selia flushed. "You are having a great time guessing what this fourth principle is all about."

"How did I get as lucky to meet a woman whose name reflects the very heart of my artwork?"

"Stop teasing me."

"I'm *not* teasing. You've given me some inspiration for a painting I've been working on. I've had an awful difficult time of coming up with a name for it. Tell me, when was the last time a pirate treated you to a date?"

"I don't know. I can't remember the last time I dated anyone."

"Yeah right."

"I'm serious. If I have, those memories are all gone."

Damien's hand fell atop hers.

Selia gazed sideways at him. "Speaking of memories, are there any other strange and unusual Scottish traditions from Clan Malloch that I should be aware of?"

Damien sighed. "Christmas holiday is always a thing. Auntie begins prepping the daises and of course plenty of thistles—Scotland's national flower. She dries them for a month at a certain time of day as to preserve their natural floral colors, then prepares them as fairy dust petals for all the kids. My sister has her kids ride their ponies in the parade in town. She decks them out with these big green bows that they can barely carry because they're so full of pixie dust, which is all of the dried flowers."

"That sounds absolutely magical. How heavy are these bows?"

"They aren't any bigger than normal Christmas decorations. But the ponies are miniatures. Do you know the Shetland ones?" He spoke in a warm tone and Selia basked in another memory that wasn't her own.

"Lovely. What else?"

"A month out from Christmas day, Auntie, she makes these fairy ornaments for the gardens. She'll make tea sets too."

"Your family is wonderful."

"They're annoying. But I love them. I consider myself very fortunate to have my clan." Damien pulled the car over to the side of the road and killed the engine.

"Why are we stopping?" Selia asked. Rain pelted the windshield, softening the sound of her question. She caught the blurry outline of a stone sign next to the road, making out the word *Cemetery*.

Damien made a gesture with his hand. "Right over that hill is where both Maria and Sophie are buried."

Selia's body tensed. Rain pelted against the car, burying the sign behind a wall of water.

Without thinking, she reached out and grabbed his hand. "I don't know what to say."

Damien stared forward at the windshield as rain began to tap along the glass. "You don't have to say anything. I want to try something." He closed his eyes, setting his head back against the car seat. "Breathe with me for a moment?"

Selia closed her eyes, focusing on the subtle sound of Damien's slow inhale and exhale. The rhythm of the rain synced with her own breath.

Rain poured now. The sound encompassing Selia's thoughts about his family. How much he still loved them. How long he'd lived alone with only their memory.

"Do you feel that?" Damien asked.

"Feel what?" Selia asked, opening her eyes on accident.

Damien was staring at her, a hopeful look in his eyes. "Look at the water."

The rain droplets dolloping on the windows began to suspend, as though levitating. Blue lights hovered there, dancing on the water. "Do you see the reflections too?"

"I do. I started seeing them a lot more when I met you."

Selia stared at the water, the lights dancing and jumping like magic. The lights did something to her heartbeat. "How is that happening?"

"I don't know."

The lights danced and jumped, coating the glass in something as crystal as ice. Was it water, or something else?

There was a pulse in the water, a subtle rhythm beyond explanation. The rhythm seemed to sync with her and Damien's breathing.

"Water acts differently around you," Damien said. "Even the water droplets in the air seem to move to your pulse. Ever since we met, I'm starting to see that water is really a magical, *healing* thing." His gaze fell on her profile. "Selia, you have a gift that I hope you don't give up on understanding."

Selia continued to watch the rain droplets drift across the windshield, trailing in different directions, as though affected by some invisible force.

Damien's hand was in her lap once again. What should she do with it?

"I can't remember the last time I've felt this way." He shook his head. "Ten years of not seeing anything but the color of the ocean, and I've finally met someone who sees the reflections only I believed were real."

Selia shuddered. How warm he'd made her belly feel again. Was Damien trying to say something to her?

"What's causing the water to react that way?" Damien asked.

*Love...*she wanted to say.

His eyes drifted over to hers, something in them Selia couldn't explain. "Ten years means that a lot of time has gone by. I'm old."

"You think you're *old*?"

Damien shrugged. "I'm thirty-nine. Not a lot of women are attracted to a washed-up artist who can't even keep track of time."

Selia laughed. "For all we know, I'm fifteen-*hundred* and thirty-nine. According to Deidra, nymphs can live thousands of years."

Damien chuckled. His lighthearted sound making Selia's heart sing. "I can't wait to remind you how young of a woman you are." He leaned sideways, brushing his lips past her ear.

Beep!

Someone honked behind them, causing Selia to jump in her seat.

"Jealous old bloke," Damien growled. He turned the key in the ignition, revving the car to life. The rain droplets trickled alongside Selia's window, and she could have sworn the water began to change form again.

As her pulse quickened, the rain began to match to her breathing. She could have sworn she saw the image of a liquid heart pulsing back at her.

PART 4
MEMORIES & SPIRITS

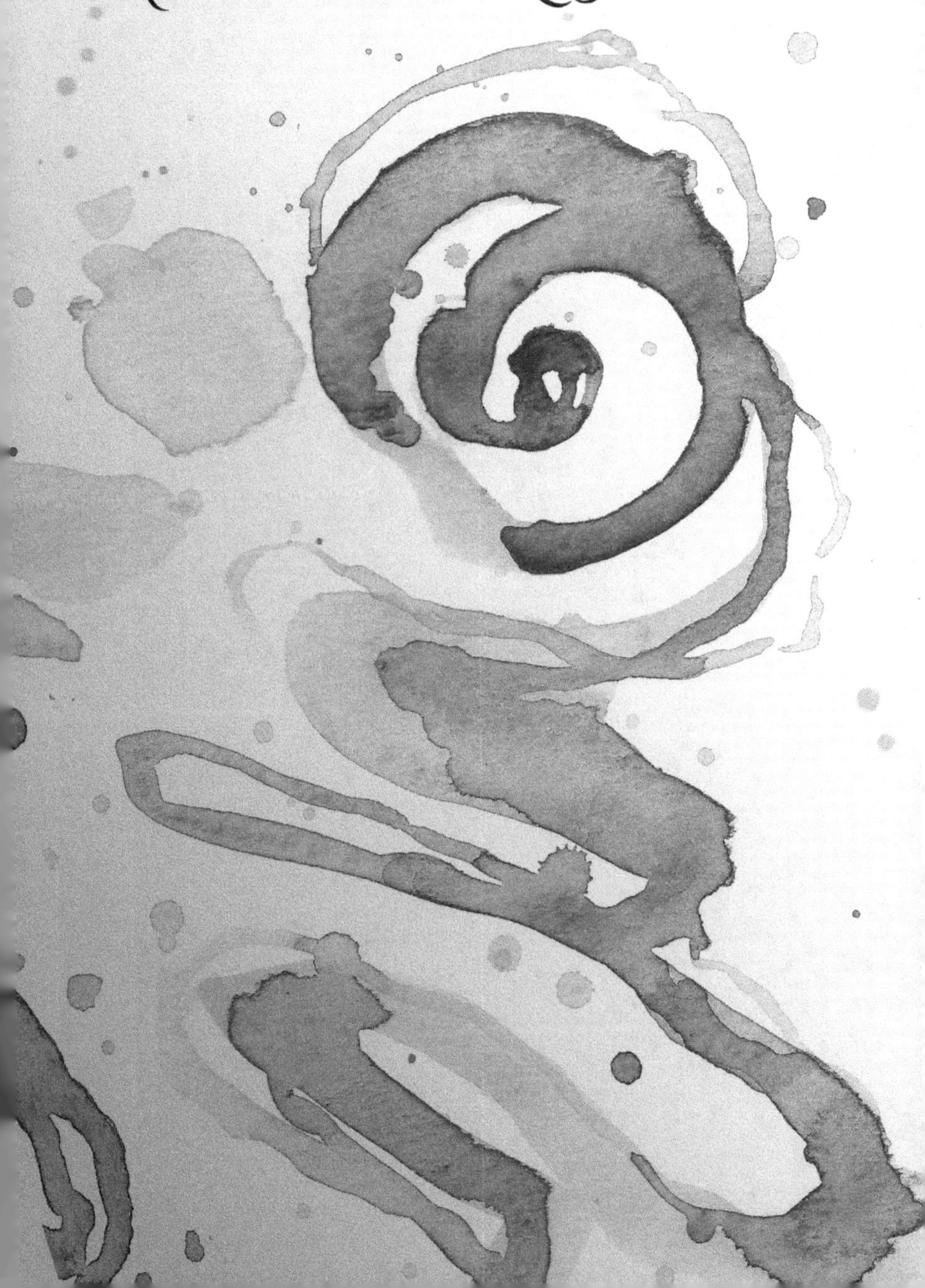

23
MERMAID PEARLS

Auntie's Pixiemobile puttered to a stop inside the city Edinburgh. Scotland's capital gave off a mighty historic vibe. With a castle in the distance and buildings that staggered next to one another, the Gothic architecture gave the impression that one had gone back to medieval times.

Damien parked the car outside the post office and opened Selia's door, helping her out of it. "Meet back here in about thirty minutes?"

"Sounds like a plan to me," Selia said as she stood.

Damien spun his heel along a cobblestone and began walking the opposite way.

"Where are you off to?" Selia said, grabbing his coat sleeve and stopping him in place.

"Well, I do have to grab something else. It's a surprise."

"What kind of surprise?"

Damien tucked a strand of her hair behind her ear. His lips brushed past her cheek, sending a shiver up her spine. "That's for me to know and for you to find out."

As soon as Damien left, Selia walked into the post office and got in line behind a couple of men she immediately recognized. Both wore dark trench coats with anchors on their backs. The air held a stench of cheap alcohol and cigarettes.

One of them swiveled on the heel of his boot to face her, but Selia ducked behind an aisle of greeting cards before being spotted.

"She won't find out. Trust me," he stammered.

One of the men shifted past a container, spilling wrapped candy all along the ground. "Oi, can't a guy find a pack of cigarettes in this bloody joint?"

He and his buddy jostled through the line of people and toward the exit.

Selia bent down grabbing the candies the men had spilled. What were they discussing about *her not finding out*?

Were they talking about Alex?

"How can I help you?" the woman behind the counter asked.

"I'm here for a message for Selia Fontaine?" she said, setting the candy back into the bucket.

The woman reached below the counter and pulled out a cardboard package no larger than a shoe box. "Here you are."

"Thank you," Selia said, turning to leave the post office. She stopped on the sidewalk, eager to open the box. She glanced over her shoulder, making sure the two men in trench coats weren't anywhere nearby.

She opened the package, finding a small silk baggie inside. She tilted the bag sideways and into her palm tumbled three shiny objects. Stones no larger than an acorn.

The little stones were beautiful. Pearls? Maybe. One side of each stone was rough and the other smooth, like it had been tumbled along the bottom of a river or stream. The shiny side was a vibrant blue, while the other was chalky and white.

Tucked inside the baggie was a small, crumpled note.

Mermaid Pearls. If not properly cared for, they disappear.

Warning. Keep away from fairies and hermit crabs.

Selia flipped over the note. Nothing. That was it?

She rolled the three little stones around in her hand, wondering who'd sent them to her. She tugged out her phone and began texting Deidra off a message: **I NEED TO CALL U ANY IDEA WHAT THIS IS?** She snapped a photo of one of the mermaid pearls and sent it off to her dryad friend.

Selia's phone rang. She pressed the speaker to her ear.

"Hey, ummmmm..." Deidra began, "you aren't trying to get *pregnant*, are you?"

Selia scoffed. "Why would you think that?"

"I thought that was a pic of one of those birth control things that tracks your fertility cycle. There are some strange ovulation rituals people practice these days."

Selia shrugged. "I don't even remember the last time I had a period of my own."

Deidra laughed. "Lucky you."

"For your information, Damien and I only kissed for the first time this morning."

"Whoa whoa whoa, you kissed? How cute! What was it like? Slow and sensual? Or is he ravenous?"

Selia's neck burned. "Back to the mermaid pearls."

"No idea. I've never seen anything like that. Maybe they act like wishing stones? Toss them into some water and see what happens?"

Selia spotted Damien strolling back up the sidewalk. "I gotta go."

"Okay. Let me know when you two finally hook up—*cough*, I mean, open the vault."

"Deidra..."

"What? *Something* needs to crack open. It's either going to be that vault or your virginity."

Selia ended the call, feeling more flustered than ever.

Selia looked up from her phone and swerved, nearly knocking into a woman standing in the middle of the sidewalk.

Selia spun, her heel catching a cobblestone. She grabbed an item that had fallen from the woman's bag—a box of paint brushes.

"I'm so sorry," Selia stammered, handing the box back to her. "Did you draw that?" she asked, noting the fairy on the box.

The woman shook her head. "No. My daughter loves drawing fairies on everything she can get her hands on." The woman brushed off her raincoat, and strengthened herself. Long locks of dark brown hair cascaded down her shoulders and back. He eyes were a deep, earthy brown.

Her eyes dipped to Selia's chest. "Oh my, what a lovely necklace! Where did you get it?"

"I sort of made it," Selia replied, feeling childish. The bottle with Damien's blue memory salt crystal in it had fallen out of her shirt.

"Well, that shade of blue absolutely compliments the color of your eyes."

Selia smiled at the woman's compliment. "Thank you."

"They say the color of one's eyes offers a glimpse into their spirit." She smiled. "My husband said that to me the other day. Men, you know how they are, always giving us their opinions when we haven't even asked for them." She waved her hand dismissively. "Anyway, I just came from the post office. Then, I became distracted by these paintings in the window. They gave me an idea on how to surprise my husband."

Selia glanced into the window, spotting a few oil paintings of the sea. While the colors were crisp and varied, she'd become a big fan of Damien's monochromatic pieces. "What did you plan to surprise him with?"

The woman began giggling. "I've been looking for a gallery to exhibit his work in."

"That sounds like a lovely thing to surprise him," Selia said, tucking Damien's bottle back into her shirt. "Where are you trying to help him start up an exhibit?"

"I know it's a long shot, but I thought about mailing a sample of his artwork to the Louvre!"

"I work at the Louvre!"

The woman's brow drew up. "You do?"

"I can say for certain that we do display art from local artists from time to time."

"Can I give you a sample of his artwork?"

"I would, however, I'm hesitant to take it anywhere close to the museum."

"Why not?"

"The Louvre is closed. There was a recent break in. Someone even stole an artifact right out of my office."

"Well then. I will make certain that when the time comes, I send a sample of his artistic inspiration to you. To make sure it *does* get into the right hands, who should I address it to?"

"Selia is fine."

"Right, then, Miss. Selia. It has been so lovely to meet you." The woman beamed at her. "You've convinced me. I'll find something of his to send."

"Hey, mom! When are we going home? I need to show dad my new fairy net!"

Selia jumped. A young girl was tugging on her mother's arm. Why hadn't she seen her before?

The woman rolled her eyes. "Your father will be ready to go on a fairy hunt when we get home."

"Mom, they'll have all gone back into their holes by then. We have to hurry, or the seashell fairies will invade again."

Selia's ears perked. "Seashell fairies?"

The girl's mother gave her daughter a reassuring and curious look. "I'm sure this kind woman has heard enough about the seashell fairies."

"This is great!" Selia said, and the little girl's eyes lit up.

Selia reached into her purse and pulled out one of the seashells Henrietta had swapped for another. "Do the fairies live in homes like this?"

The girl giggled. "No, that's a home for a crab, not a fairy." The girl held out her hand. "For the crab lady."

Selia held out her hand, and down dropped a seashell into her palm. The shell was strangely lopsided. It had three spirals in the middle, with one larger one that encompassed them all.

"Where did you find this shell?" Selia asked, intrigued by its beautiful spiral patterns that all seemed to merge into each other.

"The seashell fairies gave it to me," the girl said, her pudgy little cheeks turning red. She returned the seashell to her pocket.

"Thank you," the woman said.

"For what?"

"For fueling my daughter's imagination. It's not every day we find people who believe in the fae."

A bus pulled up, and the girl raced down the curb. "Come on, mom. Daddy's waiting for us!"

The woman's gaze lingered. "It was so lovely chatting with you, Miss Selia."

A bus pulled next to where the woman stood with her daughter and time seemed to slow. The young girl and the woman boarded. Before Selia could even say goodbye, the bus was already turning the corner down the street.

Selia blinked as a cloud of exhaust stirred in front of her. Seashell fairies? Is that what the little girl mentioned?

"Oi!"

Selia turned toward the familiar male voice. Damien was making his way toward her, carrying a large paper back under one arm. "Ready to go?"

Selia walked with him to the car, noticing the shape of how the paper bag crumpled around the top mimicked the shape of a bottle. "Did you buy wine?" she asked as she opened the door and took her seat.

"No..." Damien slid into the driver seat and tucked the mystery bag behind his seat. "What was the message from the Louvre all about?"

"You won't believe this." Selia tugged out the little note.

"Mermaid Pearls? *Really*? Who do you think they were from?"

Selia gazed at the stones, frustration billowing up inside of her. Selia held one of the pearls up to the window, making it shine. "They sort of have colors to them."

"I wouldn't know."

"I almost forgot that you can't see the colors." Selia tilted the greenish one to the side, finding a little blue sheen there. "What if these mermaid pearls go with the salt extracts that Amy gave me?"

Damien laughed. "Now you're starting to sound like a sea sorceress..." He turned the key in the ignition and pressed on the gas, steering them onto the road.

"What did you get?" Selia asked, noting the oblong parcel that made a clinking noise of glass as it shifted behind his seat.

His eyes swiveled to the side. "Nothing."

"A bottle of wine isn't *nothing*."

"Hey, can't a guy have some fun with the selkie he's crushing on?" He eyed her bag. "What did you buy?"

"Oh no." Selia said, realizing she must have picked up an item from the woman's spilled bag.

Damien's eyes got huge. "My word—is that..."

Wait a minute..." Selia held up the tiny garment. "What *is* this adorable little thing?"

Damien made a devilish sort of look. "Looks to me like someone has babies on the mind."

Selia's entire body burned with heat. She held up the little cotton garment made for a newborn. "It was a mistake," Selia said, thinking to the way the woman's eyes had thanked her in some strange, unspoken way.

"Do you want kids?"

Selia's stomach hollowed. "I just might have to give that idea more thought," she said, wishing she had a better answer. One look at Captain Malloch was enough to tell her that he would father beautiful little bundles of babies.

Damien pulled the car out of Edinburgh and onto the road that would take them north to Arbroath. Once they were through traffic and onto a country road, he took her hand in and set it on his thigh.

Selia's heart warmed. The silence felt comfortable between them. She closed her eyes and began to doze. She imagined how lovely it would be to simply drift off and have Damien's hand in hers the rest of her days, adorable little babies or not.

24

STOLEN TREASURE

A cold breeze crept by Selia's ankles as she walked down the hallway she'd walked through many times before. Her footsteps echoed off the tile floor as she walked through the Louvre to her office.

The bottle of selkie salt skin lay on her chest. It was heavy, and the weight of it made it harder for her to expel her breath. Instead of turning where she would for her office, the bottle pulsed against her skin, directing her somewhere she'd not visited in a while. She stopped in the hall of Greek marble statues.

Amphitrite's statue, goddess of the sea, and wife of Poseidon, lay before her. Her arms wrapped around the body of a fish with a gaping mouth. Amy's sculpture had been Selia's favorite in the museum for as long as she had memory of interpreting and organizing displays of sea nymphs like the sea goddess.

Alex's words rang in Selia's ears. "*The Blind Moon is helping Amphitrite to see again.*"

Movement caught Selia's eye. Something blue darted in her periphery, the shimmer glistening over the marble that was Amy's face. Amy's pupilless eyes reflected the blue lights as they fluttered through the museum, catching the daylight dappling through the windows.

Selia remembered what she'd forgotten while becoming distracted with Amy's sculpture. There had been a package delivered to her full of artifacts that she had forgotten to sort. She vaguely remembered receiving a package in the mail. Who was it that she'd discussed this with?

Panic ripped through her. What would her boss say if she forgot another meeting? Heaven forbid she forgot where that latest report on Egyptian fertility figurines went?

Her footsteps echoed in the hall as she took off in a run towards her office. Silhouettes of people passed her. Expressionless faces moved through the hall. Their bodies were drifting and transparent. Voices were hushed, too obscure to understand.

She stopped at her office, finding that the door was ajar.

Who had been inside?

The tangy scent of salt water filled her salt nodes. Light and shadow danced along the back wall where she'd seen a thread of something drifting in the wind. A cold breeze tugged at her hair, pulling her closer to the dark corner where the light had been.

Her office evaporated, and she was standing at the edge of the ocean. The water from this ocean was not salt water. It was alive and breathing. That breath synced with Selia's pulse.

The breath of the North Sea washed over her. She'd been here before. This was the ebony water with no reflections. Only a lonely moon hovered over the water, her reflection invisible like herself.

The sound of something dropping into water echoed up the beach. Selia squinted into the dark, unable to see what was making the noise.

She walked to the water's edge, crinkling her toes into the damp sand. A wave lapped at her toes, bringing an item to her attention.

The vault lay before her, water flowing back out and dragging sand with it. Light began to pulse inside of the egg-shaped vessel, blue light that was fading.

Selia's heart thundered in her chest. Why was the light fading? Was it dying?

She squatted down to touch the vault, but the waves grabbed it before she could take it into her arms. Her face appeared in the sandy pool where the vault had been. Her eyes had no pupils. Her mouth moved, but no words came out. Her reflection set her hand to her chest, and a great pulsing pain thundered through her body.

"Selia?"

A gentle shake came to her shoulder, and Selia jolted upright. The pain pulsing through her chest was gone.

"Sweetheart, are you okay?" Damien's voice steadied her. His warm hand was intertwined in hers.

"Yeah, I just dozed off," she stammered, her throat dry. Her hair was sticking up on the back of her neck. Her ears were ringing. Her skin was tingling and her heart, racing.

She wiped her hand across her forehead, finding her skin damp.

Damien pulled the rickety little car up Auntie's gravel drive.

Red flashing lights glowed in the mist.

"Why are the police here?" he said, his voice rising with concern.

Before Selia could open the door, Damien parked the car and jumped out. He darted over to the policemen, both standing with solemn expressions.

Selia's pulse raced as she ran over to meet him.

"Someone broke in," one of the officers said, and the other was busy writing on a notepad.

Damien's eyes glassed over. His jaw and neck muscles tensed. "Where is my aunt?"

Selia followed him towards the front door, which the lock had been bashed in. Garden gnome statues had been tossed aside. A couple of them had been decapitated. Many of her flowers had been trampled over.

Damien bolted through the front door, Selia on his heels.

Sobbing sounded from the kitchen, until they found his aunt as a quivering mess. She sat on one of the chairs at the tiny round table by the window. Tears were streaming down her face.

Another officer was standing next to her, but his note pad and pen were sitting on the table.

Damien darted over to her and dropped to his knees. "Auntie, please tell me that you are okay!"

Auntie gave a few blubbering sounds, that resulted in her wiping her eyes. "I'm fine."

"Who was here?" Damien asked.

"We didn't see anyone," the policeman said.

Damien's shoulders jerked back and he rounded on the officer. "What do you mean you didn't *see* anyone?" Damien growled grizzly-like, a vein throbbing in his temple.

"Damien, it wasn't their fault," Auntie stammered. "The thief locked me in my bedroom. I couldn't phone them." Her voice quivered and cracked as she spoke. "By the time I broke the lock and got out, they'd gone."

Damien pulled his aunt into a hug. "I'm sorry we weren't here."

Selia's stomach rolled with guilt. "Do you have any idea if they stole anything?"

The policeman shook his head. "Bertha insists they haven't taken anything."

"We'll file a formal report. Until then, make sure you are keeping your eyes out for any suspicious activity."

The policemen got into their car with flashing red lights and left.

Selia and Damien looked at one another.

The vault...

Selia bolted to the guest bedroom, where the door was ajar. She darted inside.

"Where did you put it?" Damien asked.

Selia's stomach clenched. "It's gone. Not only that, they took...oh no..." Selia walked over to the dresser where memory and salt had been. "They stole Amy's salt extracts!"

"What about the purple one?" Damien asked.

Selia tugged on the drawer where Damien had shoved the bottle. The wood groaned, refusing to open all the way. "I think breath has, crystallized?"

The entire inside of the drawer, including the purple bottle, had exploded into a beautiful shimmering spectacle. Thousands of tiny little salt crystals had transformed the drawer into a magical cubby.

Selia reached in to touch one of the crystals. "Ouch!" She withdrew her hand, finding a little red prick on her finger. "Wow, they're as sharp as knives."

"Did they really take everything?" Damien asked, tossing their clothes from the bed aside.

Selia began to shake. Panic ripped through her. "I don't have the vault, and now I don't even have the salt extracts that Amy gave me!"

"Calm down. We'll figure something out." Damien said, his voice dipping.

"Damien, look." Selia pointed to the wall. A crumpled napkin hung from a knife blade. She recognized the mermaid tail coiled around an anchor at the base of the napkin, which belonged to the Rusty Selkie.

She grabbed the napkin, tearing it away from the blade. A message had been scribbled there.

Good luck trying to figure out what the fourth salt trancing principle is without the help of Amphitrite's little potions.

P.S.

Steal from us again, and the fat lady in the garden will be our next target.

Damien took the note and began reading it over. "This isn't between you and them any longer. The Order has crossed a line. We're not playing games anymore."

He grabbed his pirate coat and tugged it over his shoulders, which were ridged and stiff. Next came his pirate hat, which he stuffed down atop his head rather forcefully.

"Where are you going?" Selia said.

"You don't plan on heading to the pub, do you?" Auntie asked, her voice still weak.

Damien's jaw clenched. "Nobody makes a fool of a Malloch and gets away with it."

25

DRUNKEN PIRATES

Selia tugged on the dress she'd stolen from the Rusty Selkie earlier that morning and left the cottage with Damien. She clutched the bottle of selkie salt skin on her chest. The crystal inside of the bottle clinked against the glass as she hurried after Damien toward the pub.

They had the fae treasure at their fingertips, only to have it snatched away. She dipped her hand into her purse. Her fingers scraped against the cold, smooth surface of one of the mermaid pearls. Could she somehow use them to get back at the Order?

Damien trudged ahead, his long black pirate coat swaying in his wake. After the nasty note threatening Auntie, he had every reason to want to pick a fight with someone.

"Shouldn't we head back to the shack down the way?" Selia asked, working to keep up with his furious pace.

"Knowing that lot, they're up at the pub stealing loot from people as we speak. I'm going to make sure everyone there knows what kind of scum they're dealing with."

"What's our plan when we get in there?" Selia said, having finally caught up with him as they ascended the creaking wooden steps of the pub.

"Leave it to me," Damien growled. He strode ahead of her, grabbing the rusty door handle and flung it open.

Selia stopped at the entryway and unzipped her purse to check another something that was missing. She'd not seen Henrietta since arriving back at the cottage. Even though the little crab was known to go off on her own adventure at random, her disappearance made Selia a little worried.

Perhaps Alex's cronies had stolen her as well?

She walked into the pub, spotting where Damien had already marched over to the men at the bar.

"How can we help ye scalawag?" One of the tall lanky men at the bar asked Damien.

Damien reached into his coat pocket, tugging out the crumpled napkin and slammed it down on the counter. "Listen here, you bunch of rusty *dicks*. You've picked your fight with the wrong clan." He slammed both of his hands down onto the counter. "Where's the captain in charge?"

The bar tender hiked his head back and laughed theatrically. "Sorry, Captain Short Cakes' shift doesn't start until afternoon."

Damien reached across the bar, grabbing a fist-full of the bar tender's jacket. "Then *you* will do." He grabbed the note and thrust it into his face. "You see this?"

"Yeah?"

"What does it look like to you?"

"A threat?"

"Someone in this shit-hole of a pub has gone and messed with a Malloch." He gripped tighter around the man's collar, his gravity winning him over. "I'm gonna blast your bladdered arses back to Davey Jones's Locker if you don't get the captain out here *now!*"

Two of the bar tenders erupted into a round of applause. "You're hired!"

"I'm *what*?" Damien stammered.

"Want to fill out an application? Drinks are on us!"

Damien released the bar tender's jacket, who darted off to his buddies chuckling behind the bar. He turned to Selia, tilting his hands up and his expression dumbstruck. "I was not expecting that."

She grabbed his arm. "Go with them!"

"Why?"

"This is perfect! You keep them distracted, and I'll snoop around, okay?"

Damien nodded, then walked over to where the two men were busy grabbing pens and a piece of paper.

Selia made her way through the pub, which was surprisingly empty. Rowdy laughter sounded from the back room. She stopped in the threshold that separated the main bar from a smaller room, where the voices of the men were carrying from.

Seated around a large round table were a group of gruff-looking men, all of whom were intoxicated. Between the empty steins and beer bottles littering the table, other items were scattered between them. Stacks of cards, cigarettes, and a shiny oval item that made the bottle of selkie salt skin resting on her chest tremble.

"You think Alex will find out we stole it?" One of the men grumbled sideways to one of his palls.

"Alex doesn't have any say what we do in our free time. She wanted us to toss it into the sea without knowing what was inside? Is she *mad*? We nearly kill ourselves pulling it out of the sea, and she wants us to go and throw it back? We could get thousands off something like this!"

Selia whipped around, looking back to the bar where Damien was now tending to his own stein of beer.

She waved at him.

Damien nodded at her, then made a motion to the others as he got up from his seat and walked over to her. "What?"

Selia poked her hand toward the room, keeping out of sight. "Those men in there have the vault!"

"Oi, Captain Rusty Dicks! We need to finish your application!" the bar tender called.

Selia chortled a laugh. The nickname they'd given Damien was very fitting, considering the name-calling he'd done. "Keep distracting them. I'm going to see if I can overhear what they're going to do with the vault next. It doesn't sound like they have any plans on giving it back to Alex."

"Alex didn't steal it?"

"No, her men are all talking about making some money off it!"

Damien began to move past her. "Well, I'd be happy to trade a punch or two for it."

Selia threw her hands against his chest. "Wait!"

"What? They broke into my Auntie's home and stole from us!"

Selia had something she wanted to try—something that involved the little stones a familiar hermit crab was now piling into the center of the table, stones she had three of in her pocket.

"Fine, but make sure you don't let them out of your sight," Damien grumbled and made his way back to the man waving his application in the air.

Selia inched her face back over the threshold, continuing to spy on the lot of men preparing to gamble off the items they'd stolen. They piled more stolen goodies onto the table, including something that began to scuttle across Damien's ocean map.

"What is it, anyway?" one of the men asked.

Henrietta was now being harassed by one of the drunken men. He kept poking at her with an empty beer bottle, which Henrietta was having none of. She wielded her claws like a pro and was putting up quite the fight as he threatened to smash her with the bottle.

"We could sell it to the pet store up the street and make a couple of pounds."

One of them grabbed for Damien's map. "I could make loads off artwork like this!"

"I've got dibs on it!"

"It must be a treasure map!"

"No, you big oaf! It says right here what the map is showing, can't you *read*?"

"The North Sea...ain't that the name of this here ocean right out the window?"

"Blimey, what a dumb ass you are."

"Then what's all them swirly lines about?"

The other man shrugged. "Whoever painted it must have been drunk when he made it."

Henrietta began to jostle between stolen loot and empty beer bottles. She seemed to have a plan. Whatever Amy's pet was concocting in that little crab brain of hers, Selia wanted to know. The men were just as stumped by the little mermaid pearls too, which Henrietta had collected quite a lot of. In the few moments Selia had observed Henrietta dancing between the drunken gambling bets, more of the strange little white stones began to appear like magic.

Why was she piling them onto one another?

"Oi, quit it!" one of the men. "Bloody little pest."

One of the stones topped from the pile into his half-drank pint—where it started to fiz.

"What are these things anyway?" one of the men said, holding up one of the pearls.

"Who cares? They're shiny enough to make some cash."

"What about these bottles?" another asked.

"That's mine."

"No, I got dibs on them perfumes. Women love 'em."

Selia's stomach did a flip. Both memory and salt were sitting at the center of the table.

"I'm off to get another round. This one's on me," one of the men said as he excused himself from the table.

Selia ducked behind the breasts of the wooden selkie guarding the room's entrance.

The man set his hands on the bar, spotting her crouching there. "Give us the lot."

Selia froze.

"Well? On with it, woman! Where are our drinks?" he grumbled.

Selia glanced down the bar. The other bar tenders were still preoccupied with Captain Rusty Dicks, who had a stein overflowing with a frothy beverage sitting in front of him.

She grabbed one of the empty steins from the stack in front of her and set it to the only brew in front of her—Selkie Blood.

One-by-one, she filled four steins until the head frothed on top. Then an idea crossed her mind. She dropped one of the mermaid pearls into one of the steins, then set all four of them onto the counter. "There you are."

The man flashed his gritty yellow teeth at her, then grabbed all four steins and disappeared back into the gambling room. He made his way back to his buddies with four steins, one of which was fizzing more than the others.

"Finally," a man boasted, grabbing the fizzing mug out of his hand and bringing it to his lip.

"*Pfffffttt!*"

"What?"

"You trying to do? *Poison* me?"

The other drank. "Mine is fine."

"Well, mine tastes like bloody salt water!"

Salt water?

The mermaid pearls were some kind of concentrated form of salt!

"Must have been the new girl up front. Go yell at her, why don't you?"

"I'm gonna do more than yell. I'm gonna demand we all get free drinks!"

Selia ducked behind the counter as all four men went huddling by, making their way toward Damien and the others laughing at the end of the bar.

Now was her chance!

She crept out from behind the bar and into the gambling room, where the vault, Damien's map and both memory and salt bottles lay.

The men up and left except for one, who Selia hadn't noticed.

Tucked against the wall was the giant man who had the symbol of a sea dragon climbing up his jacket—Balfour. Selia had assumed he was a statue of some kind. Had he been standing there in the shadows of the room the entire time?

Selia didn't know if she should approach him. He simply stood there, massive arms crossing his chest.

Clink!

Henrietta, however, launched herself from the table and began rolling something toward her.

"Good job!" Selia said, reaching down to grab what Amy's pet had brought her.

She grabbed both Henrietta and the bottle of salt, tucking them both safely into her purse. One salt extract was better than nothing.

"Oi!" one of the man yelled from another table. "This bloke claims to be the artist of the treasure map we stole!"

Selia looked to where the man had called. Damien was sitting there, half-way through a second pint of alcohol.

"My girlfriend and I have been hunting for pirate treasure," Selia overheard Damien say to one of the pirates.

One of the men clapped Damien on the back. "Captain Rusty Dicks, we'd love to have you back for men in kilts night! You'd fit right in!"

Through jostling bodies and heaving laughter, Damien was brought over to the table where the others were gambling.

"Oi, here she is now!"

Selia made her way over to Damien. "I think we need to go," she said, noting how each of the men were looking at her. She didn't like how dangerously close they were huddled around her.

Damien, however, remained firmly planted upon his stool. His arm looped around her waist as he tugged her closer. "How's my favorite selkie?"

Selia jolted away from his face. "What's wrong with you?"

"Don't...worry... I can keep theeese blokes entertained all night as looong as I have my prriiized selkie..."

"Are you slurring your words?"

He hiccupped. "Boys, this is my wife, Selia. Ain't she just the most beautiful...hic!...thing that you've ever...hic! Lain eyes on?"

The men downed their drinks, then slammed them to the table. "Aye!"

Damien swiveled on his bar stool, and his lips came dangerously close to hers.

Selia pulled away. "Are you *drunk*?"

Damien spun her around, the scent of alcohol permeating the air. "Come here, you seeexy merrrmaid..."

The ground began to shake.

Balfour approached the bar. His shadow cast over Damien, dwarfing him. He swaggered slightly, flexing arms that were as thick as a tree trunks.

"Oh, here comes the Kraken now!" Damien's voice cried from the bar.

Selia turned to face the drunken testosterone rooting through the pub. Balfour's hand balled into a fist. His arm slung back, slow and steady, swinging at Damien's head.

26
FAE THIEVES

Damien winced as Selia pressed a bandage to his swollen temple. While Selia hadn't succeeded in stealing back the vault or the other items the men had taken from them, she did have the bottle of salt and two other mermaid pearls to play with.

Damien sat on the stone bench in Auntie's garden. He propped his chin onto his hand, taking on a striking resemblance to the thinking gnome that sat overlooking the heather next to him. Sobering him up after being punched by Balfour had taken less than an hour.

His eyes darted up to Selia, his expression stormy. "How much longer are you going to torture me?"

Selia had to restrain herself from laughing. "You are being such a baby," she teased as she pressed a third wad of gauze onto his forehead.

"I am *not* a baby. I was just sucker-punched by a man three times the size of Goliath."

Selia giggled. "What did you think was going to happen when you harassed a man twice your size?"

Damien's eyebrows slashed. "He punched me in the head! Are you seriously taking his side?"

"You're lucky that Captain Rusty Dicks didn't end up with a concussion," Selia protested, laughing at the nickname given to him at the pub.

"I learned one thing. Don't mix the Crusty Cannonball with the Kraken."

"You and me both."

"Truth is, I could have drunk all those blokes under the table had I still been in my twenties." He gave his gut a look. "No use, now."

"I take it they didn't end up hiring you?"

"No. A bunch of the lot came over stating that my girlfriend tried to poison their drinks!"

Selia smirked. "Are you sober enough to discuss what I discovered about the mermaid pearls?"

"Do I *look* sober enough?" Damien groaned, his face looking green.

"You should be thanking her," Selia said, pointing to the seashell bobbing from one patch of flowers to the next. With each movement Henrietta made, Mr. Kisses was right behind her. His tail wagged as she dove in and out of the flowers.

Damien rolled his eyes. "Of *course*, the little crab thief gets all the credit after I risked my arse going in there to set them straight. And what do I get? A fat guy with arms as thick as tree trunks comes over and bashes me in the head!"

Selia reached into her purse, pulling out the shiny red salt bottle and set it next to the decapitated thinking gnome. "Our little crab friend stole this back!"

"What good is a bottle of explosive crystals going to do us when we don't even have the vault?"

"Hey, we would have gotten the vault had you not gotten so cozy with the men who were elbow-deep in their drinks!" Selia scolded.

Henrietta came scuttling over, waving her claws in the air in her attempt at a victory dance.

"The man who accused your girlfriend of poisoning him? I dropped one of the mermaid pearls into his drink. And the salty taste was a result."

"What possessed you to do that to a bunch of blokes who drink beer breakfast?"

"Henrietta gave me the idea."

"So, Amy's pet gives you an idea, and you just go along with it?"

Selia looked over at the red bottle, the hue enticing her. Amy had warned her that some of her salt extracts could be more seductive than others. She was willing to place her bets that salt was that one.

Selia tugged her phone out of her purse. "I never told Deidra that Alex's full name is Alexandra. Maybe that's why she hasn't sent me any new information on her yet." She grabbed her phone from her purse and walked out of the room, dialing her woodland nymph friend. A voice recording rattled through her speaker instead of her answering. *"Deidra the daydreaming dryad has gone off the grid. I'm interviewing with the National Parks Service. Leave your message at the tone. I don't promise to get back to you. I'm leaving it up to the redwoods to decide if I will ever pick up my phone again."*

Beeeeeep!

Selia rolled her eyes. It would be like Deidra to be that over-dramatic.

"Hey, Deidra. I need to know if you have any info on the Iridescent. I told you her name was Alex, but it's really Alexandra, and—"

Beeeeeep! *"Sorry, the voice mail box of—Deidra—is full. Please try back at another time."*

Click.

"Drat!"

Selia flipped through the past few months' worth of random and often drunk text message she and Deidra had exchanged. Deidra had mentioned Gaia's Order before, stating in her text the Order was *"a bunch of bodacious biker bitches who ruled the Fairy Underworld and took what they wanted from any man who crossed their path."*

Damien swiped the red Salt bottle and held it up to his face. "What's your plan with this?"

Selia took the bottle back from him. She leaned down, grazing her lips past his ear like he'd done to her in town. "That's for me to know and for you to find out."

Damien's face flushed from green to a healthy shade of pink.

Selia took the red bottle and walked through the back door of Auntie's cottage and to the guest bedroom to retrieve one of the mermaid pearls. Wedging her thumb under the cork, she opened the bottle. Nothing but a small *squeak* issued from the top.

Something about the room wasn't right. Henrietta's hidey-hut constructed out of twigs and stones from Auntie's garden had been knocked over.

Selia bustled over to the nightstand where she'd set the baggie of mermaid pearls. "Oh no, no, no, no!"

Henrietta had taken off with the last of the shimmering white stones. Something told her that it would take more than a drunk pirate to steal back this treasure.

27
HEART OF THE SEA

Selia darted into the garden, finding Damien hunched over and moping where he was before. "Damien, they're gone…" she stammered, stopping at his side.

Damien's gaze lifted. His eyes danced over her legs and chest, finally locking with hers. "Oh wow, Selia?"

"What?" she stammered. "Didn't you hear me? The pearls—"

Damien's hand reached for hers, his cheeks dimpling. "You've completely…what is this? *Magic*?"

Selia shook her head. "I don't understand what you're—"

Damien's other hand met her waist. "Have you *seen* yourself?"

She glanced down at the water in the bird bath, catching sight of her reflection. The woman gazing up at her was not her at all. Her reflection was someone else—a much more attractive and *seductive* someone who she had never seen.

Had the bottle of salt done this to her?

Damien's hand squeezed against her waist. "You are absolutely stunning. Not that you aren't *always* beautiful. It's just—" his gaze dipped to her torso, then back up. "What do I have to do to make you take advantage of me tonight?"

Selia began to giggle. "Go back to the pub with me and help me find the vault."

"The pub is the *last* thing on my mind right now..." He brought her hand to his lips, where his stubble brushed across her skin.

Selia didn't know what to do. She wasn't ready to step into this seductive, confident look that had never been part of her life.

"I can't go back in there like this alone," she said.

"You'd bring a scalawag like me to the pub? Wow! What better gift can a guy ask for?" He squeezed her around the center. "I treasure you more than this fae treasure any day, love."

After Damien tugged on his pirate coat and secured his makeshift eye-patch to hide his bruised eye, they both set off towards the Rusty Selkie. Not only did they need to track down the vault, but they also had a little crab thief to find.

The moment Selia walked into the pub, every male eye fell to her. The stench of alcohol and sweat filled the room. At least fifty people were packed into the small, claustrophobic space.

A banner hung across the bar's backdrop, framed by the bare-breasted wooden selkie overlooking the bar.

Come witness the Selkie's Treasure!
A sea spectacle worth saving your ale for.
Music and dance is sure to follow this one-of-a-kind event you don't want to miss!

"Looks like there's some kind of adult entertainment going on this evening," Damien said, his hand dropping to her waist. He pulled her closer to him as they intermingled with the crowd. He steered her toward an empty spot near the dance floor. Waitresses were dressed for the occasion, wearing Renaissance dresses and corsets. They sauntered through the guests, taking drink orders and handing out steins of frothing alcohol wherever they went.

"All crabs on deck!" a man called over by the seating area, where tables were being dressed for the evening. Little glowing lanterns sat at the center, each with an anchor.

Speaking of crabs.

Selia glanced down at the high-heeled boots of the female dancers gathering by the dance floor. Fish nets, seashells and barnacles decorated the outer section of the floor. A little lump on one of the loose floorboards was not like the other barnacles.

"Hey!" Selia said, skipping over to where Henrietta was busy camouflaging.

With a wiggle of her shell, Henrietta dove through a crack in the grimy floorboards.

"What?" Damien asked, helping Selia to stand.

"Henrietta is somewhere below us."

The heat in the room was making Selia sleepy. She didn't want to stay here all night trying to find a hyperactive crab while, simultaneously, trying to track down the vault. Her plan was falling apart quicker than she anticipated.

The chatter died down as a man wearing a long black trench coat shuffled through the crowd. Something foul stung Selia's nose as he stopped in front of her. He grinned, sporting a row of nasty yellow and black teeth. "Well, well, well. Looks like Captain Rusty Dicks has brought us a treasure indeed," the pirate said, a thick Scottish brogue rolling off his tongue.

Damien's shoulders stiffened.

"What is he talking about?" Selia whispered.

Damien sighed. "I *might* have told the lot that I would pay for every-one's drinks yesterday."

Selia caught a nasty look from the bartender. They'd both run out of the pub without paying for either of their drinks, and at least a dozen others. "You made a bet with a *pirate*?"

"Hey, get off me!" Damien stammered, but two men grabbed him under the arms and drug him back into the crowd, leaving Selia with the nasty grin of the pirate he'd apparently made a drinking bet with.

Selia backed away, but the pirate grabbed her around the arm.

"Oh, no. Yer not going anywhere but with me," the pirate said, his gaze swathing over her.

"I don't believe this selkie made any promises to a pirate," A woman said rather firmly. A whimsical tone danced like a song in her voice.

The woman shimmied between Selia and the grimy-looking pirate.

She wore a bedazzling green dress that shimmied up to her breasts. Her nose and cheeks were freckle dusted with little star fish. Her gaze flickered with emerald fire.

"*Amy!*" Selia cried as the magical muse caught every lonely male eye standing around them.

Amy turned to face the pirate who had been harassing her. "I think you need to take a swim with the fishes." She snapped her fingers in front of the man's contorting face.

His eyes hooded and his mouth dropped open. He swaggered for-ward, knees buckling, then toppled backwards.

"Oi! Another blackout!" yelled the bartender, leaving Selia standing face-to-face with the Amy's bedazzling smile.

Selia looked into Amy's emerald eyes, and calm surged over her. How good it felt to gaze into the comfort of her soul once again. Like little green flames, there was so much whimsy and wild dancing inside of them. Her freckles too, appeared much more vibrant. She counted seven prominent star-shaped ones that stuck out from the others. "What are you doing here?"

"Gambling, of course!" Amy said as she spun in place. She twirled and stopped, twirled and stopped, sending her green dress flying. "And trying out the latest fashion. The closet over there did not have the most flattering selection of selkie skins that helps accentuate our whimsical nature."

Selia laughed. She'd never had the whimsical charm that Amy had, or her confidence in a crowd. In the few seconds it took for her to twirl in her dress, Amy had already attracted every male eye in the crowd.

Amy stopped twirling and stood in place, shaking her hair out in a fit of laughter. She reached into her bosom, tugging out a green bottle. "How did my bottle of memory end up in the hands of these rowdy fishermen?"

"I'm sorry. Things got a little out of hand, and—" she swallowed. She looked into Amy's eyes. There was no room for lying. "I never could have predicted that your salt extracts would have been stolen."

Amy tossed up her hand, threw her head back and laughed. She shimmied in her dress, her wild red curls bouncing past her trembling shoulders. "Unpredictability is my *nature*. And as of late, forgetfulness." She shoved the bottle back down between her perky little breasts. "Speaking of memory, refresh my memory, love. What is it that we are searching for again?"

"You really don't remember?"

Amy's eyes met hers, and Selia could see the confusion swimming in their emerald depths. "Oh no, you really don't remember, do you?"

Amy shook her head. "I'm afraid that my memory has become as ill as yours!"

Selia grabbed Amy's hand. "I'm here to help you remember the vault! The fae treasure!"

"Ah! That's it!" Amy snapped her fingers. "I knew it involved something about a fae treasure. Let's get this party started!" Her eyes dipped to her again. "Oh, shoot. The other three principles that precede the fourth, what are they again?"

"You've forgotten the principles too?"

"That's not the *only* thing I've forgotten," she said, her eyes darkening. "Who are you, anyway?"

Selia's stomach hollowed. "You have to remember me...I'm Selia, I'm the sea nymph you began teaching the art of salt trance?"

Amy's dainty little nose scrunched into question, making the sea star shaped freckles dusting her cheeks glisten. "*Blindness* is vaguely coming to me. Oh, and the moon? I believe a full moon was involved during our first meeting."

Selia couldn't believe what she was hearing. Had Amy's memory become so far gone, that she too had forgotten everything about the art she'd taught her?

"You *have* to remember!" Selia said, grabbing Amy's shoulders and shaking them. "I haven't lived the past decade of my life blind to my past, only to find out that you too have forgotten everything!"

"What ever shall we do?" Amy asked as she clasped her hands to her cheeks, turning her sea star shaped freckles a dark shade of red.

"We need to remember the name of the fourth salt trancing principle!"

Amy didn't seem to possess the same urgency as Selia. Distraction had taken over. She swooped down, grabbing the seashell now bobbing between her dainty feet. "Oh, and aren't you an adorable little thing? Tell me, what is your name?"

Henrietta too, seemed disgruntled, even a little offended, that her owner had forgotten about her. She launched herself out of her hand, tumbling back down into a crack between the floorboards.

"Crabs are such opinionated little creatures, sheesh!" Amy shrugged. "Well, I guess my work here is done."

"Oh, no you don't!" Selia said, grabbing Amy's arm and spinning her back around. "The talismans—you at least have to remember the blue memories preserved inside of them?"

Amy nodded, her lashes blinking slowly again. "The talismans...I've collected so many up to this point, however, I've forgotten what my intention was with them." She slapped her hand to her chest and gasped. "Oh, my. Why do I suddenly feel so short of breath?"

"That's the first principle—*breath*!"

"Oh, is it now?" Amy slapped Selia's arm. "Good thing I have you around to help me remember."

Selia grabbed Amy's hand, her memory seeming to collect itself. She followed Amy toward the edge of the dance floor, where she stopped.

Amy danced the bottle of memory in front of her face. "Doesn't matter if you have these little bottles in your possession or not. It wasn't long after I sent you the salt extracts that I realized the ingredients expired long ago."

"Expired?"

Amy tucked the bottle of memory into her bosom and shimmied in her dress, giggling. "Oops! When your memory is as poor as mine, you begin to lose your sense of time." She surveyed the crowd, her pupils dilating then shrinking as her head whipped a round. Her face came dangerously close to Selia as her gaze dropped to her chest. "My love, what a gorgeous blue memory crystal you have created with the selkie salt skin! I'm so glad to see that you have been practicing with it!"

Selia grabbed the bottle, suddenly feeling possessive over it.

Amy clapped both of her hands to the sides of her mouth. "Oh, my. Have you fallen in *love* with him?"

Selia flushed. "You can read salt crystals far better than I can."

Amy winked at her. "Give it time, and you too will be reading salt crystals formed by the heart."

Amy's gaze drifted over her shoulder, then back to Selia. She dipped her fingers into her bosom once again and withdrew the green bottle. She held it in front of her face, her eyes nearly matching the green glass that seemed to shimmer more in her presence. "I recall sharing a blue memory of my own that involved us stealing pirate treasure, is that right? Refresh my memory about that night we first salt tranced together. I vaguely remember the two of us frolicking amidst a tavern full of pirates, swapping opinions on the size of cod pieces...and...oh, how could I forget! Stealing these little lovelies!" She held up a salt trancing talisman.

Selia remembered that first salt trancing experience with her all too well. "Of course, I remember. I'd been taken hostage on a pirate ship with a bunch of salt trancing talismans on board."

"Your memory is far better than my own. You might be blind to your past. You might have no idea who you are or where you come from. But a sea nymph's heart holds onto memories far longer than the minds of men have *ever* treasured." She peeked over her shoulder again.

"Why do you keep looking over that way?" Selia asked.

"I believe that bloke over there has our treasure."

Selia spun around, but Amy caught her arm. She caught the dark eyes of the man sitting at a table at the back of the pub. "*Balfour?*"

Amy nodded. "He and I go back a long time."

"But he works for the Order! I saw him with Alexandra!"

Amy's eyes dipped. "I thought about flirting my way over to him, however." Her lips pursed into a pout. "I think the hearts of two sea nymphs salt trancing are better than one." She grabbed her hand. "Before we begin, can you please introduce me to this lovely watercolor artist of yours?"

Selia spotted Damien, who was making his way over.

Amy's mouth dropped open. "Oh, he's absolutely gorgeous."

Damien stopped at Selia's side. "Sorry about that. Apparently, the guys up front still wanted to hire me, but I turned them down." His eyes moved to Amy. "Who is this?"

Selia flushed. "Amy, this is my boyfriend, Damien Malloch."

Amy's smile grew three sizes. "Charmed. Absolutely, charmed."

"Likewise," Damien said, giving Amy a small nod. "Selia had told me all about the art you are attempting to teach her. I'm intrigued with how many purposes this art seems to have."

Amy's eyes glinted. "Oh, there are more purposes than you know."

"How old is this art?"

Amy smiled. "The art is an ancient one. It predates the civilization of Atlantis. Salt trancing dates to a time preceding the memories of your ancestors."

Damien looked from Amy, back to Selia, who was just as confused by what she'd just said. Her short-term memory was obviously not the best—but long term?

Atlantis?

Amy grabbed Selia's hand. "I'm borrowing your woman for a talent show. It's time you see the creativity she possesses."

"I knew the moment I met her that Selia had a creative spirit," Damien said, winking at Selia.

Selia shook her head, heat branching through her cheeks at her boyfriend's flattering comment.

Amy curtsied in place, giving Damien a gentle bow. "I'm sure that you would come to adore her spirit even more after I am through with her."

Damien grabbed Selia's hand and kissed the top. "I'll make sure I find myself a front seat for this show."

Selia grabbed for his arm, not wanting him to leave. Damien backed away into the crowd before she could convince him to stay.

"Why are you giggling?" Selia asked as she walked with Amy toward the dance floor.

Amy wiped a tear out of her eye. "Nothing...I can just tell that the two of you are practically *made* for one another. I cannot express how happy that makes my heart." She leaned forward, her freckles catching the low light. "Selia, my dear. Why don't we show this pub the magic salt trancing has to offer?"

"Everyone, give our selkies a big round of applause!" An man announced into a microphone.

The room exploded into clapping, jeering and some high-pitched whistling that was coming from Damien, who stood at the very front of the dance floor.

Selia's heart leapt into her throat. What did Amy expect her to perform? She'd not salt tranced in such a public environment.

Amy grabbed Selia's hand, her fingers inching her forward and out onto the center of the dance floor. "Follow me, love. We have lots of magic and so little time to share it with everyone."

Selia followed Amy toward what felt like a *thousand* eyes turning to face them. Curious onlookers flocked around them. She looked from a rosie-cheeked woman to a hardy-faced man. Scottish folk had a cheerful, robust spirit about them.

She caught Damien's gaze, who was much more sober than the onlookers. He winked at her. His subtle confidence was *everything* she needed in this deep pool of a crowd.

"I have absolutely no idea what I am doing," Selia whispered, hoping Amy would call off the shenanigans now.

"The best art is expressed through pure talent, which I knew you had the moment I salt tranced with you at the Celtic Sea." Amy withdrew her hands and left Selia at the center of the floor. She walked into the middle of the crowd, gathering her energy like Selia remembered of the Celtic Sea Sorceress only a month ago.

Amy worked her magic in pubs like this. Selia had witnessed her seductive charm in a blue memory from three hundred years ago—when the two had first salt tranced together in a pirate tavern full of testosterone.

Amy turned toward her, arm outstretched. She beckoned Selia with her fingers. "I need my prized selkie to help me reveal the heart of this treasure for which you are all anxiously awaiting."

Selia swallowed. Amy wanted her to reveal something. What did she mean by *heart*?

Selia walked toward her, her feet scraping against the grimy wooden floor with each step. She hated being in the lime-light of others. She tried not to look the onlookers in the eye as she focused on Amy's outstretched hand. A single white stone lay there in her palm—one of the mermaid pearls.

"My dear, do you see this treasure?" Amy asked, fondling the pearl between her fingers.

Sweat began to bead upon Selia's temple. "I do."

Silence fell between them.

Amy's green eyes met hers, full of confidence she didn't possess. A fire behind them beckoned her, one she still didn't understand. Amy's fire was something that wasn't fueled by wood or hearth. It came from the depths of her liquid soul.

"What am I supposed to do?" Selia stammered, fear paralyzing her. Every eye in the pub was gazing upon her, expecting magic to explode from her fingertips.

Amy set her other hand on Selia's shoulder, her delicate face dipping to her ear. "Listen to the song of your heart, and every soul in this room will treasure you."

Selia's body shook with adrenaline. Amy's freckles blurred as her thoughts traveled to that special someone who might be admiring her. Damien's love for her had grown over the past few days. And that love consumed her thoughts.

Selia took the mermaid pearl and held it up into the air. "I ask you to release the heart of the sea to me…"

Her stomach churned. Damien made *heart of the sea* sound so good on his list of ideas of what the fourth salt trancing principle could be. Yet, she made it sound incredibly cheesy.

Amy turned toward the crowd, tendrils of long rebellious red hair uncoiling down her front. She spun upon her heel, gazing out into the crowd, her energy taught with poise. Hands propped upon her hips, she shimmied in her bedazzled green dress, sending a few sequins flying. "Well? Didn't you *hear* the woman? Let's get this party started! Release the heart of the sea!"

A man with a fiddle bound out from the crowd. "Heart of the sea, here we go!"

He strung his bow across the strings of his fiddle, singing out a melody. A melody that danced and reeled into something the crowd began clapping to.

Amy grabbed Selia's arm, and together they began to circle and circle, revving the jig's spirit to life.

"Heart of the sea? I've never heard of this jig in my life!" Amy exclaimed.

"I didn't know what to say!" Selia yelled back.

But the dance floor became so crowded, she and Amy had to dip away to avoid being trampled.

A couple of men flooded the dance floor.

Amy's eyes dipped to the kilt the beefier of the two was wearing. "Oh, my. This is about to get fun!"

Damien came barging over before the kilted dancers could make their way over. "Can I join in with you both?"

Amy let go of Selia's hand. "Of course!"

Damien's hand connected with Selia's free hand, and the three of them began to spiral.

Amy let go, spiraling out into the crowd. She shimmied over to the two kilted Scots, grabbing them both by their belts and tugging them aside.

Selia bumped into a very large someone who wasn't dancing. He stood stationary—his massive hands encompassing the treasure she and Amy had been after.

Balfour stood amid the crowd, forming a rift in the dance. His dark eyes lacked focus, making Selia dizzy. Balfour's eyes had storms in them.

With his bulk parting the crowd, he reached out his massive hands, handing Selia the vault. He turned on his heel then disappeared back into the crowd.

"Oh my, lookie what you found!" Amy said, swooping in and circling around her once more, taking the vault and tugging Selia aside. "I will keep this safe for now. You go and enjoy your time with Damien."

"Wait, where are you going?" Selia asked as Amy gathered Henrietta into her hand.

"To find something that you have helped me to remember, Blind Moon. I will send a message to you before long." Amy said, tilting her head forward. "Oh, before I forget! Look for the stones. They will appear when it's time for you to follow them." She swiveled on her heel and disappearing into the crowd.

Damien's arm came to her waist, tugging her back into his embrace. "You aren't leaving me now, are you?"

Selia turned to face Damien, his cheeks flush. She leaned in, kissing him on the lips as the Celtic jig reeled around them.

28

THE MOON'S REFLECTION

Orange rays of daybreak streamed through the window. Selia had tossed and turned next to Damien all night, replaying the events at the pub. She dreamt of her and Amy both dancing in the pub, the frolicking together out to the beach. Amy stood at the edge of the water, gazing longingly up at the full moon above the North Sea. A wave had come ashore, taking Amy with it, leaving Selia with her hand outstretched for the friend the sea always seemed to steal away.

Not only had Amy taken off with Henrietta, but she'd taken off with the vault Balfour had willingly given to her.

"Look for the stones. They will appear when it's time for you to follow them."

Amy's last words rang through Selia's ears like a song. She sat up in bed, wondering what the day ahead of her would show. She didn't have Henrietta to jostle her out of her sleeping cocoon any longer.

She set her hand on the side of the bed where Damien had slept. He'd already left the bedroom. She grabbed her phone from the bedside table.

Goodness—was it already *one* in the afternoon?

She and Damien must have partied at the pub *well* into the morning hours for her to have slept in this late.

She changed her clothes and walked out into the empty cottage, finding Mr. Kisses whining at the back door. Selia grabbed the handle and egged the door open, following him out into the garden.

"Selia!"

She followed Damien's voice. She spotted him around the bend of hedges, where he had his watercolor easel propped up.

She walked over to him, stopping at his side. "Where is your aunt?"

"No idea. Honestly, it's quite nice to have the quiet out here. I've been painting all morning, actually."

"How come?"

He flipped through one of his watercolor journals, shutting it and slipping it down into his bag. "I've been putting the finishing touches on a painting I've been working on for the past month."

"Can I see it?"

Damien stood up and pressed a kiss to her cheek. "You will soon enough."

The afternoon hours slipped by as she and Damien worked to tidy up Auntie's garden. Selia didn't mind the slow pace that occupied the waning hours of the day, as the moments gave her time to mull over what they'd experienced at the pub. She tasked herself with washing all the dishes as Damien had prepared them both dinner, which he insisted on serving by himself out back.

She returned outside, finding the low evening light had settled over the garden. The dipping sun cast a purple hue over the flowers, creating a colorful aura that transformed the landscape.

Damien's easel was still sitting by the garden, but he was nowhere to be found.

She walked down the hill, finding a calm wash over her. The sound of birds courting one another filled the air.

Selia caught sight of the path where a small wooden sign read: **Selkies This Way**

She followed the sign, walking out into a portion of the garden she'd not ventured into before. The flowers here were much more vibrant. Pink and purple foxglove mixed with hydrangea bushes. Even a few pixie cup mushrooms lined the stone pathway.

As evening settled in, the sky transformed into a brilliant display of colors. Pinks and oranges danced with one another, casting a colorful glow onto Auntie's garden. Yellow and purple flowers had bloomed in the late June humidity. Their sweet floral scents drifted on the air, lulling Selia's anxiety about the past few days.

Insect wings buzzed in the air. Crickets chirped along the hedges. The storm from the night before had doused the earth in a fresh blanket of moisture. She walked around the hedge, hoping to find where Damien had disappeared to.

"Selia?"

Selia turned towards Damien's warm voice. Her breath caught. Who was this man?

Damien wore a white linen shirt with loose-fitting sleeves. Lace hung from the shirt below his neck, stringing the fabric together. The garment clinging to the lower half of his body hugged him in all of the right places. His kilt had reds and greens woven over one another.

He took a few steps toward her, closing the space between them. He stopped, propping his hands on his hips. "Considering the fact I was the only Scotsman at the pub not dressed properly last night, I thought I would give you a show. What do you think?"

Selia eyed her kilted boyfriend up and down. "You are the sexiest Scotsman I have ever gazed upon."

He looped his arm through hers. "Let me show you what this Scotsman has been working on other than pulling weeds."

They rounded the corner of the garden, where a wooden table for two was already dressed for dinner. A lantern sat aglow between two dinner plates with covers atop them. Wine glasses and silverware glistened in the flickering orange light that danced across the table.

The sound of crashing waves floated on the breeze. As the sun dipped below the horizon of the North Sea, the ebony surface glowed with oranges and yellows that warmed the entire landscape. Even if Damien couldn't see those colors, he had captured the spirit of the Scottish landscape.

Damien walked up to the table and grabbed the bottle of wine.

Selia shook her head. "You are spoiling me."

Damien chuckled. He uncorked the bottle and poured her a glass, then set it down on the table. "Please, have a seat."

He pulled out the little wooden stool, and Selia sat down at the most adorably intimate spot she'd seen. The space tucked within the garden made her think they might be dining with fairies.

"What are we eating for dinner?" Selia asked, the scent of something robust filling her nose.

"Neeps and tatties," Damien said, grabbing his wine glass and filling it.

"Again?"

"My Auntie tends to make enough for a week's worth of leftovers." Damien pulled off the covers of two piping-hot plates, making her mouth water. He sat across from her and held up his glass of wine. "Cheers to many more adventures chasing after fae treasure?"

Selia held her glass up. "As long as you are wearing that kilt!"

They both drank and ate. It didn't take long before both of them had made a hefty dent in their dinner plates.

"Do you have any idea what happened to the vault?" Damien asked.

"The guy who punched you? His name is Balfour. He gave it to me amidst the rowdiness on the dance floor."

"What?" Damien said, a lump of potato falling from his mouth. "That doesn't make sense. Why would he attack me, then give you what you were looking for?"

Selia shrugged. "Beats me. Amy has it now. She told me to keep guessing what the fourth principle was. She didn't even remember my name."

"Amy forgot who you were?"

"Only after I mentioned the vault did she finally remember me."

"That is completely bizarre."

"Not only that, but she's completely forgotten the purpose of the art! I didn't realize how far gone she was. I can't let her memories disappear like mine did. If they do, I'll have no hope of discovering the purpose of the art and why she was teaching me."

Damien's cheeks dimpled. "Art only finds its purpose when it touches the hearts of others."

"I wish I had half of the magic that Amy showed everyone last night."

Damien's brow furrowed. "Are you comparing yourself to Amy?"

Selia set down her fork, doubt creeping in. Amy's personality *was* magic.

"I get the feeling that you are comparing your salt trancing talents to Amy's."

"You saw how confident she was. She can transform a group of drunks into riot of celebration without batting an eye."

"That was the alcohol, not her." Damien's eyes searched hers. "Amy wasn't the light of last night's performance."

Selia looked down at her fork, unable to meet Damien's gaze.

He reached out, grabbing her hand. "Want to know what I learned about comparing my art to the art of others?"

"Sure?"

"The time we waste comparing ourselves to others is time not spent expressing our feelings to those we love." His other hand twitched on the table. He shifted his plate aside and set his watercolor journal before him.

"Were you planning on painting this evening?" Selia asked.

Damien's eyes dipped down to her lips, then back up to meet hers. The look was almost nervous. "Possibly." He grabbed the fabric on his shirt sleeves and rolled them up, then lifted up his journal. Underneath it was a package of brown paper, which he shifted across the table to her.

"What's this?" Selia asked, taking the package that had a piece of twine wrapped around it.

Damien waggled his eyebrows at her. "Go on. Open it."

Selia unraveled the twine from the package that was bigger than most letters, the same size as the watercolor paper in Damien's journal. What-ever was inside was very light. Her heart raced as she folded back the paper.

She tugged out a letter covered in Damien's handwriting.

Selia, my Blind Moon,

Your light is very special. I can't begin to try and describe it. I can only hope this painting illustrates what you have given me. What I have lost, you have helped me to find again.

Time mends all wounds.

Reflecting   like   threads   upon   the   ocean bright.
Broken,   the   fragments   can   heal   the   deepest places   in   our   hearts.
By   threading   together   a   strand   of   moonlight.

Selia looked up at him. "Did you write this?"

Damien nodded. "I was never able to share the full folktale with you, so I ended up writing my own." He clasped both of his hands on the table. "The painting I never shared with you in Paris? Well..." He cleared his throat. "I just hope that I've done it justice."

She set Damien's note down and unwrapped the remaining paper from the package. Her fingers traced the edges of a wooden frame. She blinked a few times, the image not registering.

Her fingers trembled as she ran them along the image of someone she didn't quite recognize. A blue watercolor portrait of a woman with long dark hair. Her gaze fell foreword, captivated with a reflection of the moon below. The reflection dancing on the water spiraled and danced around her heart.

Selia traced her fingers around the woman's face, which he'd accentuated in an Art Nouveau style. How intricately he'd paid attention to her features. Her eyes were dark, luminous pools of emotion.

She looked up at Damien, tears stinging the corners of her eyes. "You painted...*me?*"

"Do you like it?" he asked.

"Like it? Damien, I am speechless..."

"I didn't show it to you because I hadn't added the final details I felt it deserved. When I learned that your name meant blind moon, everything became easy after that. I bought the frame when we went to town, knowing I had to finish this sooner than I had planned. I was able to complete it this morning." He tugged out his detail brush and waggled it at her. "You found this brush that I lost. And I wasn't about to add the finishing touches without it."

Selia looked down at her portrait, then back to the artist who'd painted her. "I don't know what to say."

Damien reached out and took her hand. "Selia, you've helped me see the world in a way I've spent the past decade trying to *forget.*"

Selia tried to say something, but all she could manage was a little squeak. Tears in her eyes stung a little less, and she wiped the back of her hand against one of them that had begun trickling down her cheek.

Damien squeezed her hand. "I hope the crying is a good sign that you like it?"

"Like it? I *love* it...I love her..." she blurted out. She wiped a tear from her eye and placed her portrait back into the envelope.

Damien stood up from his chair and held out his hand, which she took.

Selia walked with him toward a bench that overlooked the North Sea. Damien sat down first, and Selia sank down next to him. The full moon was rising above the horizon, her reflection mirrored in a spectacular way. A lighthouse lit up in the distance, the beacon light flashing as it spun.

Damien wrapped his arm around her, resting his chin on her forehead. "I adore you, Selia. I will cherish you always."

She closed her eyes, savoring in his words and affection that bundled her up into the Scottish countryside. This feeling of warmth and kin she couldn't imagine ever leaving.

Down the hill, the lights of Auntie's cottage lit up. Little wisps of smoke climbed through the chimney and drifted out to sea.

Damien sighed, slouching next to her. "Looks like Wilson and Auntie are going to be discussing the vixen sprites well into the wee hours of the morning."

Selia laughed. "It's about time your aunt found someone that she got along with." She set her hand on his kilted thigh and began inching her fingers towards his knee. "Are you suggesting that we find another place to stay tonight?"

Damien's lips brushed behind her ear. "Where should we go?"

Selia gazed out on the horizon, and the lighthouse beacon flashed once more.

29
REMEMBER WITH ME

Dark clouds began to roll on the horizon as Selia walked with her kilted Romeo through the garden. The storm was no match for the electricity jolting between her and Damien as they made their way up to the Lighthouse Inn.

Damien opened the door and they walked inside. An elderly woman sat behind the counter, reading a newspaper. Pacing back and forth along the counter was a plump tabby cat.

Selia approached the counter. "Do you have anything to accommodate two adults?"

"I'm afraid I am all booked up for the evening," The woman replied, not looking up from her paper.

Selia eyed the empty key hooks behind the woman, spotting one that was stuffed under a pile of postcards in the outgoing mail. "What about that one over there?"

The lady looked up from her newspaper. She hobbled over to the mail box and plucked a key with a silver crescent moon hanging from the end. "How about the honeymoon suite?"

Selia grabbed the key from her.

Damien grinned as he slipped the woman payment.

Selia grabbed him by the belt and tugged him towards the stairs. She started to run, and he grabbed her around the waist before she could dart ahead.

Once at the top of the stairs, he pinned her against the wall. "You lead the way," he breathed in her ear, finally releasing her.

Selia took his hand and walked toward the door at the end of the hall with a giant crescent moon on the front.

She pressed the key to the lock and walked inside. A king-sized bed lay by the window, which the curtains had been drawn. The warm air was swollen with moisture, pregnant with the electrical energy that always manifested before a thunderstorm.

She glanced sideways at Damien, then back out to the water in all its dark, settling calm.

"What are you feeling?" he asked as he closed the door and locked it. He walked to her side, his hand falling to her waist. Damien's touch warmed her in ways she'd never known. His warmth was the only feeling she craved.

She wrapped her arms around herself, her body cold. In some strange way, it felt like she was violating that memory of his family. That space and time he had spent grieving and alone. If she was to step into the void of loss in Damien's life, what would happen to Maria and Sophie's memory?

"Losing them, Maria and Sophie," she said, her words louder than she expected them to be. "How do you move forward with your life after something like that?"

"You make the choice to do so," he said, turning to face her. "Losing them was the most difficult thing I have ever experienced."

She looked into Damien's eyes, the desire there threatening to turn her inside out. "I know you want a family. I know that from seeing what you paint and what you love. I know you want to experience that joy in your life again."

His eyes fell heavily onto hers. He brought his hands to her chin, cupping her face. His eyes hooded as his lips grazed against hers.

Once, then twice, until the hotness of his tongue was inside of her mouth.

Selia leaned into his kiss, savoring every sensation his lips gave her.

As their kiss ended, one of his hands caressed her face, while the other dropped to her hip.

Selia's body was flush with passionate heat. She turned, yet his grip on her hip did not give.

"Why are you distancing yourself from me?"

Selia allowed the void of her thoughts to drag her away from Damien's comfort. She walked to the window, clasping her arms in front of her. "I'm afraid that I won't be able to give you what you've lost."

Damien's hands came to her shoulders. She gazed out the window, wishing the North Sea could answer why she felt so lost here in the shadow of Damien's past. Her vision began to blur. "I've felt the pain you've experienced; the void that loss has left in your life."

"Selia…"

"I've learned from your experience that sadness and the grief never really leave you. Once you lose someone you love, *you* are alone." She felt so small next to him, so vulnerable, and a bit lost. Anxiety trilled through her. She had no memory of making love to anyone before.

Damien grabbed her, pressing her against the wall. His lips met hers, hot and passionate against her mouth. "Selia…I want you…" he whispered against her neck. He locked his gaze with hers, his eyes dark and magnetic. "Can't you see that I've fallen in love with you?"

Selia grabbed his hands. *Love*, he said. When someone left you, did their love also slip away? "I don't know if I can ever give you what you're looking for. If there is one thing that blue memories have shown me, it's that memories of the heart are far more powerful than those of the mind." She looked away from him, unable to grasp the loss swimming in his eyes. "I would be vain to say that you don't still hold a place in your heart for Maria and Sophie."

"What are you saying?"

Her heart ached. "I can't step into your life like this, when you still love someone else so very much."

Damien dropped his hands to her waist, holding her in place. He leaned in, kissing her lips softly, then began exploring the spot behind her ear. "Selia, please. I want the chance to love someone again." He took her other hand. "Make memories *with* me?"

Selia closed her eyes as his lips moved down her neck. He moved behind her, dropping his hands to her hips again. His hands worked to her front, where he caressed her navel, then worked his fingers lower.

"What do you like?" he whispered.

Selia's breath caught. What *did* she like when it came to the art of seduction?

Damien's hands continued to wander. "Faster?"

"Slower," she breathed, wishing he would move those wide artistic hands of his to the part of her that ached for his touch.

He chuckled, his stubble grazing past her earlobe. "Baby, I can make this last all night."

Selia closed her eyes as he worked his magic over her body, draping sweet hot kisses down her neck and shoulders.

Her salt nodes were on fire with a pleasure she'd not experienced before.

She turned in his arms, facing him. "What do I do next?"

He smiled, kissing her forehead. "I want *you* to paint this evening, not me."

Selia's heart thundered. Tell the artist how to make love to her?

He grabbed her hand. His fingers intertwined through hers as he walked with her back over to the bed. He stopped at the side of the bed, gathering her around her hips again. He faced her, pressing his loins against her. That kilt she'd fantasized about was suddenly a barrier she wanted gone.

Damien's hazel eyes met hers, so inviting, patient and warm.

She touched the hem of the fabric instead, searching for some way to unravel this confusing garment from Damien's body. A groan escaped one of them, while Selia kept exploring the thick fabric that clung to his waist.

Damien's kilt landed at his bare feet. If only she knew what she was to do with *so much man*...

His hand came to her cheek, brushing a lock of hair away from her face.

Selia searched his eyes, wondering how such an expressive person could only see one color. "I'm going to need you to undress me first."

He reached for her blouse, which Selia quickly tugged over her head. She sloughed off her pants, kicking them away. Doing so made her lose her balance, and she fell back onto the bed. Her panties and bra still on, Damien stood in front of her, the desire in his eyes making her flush.

He wrapped his arms around her center, tugging her up onto the center of the bed. He knelt between her legs, lowering himself down to place another kiss on her neck.

Selia raked her fingers across his back, grabbing a fist-full of this thick hair. She tugged his neck to the side, and Damien fell next to her. She pressed his shoulder away, persuading him to lie on his back.

She reached across, grabbing his other hand while kicking off her panties. She sat atop his belly, straddling him. The heat from his body warmed her legs, and that spot that ached was so much hotter.

He reached behind her back, undoing her bra. He grabbed her breasts, working his thumbs over her skin. She let out a moan, hoping that he'd respond to her pleasure.

She fell to his side, afraid the spot that ached for him would ignite too soon.

Damien sat up next to her on the bed and grabbed one of her legs, resting her calf upon his shoulder. He worked his mouth down her leg. He stopped at her foot, where he draped his kisses along her toes.

He set her leg against his neck, locking his eyes with hers. "Relax, sweetheart. I want you to enjoy this."

Selia shivered. Damien was so generous with his touch.

He worked his kisses down her foot, her leg, toward her inner thigh.

She closed her eyes, surrendering to every hot flick of his tongue against her skin.

That aching spot set on fire.

30

ALEXANDRA

amien's subtle breathing awoke Selia from her dream. Their night spent twisting and turning beneath the sheets had left her exhausted yet energized. She lay on her side, facing away from him, his arm draped over her center under the blankets. She grabbed his hand, brought his fingers to her lips, and kissed them.

She twisted in bed, turning over to face him and tucked herself under his arm.

Damien's eyes opened. He worked his arm down her side, pressing his hand to her lower back. "Want to fly away to Neverland with me?"

Selia giggled. "Why would I fly away when I have what I want right here?"

Damien kissed her forehead. "I love you, Selia. Don't you ever forget that."

Selia buried her face into Damien's chest. "I love you too," she whispered back.

Ching!

Selia grabbed her phone from the nightstand. Deidra had texted her a string of eggplant emojis, followed by a heart. How that dryad knew what she and Damien were up to was beyond her.

She and Damien packed up the few things they brought with them to the inn. Selia tied the bottle of selkie salt skin around her neck.

Her phone was exploding with text messages from Deidra. "I just need to call her."

"You go ahead. I'll go return our room key, and meet you back at the cottage?" Damien said.

Selia kissed him on the lips. "Don't keep me waiting."

She made her way down the hall and outside to the back before her phone. "Look, I'm not going to give you all the details on our first night—"

"The artifact Alex stole from your office, did it have a counter clockwise spiral?"

"Yes, why?"

"That's not good..."

"How is that not good?"

"I did some digging on my end. The Order has apparently been hunting down and confiscating these talismans for a long time. They date back to a nasty plague that occurred in ancient Egypt."

"A *plague*?"

"The ones with a counterclockwise spiral are labeled as sick, or diseased. They are known for absorbing memories that are not so happy ones. Dark memories that are so painful that prolonged exposure can result in illness or, even, death."

"What does that mean?"

"I have no idea, but I thought you might want to know, since you'd been in contact with the one in your office for, how long again?"

"A decade."

"You haven't been around anyone who has experienced painful memories now, have you?"

Selia's heart jumped into her throat. "No, I—"

"—I'll call you back when I find out more."

"Deidra, wait..."

Deidra ended the call.

Selia made her way down the hill, following the path she and Damien had trekked up the prior evening. Deidra's root readings had been wrong before. Maybe she had tapped into some reserve of knowledge that wasn't quite accurate.

A cool morning breeze drifted in from the North Sea, cloaking the horizon in a fine mist. Something glinted in one of the hedges not far from where she stood observing the water. The ground had been disturbed. She walked over to the hedge where little stones had been tossed and turned over.

Amy had told her to keep an eye out for the stones when the time came for her to meet with her.

"Well, if it isn't the Blind Moon."

Selia turned toward the cold voice.

A cloaked figure stood on the path, blocking her. A pair of grey eyes darted down, leveling with her. It was the Iridescent who worked for the Order, Alex.

Alex held out her hand, her fingers clenched around a familiar item—her salt trancing talisman. "Doesn't it seem a bit peculiar that your memories go back to when you first discovered one of Amy's little toys? There are plenty more just like this. Amy has been collecting the talismans and using them to manipulate the blue memories of those whom they come into contact with."

Selia bit her tongue. Amy, *manipulating* memories?

Selia's fingernails dug into her palms. "You're trying to scare me. Amy is my friend."

"Amy works her magic in manipulative ways. She sings to the talismans, and the salt obeys her. The salt they hold can carry her voice anywhere she desires. I am sure that before you met her, the talisman said a few choice things to you about an illness?"

"Stop it."

"Amy's memory is fading with each passing day. Before long, not even the talismans will be able to help her." She held out the talisman. "This talisman has more power over you than you think. I stole it from you because it would force Amy to rethink her plan on how she would use you to find the vault."

Selia shook her head. "Why would Amy use me?"

"Amy gave this talisman to you, so she could infect you with an illness for which only she has a cure." She grinned nastily. "That illness has your name tied to it, blue memory *blindness*?"

"No, you're wrong. Amy didn't give me the talisman!"

"Then tell me, who did?"

Selia glared at her. "I can't tell you who. But I refuse to believe the lies you are throwing at me."

Alex laughed, high and cold. "Can't you see the trap you've walked into? Blue memories are what Amy manipulates! She has forgotten the fourth principle. She needs the Blind Moon to help her remember. Once you've helped her, she will toss you aside like she's done with countless others."

"You're lying!" Selia spat.

"The one thing Amy remembers about the art is how to manipulate the hearts of others. Dare I say, the blue memories of the man you are falling in love with?"

"Stop it!"

"You should not have subjected his heart to the depths of Amy's wickedness. Memories of the heart are so easily manipulated. This symbol has moon magic threaded within it." Her eyes dipped to the bottle tied around her neck. "I pity the heart of the host you subjected to her poison."

Selia grabbed the bottle, the crystals inside of it pulsing against the glass. "Leave Damien out of this!"

"Amy's heart has been corroded by something you are immune to."

"*Immunity?* To what?" Selia asked.

"Amy needs you because your heart is immune to a substance that resulted in a plague so dark, that not even the Egyptian Book of the Dead has record of it."

"What kind of plague are you threatening me with?"

The corners of Alex's mouth turned up into a sinister grin. "Why don't we allow this talisman to share that memory with you? I can't promise that you won't be haunted by it."

Selia blinked. It wasn't a chunk of limestone she remembered. Something was different about this talisman. It had *legs.*

Spider webs branched from Selia's periphery. The threads gripped her legs and arms, binding her in place. A thrumming rhythm coming from the web made her wonder if she wasn't the only one caught in it.

Something jostled against Selia's ankle. When she tried to move, whatever the creature was attempted to scurry away.

"Be patient," Alex whispered, her voice darkening. Her fingers coiled back and the phantom creature withdrew its many legs from her ankle. "I think Selia needs something more potent to help stir her memory."

Something sharp emerged from the spider web. A barb the size of her fingernail danced dangerously close to the veins in her wrist.

Selia sucked in a breath, her lungs working hard against the paralysis cocooning around her. She couldn't move her arms or her legs as Alex held her in place.

"Wait," Selia whispered, but her voice was drowned out by her blood pounding in her ears. She splayed her arms out in front of her as her vision went black.

The ground fell out from beneath her feet as the landscape around her evaporated.

A flicker of blue light darted in her periphery. Something sharp grazed past her cheek.

Selia brought her fingers to her skin, finding them damp. Her own blood glistened back on them. She was swimming now, swimming in this liquid her heart and mind combined in.

The distant sound of a child crying filled her ears.

Selia's feet hit a hard surface. She was standing in the hallway of a familiar cottage. The scent of the ocean drifted in the far window that was cracked open, bringing with the scent the sound of the waves of the Celtic Sea.

Damien's art studio lay before her, long before the Order had ransacked it.

Paintings covered the easels, tiny paintings full of layers of color.

These paintings were different from the ones she'd seen torn apart in Damien's studio. They were not blue monochromatic seascapes. These paintings illustrated all colors of the rainbow.

In the far corner were images that stacked upon themselves. A collection of blue images with a piece of paper painted above it.

Sophie's Blue Magic

Selia's breathing caught. Had Damien been preparing something for his daughter?

A child crying echoed from inside another room. Selia followed the distant cries, stopping at the threshold of a door where the crying was coming from.

Inside the room, Damien's paintings covered the walls. There were only blue paintings in this room.

In the corner was a cradle where the crying child would surely be found.

Selia took a step into the room.

"Hi there, beautiful..."

A woman's voice filled the nursery.

Maria was there, looking down into the crib.

"She's color blind, isn't she?"

Selia jumped. Damien's voice echoed behind her.

He stood next to her, his liquid blue aura blending with her space. His memory stood there. His hair was more colorful. No strand of moonlight yet threaded behind his ear.

She watched Damien walk into the room by his wife, who had tears in the corners of her eyes. "Will she ever see color?"

Damien wrapped his arms around Maria as she took their baby into her arms. "I don't think she's blind to *every* color," he said, holding out a blue seashell that caught the baby's attention.

The room changed again. This time, an aquatic whisper drifted past Selia's salt nodes as the memory swam around her.

Damien sat in his studio, hunched over a stack of blue monochromatic paintings. He was holding a small blue paint brush, the one Selia remembered from when she first salt tranced with him.

Maria walked in, setting her hands on her husband's shoulders. "You've created her something so magical. What's this symbol about?" she asked, pointing to the signature Damien draped across the bottom of the miniature moonscape.

"It's from the Scottish folktales my aunt has."

"You should illustrate a children's book!"

Damien dabbed his brush into a glass of water, which turned blue. "You think?"

She kissed him on the cheek. "You would be spectacular at it."

Another thread of smoke drifted, and the sea manifested before her.

"Look, dad. I found a fairy egg!" Sophie cried, her pudgy little arms flailing toward the sky. Wild blond curls trailed out from her head.

"Maria, come look at what Sophie found," Damien said.

Maria walked over to her daughter, crouching down. "What on earth is it?"

Maria took the item from her daughter's wet hands. "Doesn't it look like the symbol from those Scottish folktales your aunt had?"

Another tendril of smoke drifted in front of Selia, washing the memory away, and replacing it with the sound of a car engine.

Sophie sat the passenger seat of a car. Her fingers clung around a stone. Her hands weren't as pudgy now, and her blond hair had grown out, with two pigtails tied in front of her ears.

She had her mother's warm brown eyes and Damien's subtle dusting of freckles. "Mom, how many packages do we have to send to the Louvre before they write you back?"

Maria shrugged, smiling as she gripped tight on the steering wheel. "As many as it takes them to believe in the fairies you and your father are seeing."

Sophie held up the cardboard box she was busy scribbling a blue crayon against.

"Shouldn't you put a return address on the label instead of drawing a fairy?" Maria asked.

Sophie shook her head, her pigtails flapping against the sides of her face. "No. The fairies will make sure it gets to the right place."

Maria nodded. "I think the two of you need to create a children's book. You write a story, and your father illustrates it."

"That's a great idea! I'll ask him when we get home. You want to know what the best birthday gift would be?"

"What's that?"

"That dad has his artwork put on exhibit. Then everyone in the entire world can come and see how talented he is."

Maria laughed. "We've been doing this every year on your birthday. But this year, somehow, I feel like it's going to be different."

"Seven years today," Sophie said, adding the last of the details on her blue fairy. "I'll keep mailing them stuff until his art finally gets chosen. Why can't we just go to Paris and show them the paintings dad made?"

"Because not everyone believes in your father's imagination. He's an artist. He sees the world differently than most people do. You must always remember that."

Sophie sighed.

"We are going to surprise your daddy," Maria said.

"How?" Sophie asked.

Maria smiled, touching her daughter's hand clasped around the stone. "Don't tell him, but I'm sending a sample of his paintings to the Louvre."

Sophie held up the stone. "I know this stone is a gift from the fae. I hope it convinces them to show daddy's artwork."

Sophie dropped the stone. It fell onto the ground.

"Sweetie, be careful with it," Maria said.

Sophie reached for it.

Maria's hand left the wheel...

Scrrreeeechhhhh!

The car swerved from the road, plunging over the rocky cliff.

"Noooo!" Selia screamed as the blue memory evaporated before her.

She stood at the edge of the field where she'd seen the car disappear into the fog. "Please, no!"

The fog cleared, and another memory threaded in front of her.

A man stood at the edge of the water, holding a soggy cardboard box. "What's this?"

"This was the last item we salvaged from the car," the man replied, rubbing his finger across the fairy drawn on the box. "It's addressed to the Louvre."

PART 5
FORGOTTEN

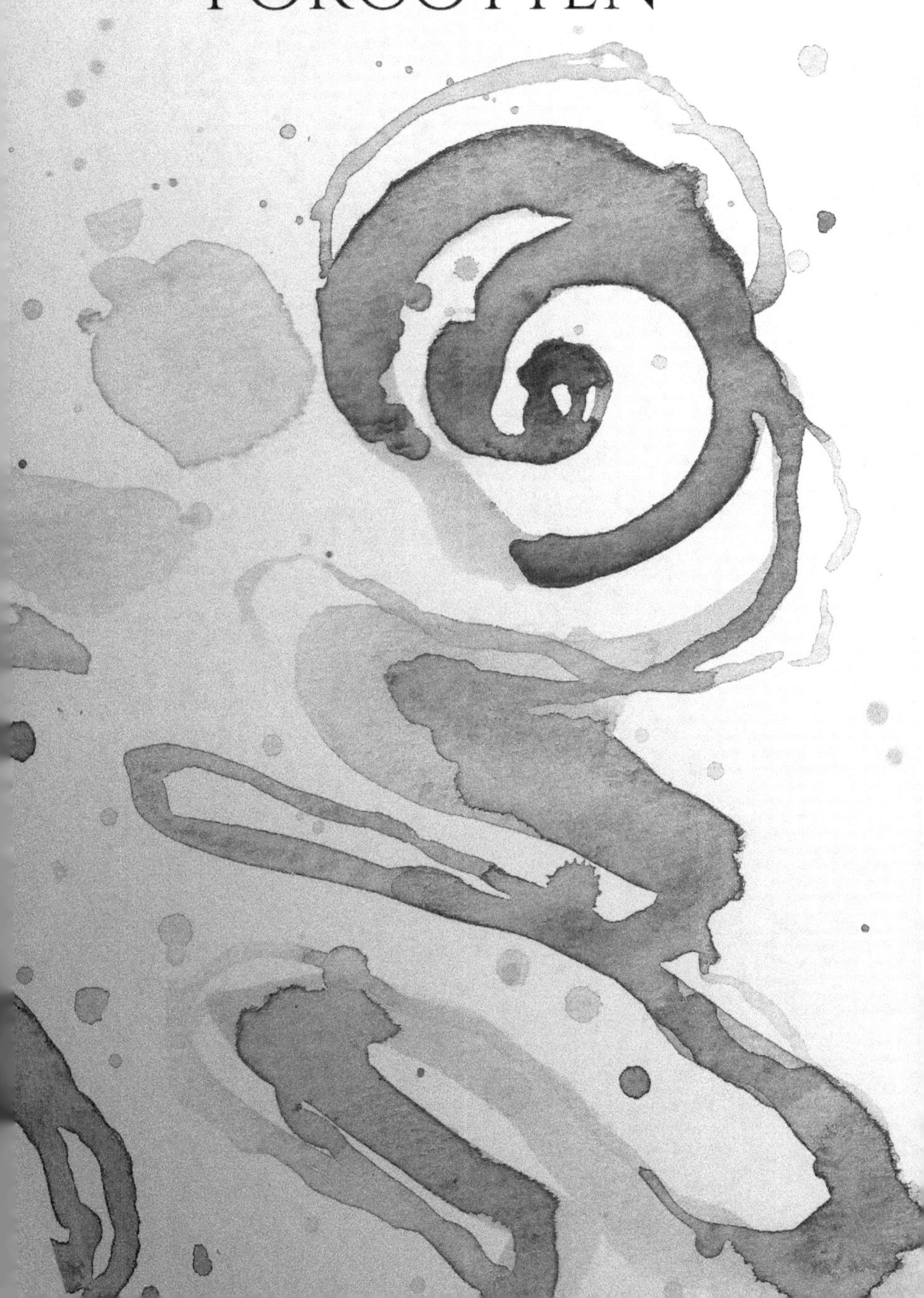

31
BROKEN

The blue memory inside of the salt trancing talisman had vanished. Selia's knees buckled as she fell to the ground. Alex was gone.

All that lay before her was the shattered body of the talisman.

Maria and Sophie were going to send it to the Louvre, but instead…

Deidra was right about the darkness locked inside of the talisman. The memory it had preserved had been of Maria and Sophie's death.

She sucked in a breath, fighting back the urge to wretch.

"Selia?"

Damien was walking toward her. "What happened? Are you hurt?"

She couldn't think. She dusted herself off and stood, her legs like jelly. "Alex was here."

Damien stopped before her. His eyes widened. "What?" He glanced over his shoulder, then back to her. "Where did she go?"

"I don't know." Her heart ached as she gazed into the hazel eyes of her love. "I know how the talisman came into my possession." She swallowed. "I saw the entire history behind it before it came to me at the Louvre."

"What do you mean, the history behind it?" Damien asked, closing the space between them.

Selia's arms trembled. She felt so *sick*. Had the woman and young girl she'd bumped into in town really been Maria and Sophie? They had both been returning from the post office when she'd run into them.

She sucked in a breath, exhaling the air. She had to tell him the truth. "The talisman showed me a memory owned by *you*."

"What?"

"Maria and Sophie were the ones who mailed the talisman to the Louvre."

Damien's eyes widened. His mouth opened, but no words came out. "That's not true."

"It *is* true," she said as her throat tried to close. "I've known for a long time the talisman had impacted my memory somehow, but now I know why." She blinked, unable to look him in the eye. "I had no idea that your family's death was tied to it."

Damien shook his head. "Prove it to me. Tell me what you saw from that memory."

"Sophie was color blind to every color *but* blue. Sophie inspired you to paint seascapes in the one color she could see. When they found the talisman on the beach, they saw how similar the symbol was to your artwork and sent it to the Louvre.

"Why would they send the *talisman* to the Louvre?

Selia grabbed his hand. "Your wife and daughter wanted to *surprise* you. They were hoping to convince the museum to display your artwork."

Damien tugged his hand away from her and backed away. His shoulders rounded. His eyes centered onto her, fear glinting in them. "How long have you been looking into my mind?"

"Damien, this isn't your mind. These blue memories are in your *heart*. That's the power of them. They live on even after—"

"I don't care *what* they are. I don't ever want to visit that day again..." Damien shook his head. "I want nothing more than to bury that day, and for some reason, you want to dig it up."

"I can't get close to you if you don't share that part of your life with me, don't you see?" she reached for him, but he took another step back. "I won't be blind to the past of the man I'm in love with!"

"I don't care," he said, his voice lowering.

She reached for him. "No, you need to know the truth. What you've blamed yourself for is only—"

"I said stop it!" he bellowed.

Selia backed away from him. Why couldn't he see that she was trying to help him?

Damien's gaze didn't meet hers. Not seeing the greens in his eyes was all the sign she needed to know that Damien Malloch would rather stay blind to his past, instead of moving forward with her like he'd promised.

She turned, heading down the hill where Alex had gone. She didn't care anymore. She didn't care about the vault or the art of salt trancing any longer.

What good were memories of the heart if you didn't reflect on them with someone you loved?

32
LOST

Gravel shifted under Selia's feet as she raced into the fog. Damien's footsteps weren't echoing behind her, and she didn't care. She never should have gotten close to a man who couldn't keep his promise.

As the gravel shifted under her shoes, Selia tried to focus on the earth shifting beneath her soles. She needed to ground herself in something that wasn't the painful past Damien didn't want her to know.

She could go back to the Louvre and take back her job. Now that the talisman was out of her life, she could go back to the life she knew, right?

Not having memories of your own past was easy. After everything she'd learned about Damien, she didn't want to know any more about her own. Memories of love meant pain.

The terrain changed from green meadow to rocky outcropping. A cold wind billowed past her face, drowning out any sound of the waves. As Selia's path descended to the beach and the terrain transitioned from mossy soil to beach pebbles and driftwood, her pulse rose into her throat. Her breathing was so fast, her own blood was now pounding in her ears. The necklace on her chest full of Damien's blue memory salt crystals were pulsing against her own heartbeat.

She met a fork in the trail—one that lead back to Auntie's place, or the other down to the Rusty Selkie.

The flowerbed shifted behind her. Henrietta had scuttled after her.

Selia rounded on Amy's pet. "What do you want? You're no help at all."

The little crab wiggled her shell, then dove back into the flowers.

Selia fumed. Good riddance! She didn't need Amy's pet to point her down another dead-end trail. The vault and whatever fae treasure was inside could sink back to the bottom of the North Sea for all she cared.

Fog settled over as she continued walking down to the Rusty Selkie. She'd lost any hope of staying here in the land Damien said fairy tales were practically born from. Those words, his words, were full of imagination and magic. When he'd said them, they'd not made any sense to her. A watercolor artist who believed in fairies? And wanted to share the fae world with his daughter?

This salt trancing art was ridiculous! Who wanted to subject their own heart to that kind of pain? This wasn't magic. It was insanity!

Big salty tears streamed down Selia's face. She wrapped her arms around herself. The salt trancing talisman had been in the possession of Damien's family. The memory behind it, the blinding, grief-filled memory had settled deep into her heart. Had Damien's daughter never found the talisman, she and her mother never would have...

She forced that memory out of her mind and kept walking. She didn't belong with the spirits who still existed in his heart. The memories of his family were for his eyes only. Damien hated that she'd seen them. And he didn't want her to venture back to that painful time in his life.

"Oi! Get a load of this!"

Selia slowed her steps, stirred by the obnoxious voice of a man upon the dock.

A couple of motorbikes were parked next to the dock where a few fishing boats were swaying in the water. She walked past the tugboats and behind a wooden crate full of lobster traps.

Balfour was standing on the dock with the two others. His arms were crossed in front of his chest as he scanned the water.

Great, just what she needed—Alex's henchmen.

Selia ducked behind one of the crates as Balfour's gaze dipped toward her.

Footsteps approached from behind.

Selia's hair stood on the back of her neck.

A pair of familiar grey eyes glinted in the lamp light. "I can see that you two are doing a splendid job of guarding the port."

The two bickering men straightened and snuffed out their cigarettes as their boss approached.

Alex walked past them, stopping next to the crate where Selia was crouched.

The sound of metal cut through the air, and flash of silver from a knife glinted in the lamp light.

Alex walked the length of the crates, she tilted the blade against the wood, her blade thudding against the unevenly stacked lobster traps. She sliced through fish nets, spilling a few fish, where they splashed back into the sea.

The silver knife blade dangled inches above Selia's head, fresh fish guts dangling from the end.

Selia pressed herself against the wooden crate as Alex dug her knife into the wood. Metal creaked above her, and a chest fell onto the dock. It was the same chest Selia remembered Alex's henchmen carrying to the water when they tried to destroy the vault.

Alex kicked the chest open, revealing nothing but saltwater sloshing around the base with a few sea stars scrambling to escape. "If my memory serves me right, I believe I told the both of you to dispose of an item that was in here." Her eyes moved between them. "Well? Where is the vault?"

The men's eyes darted towards one another.

Selia held her breath, fearing that her pulse would give away where she was hiding.

Alex approached the beefier of the two. "I'll ask you again. *Where is the bloody vault?*"

"It...well...it's..."

Alex grabbed the man by the throat. "Answer me!"

"We were just making s-s-s-s-ure that i-i-i-itt was getting c-c-c-c-ozy down there with the f-f-f-fishes...no harm d-d-d-one."

Alex held her knife to his throat. "I let you pocket *thousands* of pounds worth of treasure that comes into my possession, and the lot of you can't dispose of something?"

Splash!

Selia shook her face as sea water splashed into the air.

The man's body fell into the water, face down.

Alex returned the knife to her pocket, retrieving a cigarette and a lighter. She stood puffing on the stick for seconds, dragging on the smoke and blowing it out again. "I'm getting real tired of this game. Jenkins, let's hope that next time you'll do a better job of disposing what I ask you to better than Angus did."

Jenkins nodded, the whites of his eyes glinting with the orange ember of Alex's cigarette.

Alex held her cigarette out over the water, tapping the soot loose with her finger. "I need to discuss your time at the pub—specifically what you've been gambling."

Jenkins swallowed. "We were just having a good time."

"I don't think a single one of you asked me about gambling with the talismans, now did you?"

"But you said yourself they'd done their job finding the vault! We thought they were up for grabs when—*uhhhhlp!*"

Alex dropped her cigarette, rounding on Jenkins. With a jerk of her arm, she snatched a fist-full of Jenkins's coat, buckling him by his throat. "The talismans are not to be played with by simple men like yourself." Alex gripped his throat tighter, bringing his face down to meet her. "Who were you swapping the talismans with?"

"A woman at the pub..." Jenkins wheezed, his knees buckling.

The scar on Alex's lip twitched. "What did this woman look like?"

"She was wearing a cloak. I could barely see her face. She had red hair, that's all I remember."

"Did she have green eyes and freckles that resembled little starfish?"

Jenkins trembled, nodding.

Splash!

Jenkins's body bobbed in the water next to Angus, who was now sinking.

Alex spun on her heel, heading for the boat at the end of the dock. "It's time that I put Amphitrite's poisonous pranks to an end."

Something shiny and white floating in the water caught Selia's eye. A little white pearl was floating there. Scuttling along the length of the boardwalk was a familiar little hermit crab shell. A trail of white stones glinted in the light, leading down the path and up toward the hill.

33
RISING TIDES

Selia raced off the dock, her feet slipping on the soggy boards as she launched herself back toward the hill. Amy's pet had left her a trail to follow. Apparently, the green bottle of memory wasn't the only thing Amy had swiped from the pub. She'd been working her charm on the fishermen who worked for Alex, gambling and stealing salt trancing talismans.

She ran up the hill that led back to the fork where Henrietta had darted off the trail. Something was sitting there, glinting up at her.

A line of shiny white mermaid pearls.

Woof!

Selia stopped as Mr. Kisses bound up the path.

"Oi! Down, boy!" called Mr. Wilson as he followed the dog's lumbering pace. "Oh, hello, Miss Selia. Enjoying a brisk morning walk?"

"I am," Selia said, her eyes drifting over to where the line of white stones shimmered. "Ah, I see you've found a fairy ring!" Mr. Wilson said, pointing over to a patch of mushrooms that seemed to have sprouted in the few moments since she'd discovered the stones. "Bertha has been complaining about something digging up her garden, hence, I'm taking the dog for a walk while she gets it sorted out."

The garden, that's where she needed to look!

Selia patted Mr. Kisses on the head. "It was good seeing you both!"

Selia darted up the hill, finding what appeared to be a set of bunny ears flopping around the hedges. When she got closer, she realized her mistake. She was looking at the bow of an apron. Auntie had her backside stuck up into the air as she maneuvered through the disturbed earth.

"Wait till that bloody selkie gets an earful!" Auntie said as she grabbed a root, tossing it in a fury behind her. Had the garden gnome not already been decapitated, it would surely have lost its head.

Selia stopped, bracing herself.

Auntie turned, her face as bright as a beet. She stood up, facing her, hobbling back and forth on her pointed little boots. "Would you get that blasted creature of yours under control? She's done nothing but make mischief ever since you let her have her way with my garden."

Clearly, Henrietta was on the trail of something.

"What's she doing now?" Auntie stammered. "Taking off with the heads of my garden gnomes? Before I know it, she'll have summoned her kind, and my entire garden will be swarming with vixen sprites!"

But Auntie had given Selia a clue. "These vixen sprites, how long have you been dealing with them?"

"For at least a decade, why?"

Decade was all Selia needed to know.

Selia darted through the garden, hot on the trail Henrietta had left her to follow. The crab led her to a dead-end at the Rusty Selkie before. However, she didn't return under the building a second time. When she and Damien had been down there, they'd found the secret hiding place where Alex and her men had been holding onto the vault.

Something told her that these little stones were going to lead her back to the crypt beneath the pub. The same place Amy had had been working with Henrietta to lay a trail for her to follow.

She reached the fork in the trail, spotting the hunched outline of two other men who were walking her way.

She crouched down behind the hedges, holding her own breath.

"Alex is on a rampage now," one of the men said, his words quivering as his footfalls muddied his voice.

"Those stupid talismans? We never should have gambled with them."

"Who gave us away?" the other grumbled.

"Jenkins, and now he's paid a visit to Davey Jones's Locker."

"We'd better get to the dock. She'll be slitting all our throats if we don't find the vault again."

"Where is Balfour?"

"No idea. That bloke is always disappearing at a moment's notice."

The men moved out of earshot before she could overhear anything else.

With each step Selia took toward the Rusty Selkie, more of the glistening white stones appeared. She imagined it would have taken Henrietta all night to lay this kind of trail for her to follow. It was apparent by Auntie's outrage that these strange fae pests she called vixen sprites were up to something. Were the fae perhaps associated with the strange stones that Henrietta was busy collecting?

The roof of the pub came into view as she descended the path, on which a little hermit crab went darting across.

Selia slid to a halt, almost trampling the little crab.

"Hey!" She said, but Henrietta had disappeared again.

Selia crouched down, hoping to find where Henrietta ran off to. The brush had been disturbed. Dog prints zig-zagged across the trail.

Mr. Kisses had been here too, most likely inspecting the work of the enthusiastic hermit crab.

A white stone lay out of reach, which Selia grabbed for.

Selia tumbled forward as the ground gave away. Roots, moss, and lichen exploded in her face as the earth crumbled and she fell deeper down the hidden path.

She grabbed for a root, which tore away from the ledge that had given out.

Her fingernails scraped across the cool damp surface of a moss-covered stone.

The face of something had been carved in the stone; it was the same face of a selkie she had seen beneath the pub. An ancient dolmen? Maybe. Scotland was full of burial mounds and stone circles that had yet to be unearthed.

She ran her fingers down the sculpture's side, finding more places where the earth had eroded away. The serpentine body of the stone lead her further down the hill toward the North Sea.

At the base of the selkie's moss-covered tail was a stone with a counterclockwise spiral etched into it.

A moon, perhaps? Whatever the petroglyph, Selia's salt trancing talisman came to mind.

She ran her finger through the spiral where the moss had refused to grow.

The sound of earth and stone shifting disturbed more of the earth.

As she backed away, the stone shifted.

The scent of sea water came wafting from deep inside a hidden passage.

Selia crawled down into the passage that filled with the sound of dripping water. Elbow and kneeing her way in, she found another glittering white stone.

Henrietta had undoubtedly used this secret passage to move between Auntie's garden and the pub, illuminating what path she could for Selia to follow. Damp soil and roots brushed past her arms and knees as she crawled forward. The chamber was much better suited to a hermit crab or a cat, not a sea nymph who could barely see. What light did filter down into this secret passage was strange. It didn't come from above or below, but from places in between the stones.

How was that possible? Was the light source from the fae?

The chamber was ancient, possibly from neolithic times. She imagined ancient Scottish people traveling back and forth from the hill where Auntie's cottage now sat and the sea.

Finally, the ceiling opened, and Selia had enough room to hoist herself up to a crouched position.

She pressed her ear to the wall of soil and roots, listening for trickling water. Pale light crept in through a small hole that appeared to be perfect hermit crab size. Not one, but dozens of little holes. Maybe Henrietta had burrowed through here. Had she really crafted all these holes? She hadn't been in Scotland that long. Either way, whatever mysterious force in nature had crafted them, they were letting light in from the outside.

Selia walked alongside the wall, following the trickling sound. The musty scent of earth gave way to fresh air. An opening to the sea appeared.

She took off in a jog toward the North Sea when the silhouette of someone appeared in front of her. Selia stopped, backing up against the wall.

It was Balfour.

Henrietta's little shell bobbed up to his boot.

"No!" Selia whispered, catching her scream before she gave her position away.

Balfour's gaze dipped to the shell, and a deep throaty chuckle escaped him. Selia could have sworn she saw him shrug.

Was he communicating with the crab?

How Amy's pet was so brave was beyond her. A crab slipping past giant who could squash her in an instant.

"Oh, look. A stowaway..."

Selia jumped as another male voice broke her observation of Henrietta and Alex's henchman.

Another man bent down to grab the crab, But Henrietta would have none of it.

"Ouch!" he said, flinging his hand away as a pair of claws flailed in his face. Henrietta retreated back to where Selia was hiding.

Selia swooped little Henrietta back into her hand as the two men cursed at one another and walked away. Her hair stood on end as Balfour's gaze dipped toward her as she crept into the passageway.

With each step Selia took toward the dark passageway, Henrietta's body began to shudder. It would be impossible to keep her tucked away, so Selia settled to have her perch atop her shoulder. Leave it to Amy's pet to help her navigate the dark cavernous space beneath the pub.

Selia reached the stairway to the dock, which was slick with condensation.

She ducked inside the passageway she and Damien had discovered beneath the pub. Back then, she and Damien had been a pair on a mission. Now, it felt like a piece of that mission had been lost.

"*Ooof!*"

Selia turned, finding two men striding her way. One carried a fishing net in his arms and the other something large and bulky on his shoulder.

She shifted to the side as the men walked past her toward a boat at the end of the stone archway.

Selia remembered this passageway. It was a tidal controlled system that changed depending on the sea level. With the tide so low now, the boats had shifted. She walked up to the stone archway, watching the water streak down the selkie's oblong face—her mouth a gateway into a watery chamber the tide had exposed. She treaded carefully, her heels slipping on the stones slick with algae.

"Get him over here!" a man yelled, his voice echoing off the water-logged stones.

Selia ducked behind one of the boats as two of Alex's henchmen staggered over to the boat, lowering what appeared to be the body of someone into the bobbing vessel.

They took off into the dark, unknown passageway that led under the pub. Henrietta launched herself from Selia's shoulder, darting over to where one of the boats bobbed in the water.

A couple of little white stones were there floating next to the boat. They sparkled little pearls, reflecting bursts of blue light as the water tossed them.

Selia jumped into the boat, tucking Henrietta's shell away. "Okay, little crabby cakes. I'm going to trust you on this one."

She untied the boat, dropping the rope behind her. She sat down and held her breath, terrified as to where this chamber might lead. Who knew if she would end up in some ocean trench beneath the North Sea, lost to the world above for all eternity.

Selia lay back on the damp wood, praying that she wouldn't be dumped out. Henrietta dove into her cleavage as the boat tipped forward.

34

AMY'S SECRET

Water erupted from either side of the boat, drowning any scream Selia tried to muster. She quickly snapped her mouth shut as the spray exploded around her. Deeper into the passage she went, until daylight no longer existed. The chamber went deeper and deeper, her coffin-like vessel whizzing through the claustrophobic passage beneath the pub.

The boat shuddered violently against the stone channel, sending a wave crashing over Selia's head. Fortunately, that wave caused her boat to slow.

Selia opened her eyes, finding her vessel was no longer traveling alongside a canal. She wasn't surrounded by choppy water, but a surface as smooth as glass. She sat up as the boat leveled, floating out into a glistening black sheet of water, one that had no reflections dancing upon its surface.

Yet something was glittering above her. Were they stars? Had she discovered a cavern beneath the pub?

What time of day was it down here in this mysterious cavern that seemed to fill with its own moonlight?

Henrietta scurried to the front of the boat, perching herself on the wooden edge. Even she seemed in awe of the lights glowing above them. Glittering blue lights danced and reflected above, shimmering in the dark. The blues came in a thousand different variations, all shimmering like diamonds. Ultramarines danced with cerulean. Strangely, the lights did not reflect on the water beneath her boat.

What made those shimmering blue lights? Creatures, perhaps? She knew there were species of insects that burrowed into glaciers. Their bioluminescence appeared after they emerged from a year of frozen hibernation.

The bottle full of Damien's blue memory salt crystals began to warm, then cool. Were the crystals reacting to this otherworldly cavern? And why were they humming, almost singing to the pulse of the mysterious blue lights shimmering above?

The boat bumped against a rocky bottom, shuddering to a stop. She'd stopped next to a rocky outcropping. It had apparent ancient symbols on it similar to the salt trancing talisman.

Selia climbed out of the boat, grabbing stubborn little Henrietta as she shuffled up the damp dark stones that were stacked atop one another.

What was this place deep beneath the Rusty Selkie. A cave? Absolutely. What she assumed should be musty, was remarkably clean. An air that was wind-blown, fresh, and crisp enough to make her salt nodes relax.

Her steps echoed through the cavern. Down at her feet were glittering, damp *footprints?*

Selia's heart leapt. The prints had been made by a pair of bare feet—dainty feet that had scurried up the path.

Selia took off in a jog, but her boot met a slick patch of algae. She slowed her pace, treading lightly on the path that narrowed next to the water. One wrong step, and she would fall into the pool that seemed to have no bottom.

She kept walking, focusing on the blue lights that were brightening. The further she walked, the more she noticed the sounds they were producing. Some hummed, while others trilled a high-pitched ring.

Were the lights communicating?

Selia's boots scuffed a dry patch of stone. The air was colder here, making her tug her jacket around her center.

Something shifted on the path before her. A figure wearing long grey cloak was crouched low to the ground.

Selia's stomach hollowed. Alexandra had beaten her to the punch!

The figure stirred, turning toward her.

A thread of rebellious red hair uncurled from the hood.

The figure stood up, and the most beautiful impish smile made Selia's heart tremble with excitement.

"Amy!" she cried, darting over to her friend.

"Shhhhhhhhhh!"

Selia slowed, skidding to a stop inches from Amy's trembling face. "What?"

"Careful, we have an entire audience!" Amy turned and held out her hands, palms facing up. Her fingernails curled around the base of a vibrant blue bottle.

Selia glanced over Amy's shoulder. What was she doing with all these shimmering blue lights reflecting across the cavern wall?

And why were the crystals in the bottle on her chest pulsing?

Amy's free hand reached for Selia. "Come and bathe in the moonlight with me. There is so much to remember and so little time."

Selia grabbed the bottle, wondering what it was about this cavern that was bringing them to life.

"Oh, hello, my little crustacean friend." Amy bent down, gathering Henrietta into her hand. She held her in front of her face, Henrietta's little seashell reflecting in Amy's eyes. "Wouldn't *you* love to be part of my moonlight experiment?"

Henrietta snapped her claws in agreement.

Amy set the crab onto her own shoulder, grabbed Selia's hand again, and turned once more to the cavern wall.

"A moonlight experiment during the daytime?" Selia asked, wondering if she had lost track of time.

Amy's smile became a mischievous one. "Oh, the magic of these little fae creatures you have yet to experience." She set Henrietta next to one of her strands of rebellious red hair and took Selia's hand in the other. "Say a few words to them with me and see if they agree?"

Selia nodded as the bottle on her chest throbbed.

Amy closed her eyes and tilted her chin up toward the ceiling of lights. "North Sea, bring to us your eternal night. Without your darkness, we would not be able to see the moonlight."

Selia wondered if she too, should be reciting the words Amy was reciting. A sea sorceress had an intuition that she had yet to trust in herself.

The lights dancing on the wall began to spiral.

Selia's heartbeat began to slow. With her eyelids falling heavy, she became hypnotized by the pulsing blue lights that seemed to sync with her own heart.

Fwip!

Selia turned, startled as to what had landed on her shoulder.

"Don't be alarmed," Amy whispered, thrusting the bottle into her hand. She snatched Henrietta away from the glowing creature inching up Selia's hair. "Quick! Dab some of the salt extract onto your wrist."

Selia uncorked the bottle and tipped the glowing liquid onto her left wrist. With a brush of its wings past her ear, the creature fluttered down, exposing itself to her.

What a beautiful creature it was. It was not a butterfly or a moth, but something in between. It was the approximate size of the mermaid pearls Henrietta had been collecting. Its triangular wings were stiff and transparent, like looking through a piece of glass.

Amy clasped her hands together and squealed with delight. "Oh, what a marvelous little boy you are!"

"*Boy?*"

"This is a male minca moth! He, along with many others, have migrated *thousands* of miles for this moonlit occurrence. The males carry moonlight in their wings wherever they go. They are nocturnal by nature, meaning it is easier for my salt extracts to absorb their moonlight when they are dazed with sleep."

The moth's little feet tickled Selia's skin as it scurried over to the drop of salt extract on her wrist. Once discovered, it circled around the drop, unraveling a tiny black tongue. The drop began to shrink as the minca moth slurped it up.

"Do they drink salt water?" Selia asked.

"They do. Many fauna fae species related to insects feed on minerals."

Selia wondered how such a magical little creature could survive on a diet of *salt*. Then again, fae creatures had all kinds of quirks Henrietta had made her aware of.

"These are the reflective blue creatures I've been seeing, aren't they?" Selia asked.

"Have you been experiencing blue lights darting in and out of your periphery?"

"I have ever since I left the Celtic Sea."

Amy smiled. "Minca moths are invisible in most light. Night is when they are spotted easiest. Only when a sea nymph begins to salt trance will she begin to see them in daylight."

Selia marveled at the creatures that had remained invisible most of her life. It would explain why she started seeing them after Amy had started teaching her the art. With the drop of salt water gone, the moth began to circle on her skin again. It began to spiral out, tipping its wing against her wrist.

"Ouch!" Selia said, jumping as the moth grazed her skin with its wing.

"Careful, their wings are razor sharp. They become dangerous when swarming together in flight," Amy said, reaching out and grabbing the scurrying creature. She threw her hand up, tossing him up into the air. He circled around their heads, fluttering to where the other pulsing blue lights were gathered.

Selia remembered the cut on Damien's forearm. For how small the cut was, it bled profusely. Just getting the bleeding to stop had taken him a few days for a scab to form. Did he have an infestation of male minca moths hiding away in his art studio?

Amy bent down, gathering a salt trancing talisman that had floated up from the pool at their feet.

She dropped the talisman into Selia's hands. "Want to see the moon magic in action?"

"What do I do with it?"

Before Amy answered, the talisman began to morph between her fingers.

Selia rubbed her thumbs over the surface, which was soggy with water. The rough exterior began to dissolve. Limestone flaked away, revealing a tiny pearl of an item Selia recognized. One of the white mermaid pearls lay at the center of her palm. The surface reflected the fluttering blue wings from the minca moths circling above.

Amy's eyes lit up. "Hermit crabs *adore* the salt chrysalises left over by the male minca moth. When he molts and his wings form, he leaves this little salt chrysalis behind."

"Wait a minute. The talismans are created by a fae creature?"

"Partially. The sea then transforms them into the talismans after time."

Selia thought about Deidra's root readings and her claims of a *mass gathering* of some kind. She was right about that. There were millions, if not *trillions,* of little lights now pulsing down from the ceiling. "But I thought the talismans were made of limestone."

"Given the right circumstances they are. Many of the salt chrysalises dissolve back into the ocean. Ancient ones like this that are buried under layers of sediment find themselves transforming into the talismans that absorb the memories you and I are familiar with."

Selia marveled at the pearlescent core of the talisman. There was a hidden treasure inside of the chalky exterior the entire time. Like a geode, it was rough on the surface, but contained a glittery center full of light.

"Where do minca moths live?" Selia asked, looking up at the moths dozing on the cavern walls.

"Oh, very far out at sea where the vast groves of minca kelp once grew. Minca moths, like many other fae species are *ancient.* They have existed on the earth longer than us sea nymphs." She eyed the talisman. "I'm afraid that with minca's extinction, these fae creatures too, are losing their home."

Selia marveled at the fae moths above, wondering if moonlight was what made the male's wings shimmer so brilliantly. "Why have so many of them gathered here in this cavern?"

Amy's eyes dipped to the vault, then back up to the fae moths beginning to spiral above. "They happen to have romance on the mind. Romance does not occur for a male minca moth unless he provides an offering."

"An offering to what?"

"To *whom,* my dear. Their queen is inside the vault."

"A fae *queen?*"

Amy nodded. "Minca moth queens are a rare occurrence indeed. For every thousand males born, there is one queen. Soon after she is born, she goes into hibernation. A queen does not emerge from her chrysalis unless the perfect environmental circumstances are present." She crouched down to the pool and propped her chin onto her hand. Her expression became child-like as she gazed down at the dappling blue light in the pool created by the moths. "The minca moth's mating cycle has fascinated me for eons. Some of the most powerful beings in existence are those we often overlook. Many of which, belong to the fae kingdom."

"What does the male offer the queen?"

"Once the males locate a queen, they will molt, depositing their salt chrysalises in a cavern close to her, hoping to coax out of hibernation. That is why there are so very many of them. However, no matter what they do, they cannot convince this queen to emerge. I in fact sealed her away long ago for reasons the Order does not agree with."

"What were these reasons?" Selia asked.

Amy's eyes did their mischievous flair. "Reasons I cannot remember. The queen's emergence relies on the fourth salt trancing principle *you* are going to help me with. This fae queen is very special. She dates back to a time when the art of salt trance was being taught in ancient Egypt, when a friend and I..." Amy looked away, pain darting across her face.

"Your friend, you mentioned her to me before." Selia reached out, touching Amy's arm. "What happened to her?"

"I wish I knew." Her eyes dipped to the vault. "All I know is that her memory has started to impact my heart in a way I cannot continue to endure."

Selia looked from the vault, to Amy. Her face started to pale. Her starfish freckles began to dull. Secrets were to be had that if Amy was telling the truth, and her memory really was as faulty as her own. The mystery plague came to mind, a plague that Deidra had mentioned her research dated back to ancient Egypt.

One of Amy's red eyebrows arched up into her wild curls. "Well? Are you going to help me?"

"Alex told me that you whisper to the talismans, and the salt obeys you. Is this true? Can you manipulate the blue memories of others by practicing the art of salt trance?"

"That depends on how long ago the memory occurred."

Selia bit her tongue. She didn't like the sound of Amy's response. Memories were important to the heart of the individual who held onto them, no matter how long ago they occurred.

Amy's expression darkened. "I sense hesitation. I can see now that Alexandra has attempted to turn you against me."

Selia locked eyes with Amy's emerald gaze that if stared into for too long, could make her nauseous. "The talisman Alexandra stole from my office, I learned how it came to me."

"Let me guess. It dissolved as soon as it revealed the memory locked inside of it?"

Selia pulse jumped as Damien's hurt face flashed before her. "It doesn't matter *what* it showed me."

Amy grabbed her hand. "He's lost someone, hasn't he?"

Selia's pulse thundered. "How can you tell that? How did you know that the talisman had Damien's blue memories preserved in it?"

Amy's eyes dipped to the bottle resting upon Selia's chest. "The salt crystals show me everything from his heart that you have experienced."

Selia grabbed the bottle on her chest, forgetting it was even there. A burden now she wished she'd never accepted. She wanted to rip it from her neck and toss it away, never to feel those emotions again.

Amy's hand came to hers. "Keep it. *Treasure* it. You never know when a man's heart will benefit your own. Moonlight will always show the love it reflects."

Selia shook her head, trying to ignore the pain in her chest. "The moon hasn't shown me *anything*. The one thing blue memory blindness has made me blind to is *grief.* Without having memories of my own, I will never be able to understand that emotion fully."

Amy removed her hand from Selia's hand clutching the bottle, grazing her fingers past her cheek. "You *are* that moonlight, Selia. Your light has yet to shine on what the heart of salt trancing reflects."

Selia swallowed. Her feelings for Damien were not the priority right now. She needed to help Amy remember the fourth principle so she could get the vault open. From there, perhaps she could reconnect with her own memories and past.

Selia shook her head. "He doesn't want me to know his past. He's angry that I ever used the art to uncover it."

"I'm sorry, love. Salt trancing is what allows us to illuminate memories that have long been buried in our hearts. Not every strand of moonlight we see is destined for us to enjoy."

Silence fell between them. The gentle hum of the minca moths wings filled the cavern.

Selia looked down at the fluttering blue light from the fae moths reflecting on her skin. Her eyes stung. Why couldn't Damien see that she *wanted* to be part of his life, understanding his past and being part of his present and future?

"Do you remember the art's purpose at all?" Selia asked.

"My friend and I discovered that restoring the art to its original purpose demanded much more than either of our hearts expected." Amy grabbed her hand. "Help me to remember her face. I can feel her heartbeat here with me. Her pulse is present *inside* of you. After all this time, her memory is reaching out to me through the Blind Moon."

Selia wished she could help, but this unknown sea nymph Amy was determined to remember was just as much of a mystery to her.

"Damien and I narrowed down what we believed the fourth principle could be," Selia said as his moonlit paintings danced in her memory, her portrait specifically. "Moon, tides, the voice of the sea."

Amy closed her eyes. "And with their reflections, you will discover your fertility."

Selia jumped. "You *did* mention fertility as one of the items in the message you sent me."

Amy's eyes burst open. "Did I now?"

"Yes!"

Amy glanced up at the wall of minca moths now synchronizing their blue glow. "Fertility..." Amy closed her eyes. She tilted her chin against her chest, her face riddled with concentration.

She threw her head back, eyes opening wide. "I remember now! It is the *fertility* of the sea that the heart of this fae creature reflects!"

Selia looked at the vault, then up at the male minca moths, waiting for their queen to emerge. She bent down and grabbed the vault. "Follow me."

35
DAMIEN'S WOUND

A reverberating hum filled the cavern, making Selia's salt nodes swell with heat. She gripped the vault in her hands, keeping it close to her heart. With each step she took, her own pulse became a little sharper.

She slowed her pace, realizing that Amy was no longer walking behind her. She had stopped ten paces behind and had collapsed to the ground.

"Amy!" Selia cried, turning on her heel and darting back to where Amy was crippling to the ground. She dropped to Amy's side and grabbed her trembling hand. "What's wrong? What's happening to you?"

Amy's eyes were rolling into the back of her head. Her hands clenched as a sickening, rasping sound escaped her mouth.

She dropped the vault. It rolled around the bend, slowing to a stop.

Selia threw herself over Amy's body as the moths began to swarm, dipping down to the vault. Their wings clipped past Selia's ears, slicing off pieces of her hair. Their movements were no longer fluttering and soft, but cutting and swift. They brushed the sharp edges of their wings closer and closer to Selia's face, some dangerously close to her eyes.

"Stop it!" she yelled, but her voice did nothing to persuade the fae creatures to cease their attack. She brushed her hand past her cheek, her fingers becoming damp.

Crimson liquid glistened on her hand.

The minca moths had spilled her blood.

Movement caught her eye as a familiar figure rounded the bend.

Alexandra walked toward her, a scowl upon her face. The scar on her upper lip twitched. In her hand she held a salt trancing talisman. Her gaze dipped to Amy. "It's so good to see you again, Amphitrite."

Amy's body began to thrash beneath Selia, who fought to keep her legs from kicking against her.

"Stop it! You're hurting her!" Selia screamed, but another moth dove in front of her, slicing her hand with its wing.

Alex grinned nastily, holding the talisman out in front of her. "Oh, I'm not the one hurting her. A thousand little heartbeats of the fae moths who want their queen are the ones hurting her."

Selia glared at the talisman, then to the blue lights pulsing around her. The lights were sharper, dagger-like and threatening. Was Alex controlling the heartbeats of the moths to harm Amy?

Alex continued to hold the talisman in front of her, the spiral at the top glowing blue. "Fae instincts are some of the most powerful forces in nature. You would think that a goddess of the sea would respect such things and not attempt to tamper with them."

Amy's head arched back, her face contorting in pain.

Selia closed her eyes, envisioning the moonlit symbol on the talisman in her mind's eye. The spiral glowed, with three strands of moonlight rippling beneath it. She held her hands to her chest and took a breath. Memories of Damien's moonlit paintings flashed before her. The taste of salt filled her mouth as memories of paintings flooded her heart.

"I said stop!" Selia screamed, her voice echoing off the walls.

The bottle of selkie salt skin chest vibrated, and the entire cavern shook.

Selia focused on the humming reverberating from the crystals in the bottle around her neck. That dangerous sharp light Alex had been controlling with the talisman softened.

Amy's violent movements ended. Her body lay still on the ground. Her wild red hair spilled over her shoulders and her hands unclenched. Blood formed on her palms where her fingernails had dug into her skin.

Alex glared at Selia, the sneer returning as she lowered the talisman. "I see you've been practicing."

Selia wiped the back of her hand against her cheek, smearing her blood. "I'm not going to let you hurt my friend anymore." She climbed to her feet. "I'm going to open the vault, whether you like it or not!"

Alex's gaze dipped to the vault, where the minca moths were swarming. A dozen of the razor-sharp creatures hovered around it. "These fae creatures will do anything they can to ensure the safety of their queen. That includes killing a sea nymph."

Selia shielded her face as another wave of the angry moths dove for her again.

How could she convince the moths that she was trying to *help* them?

Alex held the talisman up into the air, and Amy's body began to thrash on the ground again. "I've had a long time to practice this."

"What are you doing to her?" Selia yelled.

"Something I should have done a *long* time ago," Alex said, moving her hand, and Amy's body thrashed again. "Making sure that her wicked heart is crippled for good."

Selia looked from the vault down to Amy's face, which appeared frozen, then back to the salt trancing talisman Alex was holding. She was triangulating a pattern she'd seen so many times.

The strands of moonlight dancing on the surface of the water.

The reflection Damien signed his moonlit paintings with.

The Blind Moon is helping Amphitrite to see again.

Selia's fists clenched. "I know who has been whispering to the talismans. It hasn't been Amy. There is no crime against the fae you convicted me of." She sucked in a breath, anger ripping up her spine. "There is no blue memory blindness! *You* were the one who made it up!"

Alex laughed high and cold. "It looks as though the Blind Moon has finally opened her eyes." Her eyes dipped toward the shadows. "However, I am not responsible for your memory loss. I have done nothing to make you forget who you are. Balfour?"

Balfour emerged from the shadows, his steps rattling the walls. The hulk of whatever he was carrying his shoulder sloughed from his body, landing in a heap before him.

Selia's stomach hollowed. "Damien!" she cried, launching herself toward Damien's lifeless body.

Balfour took one step forward, and Selia slammed into him.

"Leave him alone!" She screamed, slamming her fists upon his burly chest. Fight as she might, Alex's giant henchman didn't budge.

Balfour grabbed her around the waist, and picked her up, arms still flailing through his beard and fingers scratching across his face.

Even the moths didn't venture near him. They dove through the air, spiraling around him.

"Damien has nothing to do with this!" Selia screamed, watching Damien's head roll to the side.

"Ah, but he does. I discovered that the memory of his family was absorbed by the talisman. The individual responsible for erasing your memories, is in fact this artist."

"How?"

"Blue memories live in the heart, not the mind, do they not?" Alex asked, and the bottle on Selia's chest pulsed again.

Selia grabbed the bottle, fearing it would burst open.

Alex held the talisman over Damien's face, casting his features in a pulsing blue light. "The loss his heart has endured has in turn, reflected onto you, Blind Moon. His loss has impacted your *own* memory. He has spent ten years painting this moonlit symbol with moon magic behind it. Moon magic that is reflected onto any sea nymph who touches it."

Selia swallowed. Deidra had mentioned the Order had been collecting these diseased talismans that could absorb painful memories. Amy had *also* come into contact with the talisman. After she did, she too began to experience memory loss.

Had Damien's grief really impacted both of their memories?

Alex held the talisman above her head. "Salt trancing is a double-edged sword. One edge reveals the heart of the individual. The other edge reflects what heart has suffered—in Damien's case, death of those he loves. If you choose to open the vault, Damien's heart will drown in the memory you have experienced."

Selia looked from Damien's white face back to the vault. The bottle on her chest was humming so violently, the glass was in danger of shattering. "The fourth principle has something to do with the *heart*?"

Blue light flashed across Alex's face, illuminating the scar on her lip. "Reveal the fourth principle, and watch Damien Malloch's heart give up."

36
EMERGENCE

The bottle resting on Selia's chest began to warm. The crystal inside was glowing with the same light filling the cavern. Dozens of tiny blue flecks drifted in the air, raining down like snow.

She reached out and grabbed one of the flecks, bringing the shimmering blue substance to her face. It was a tiny scale from a minca moth's wing. Thousands of them were raining down from the dark ceiling of the cavern. Each scale was as sharp as glass and like an ice crystal, as frigid as the vault.

"You are the moonlight, Selia. Your light has yet to shine on what the heart of salt trancing reflects."

Maybe her choice had been made for her. The males were coaxing their queen to awaken.

"You're *wrong*, Alexandra..." A gravelly voice said behind her.

Selia turned, finding that Amy was now climbing to her hands and knees.

A look of hunger stretched across her face. It was the look of a caged, wild animal who had been released.

The pointed edges of her freckles were sharper. Even her hair was curling out. Her pupils had become vertical slits, giving more fire to her emerald eyes.

"There is one thing you've forgotten to tell Selia about the art," Amy growled as she stood. "The heart of a sea nymph has more power over the sea than the Order can know." Amy didn't break her gaze with Alex. She grabbed what was left of her cloak that had been torn to shreds from her violent seizure and tore the remaining fabric away from her shoulders.

She stood with her hands held in front of her heart and her fingers curled against one another. Her skin cloaked in the shimmering blue light as the wing scales of the minca moths coated, trembling around her. "Only the moon can dictate the power of the tides."

Alex laughed. "I pity you for feeding Selia such lies."

Amy held her hands out wide, tossing her head back. "I am the sea!" she cried, clapping her hands together.

The sound ricocheted off the water, rattling the cavern walls.

Selia batted her eyes as one of the sharp wing scales landed on her eyelash. It fell to her lip, which her tongue grazed against.

Bitterness bit her tongue.

The tiny blue wing scales dancing in the air were coated in salt.

Selia kicked out against Balfour's leg, jabbing her toe into his bulk of a shin. "Let Damien go!"

But Alex wasn't going to give in. She tipped Damien's body over with her foot, making him slump toward the edge of the pathway. "One wrong move, and lover boy here finds his end in a place deeper than the Mariana Trench!"

One of the moths dipped past Alex's face, grazing her cheek.

A red line as thin as the scar on her upper lip appeared.

Amy's gaze found Selia. "You can do this! I know you can! Think back to all your memories since meeting Damien." She held out her hands, and Selia knew she'd begun to enchant the tiny particles of salt in the air.

Fwwisshhhhh...

Balfour reached for one of the wing scales that landed on his shoulder. He released his grip on Selia's core.

Selia kicked off his body, launching herself toward the vault. She snatched it up and darted toward the water.

Even with the hurtful things Damien said to her, she didn't want him to *die* over it...

"You fool!" Alex bellowed, slapping away the moth that had distracted the giant.

One, by one, the little males dive-bombed Selia, swooping in and out of her hair. She had their queen in her arms, and they were likely to kill her over it.

She skidded to a stop, water lapping at her feet.

The tide was coming in fast.

Splash!

Damien's body fell from the rocky outcropping, disappearing into the water.

Selia jumped into the water with the vault in her arm, her feet hitting the water first.

The cold that slammed against her body forced her to release the vault. Water swirled around her as she sank down into the ebony abyss. She whipped her head around. Where was Damien?

The minca moths dove through the water, their razor-sharp wings spiraling around her.

The vault began to drift, sinking down into the blackness of the North Sea.

With each moth that dove past her face, Damien's sinking body began to illuminate.

The bottle with his blue memory salt crystal floated up in front of her. The crystal inside of it was glowing.

Damien's face was a canvas of glowing blue lights as the moths continued to dart down into the water.

Selia's body cramped with cold. Her ribs constricted, gripping around her lungs. The water was forcing her to surrender to it.

She wanted to scream. She had to choose. She could save Damien, or the vault.

She kicked into the water to force herself forward, grabbing Damien's hand.

The bottle settled once again onto her chest.

All at once, the memories around her unfolded as liquid silver threads around her.

Each thread had a pulse of its own. Each blue memory of his grief blinding her.

The fear in Damien's eyes when she'd seen something he couldn't forget.

His painting of her, *Blind Moon.*

Sitting in the car, with the crystal light of raindrops dancing on the windows.

"Water acts differently around you. Even the water droplets in the air seem to move to your pulse. Selia, you have a gift that I hope you don't give up on understanding."

Him jumping into the water to save the vault.

The kiss they'd shared after she'd seen the strands of moonlight—of grief—threaded behind his ears.

Discovering the maps he had stopped painting after his heart had given up.

The night at his art studio, when the moonlight first caught her eye.

The talisman stolen from her office.

Damien's signature, and the moonlight reflecting over water—the moment his paintings captured her heart.

Selia's heart rate began to slow as each memory pulsed through her, back to the moment he'd met with her in the City of Lights.

Outside the Louvre, when the water from the fountain caught the light in a magical way they both noticed.

His hazel eyes glinting up at her. The colors reflecting in the water droplets glistening on his eye lashes. *"Do you see them too? The lights that look like fairies?"*

Selia's pulse stopped.

Time itself seemed to lose flow.

Damien didn't only see the mysterious reflections, he *felt* what all the strands of moonlight connected to—the *heart*.

Breath.

Memory.

Salt.

Selia opened her eyes as the heartbeat of those memories pulsed through her.

"Pulse!" She screamed, bubbles billowing out of her mouth.

The bottle resting on her breast shattered, sending blast of white-blue light out into the water.

Siphoning, the water began to spiral. A trillion little heartbeats swarming through the water synced with Selia's pulse.

The force took Selia's body with it, ripping her and Damien away from the vault.

The vault began to rise into the spiral of water.

She grabbed Damien's hand and kicked her legs, forcing them to the surface.

Amy was standing there, her hands outstretched. "You did it! Selia! You did it!"

"Pulse! The fourth principle is *pulse*!" Selia yelled, coughing as the wave brought Damien's body onto land again.

Selia looked from the vault to Damien when horror washed over her.

What had she done?

The vault began to dissolve, revealing a much smaller orb that had been inside of it. The orb shook and trembled. The shiny white surface began to peel away, revealing a creature as bright as a star.

"Oh, hello beautiful!" Amy said, lowering her voice to the tone one would use with a child.

A brilliant blue creature emerged from the pulsing light, her little legs gripping onto Selia's arm. The hairs on her six little feet tickled her skin as she perched herself atop her wrist.

Two fuzzy antennae uncoiled from the queen's glowing face. Her body shook, sending dust of some kind into the air. A complete sense of calm washed over Selia as the fae queen gazed up into her eyes.

She was so different from the males. Her body was three times as large, and she had more colors shimmering about her body. Her wings, however, were not developed at all. They crossed atop her back, the membranous veins holding them together giving off their own blue light.

"She is absolutely lovely." Amy whispered.

Selia marveled at the little queen, whose eyes seemed like a trillion little glass diamonds that reflected all colors.

"No!" Alex bellowed.

The minca moths came spiraling up from the water, their swarm guiding the wave behind them. The swarm exploded out of the cavern wall, bringing with them a trillion tons of salt water.

Amy cupped the fae queen in her hands, then backed into the wall of water.

"Amy!" Selia cried, but the tidal wave swallowed her.

Balfour was standing in the way. His body became a shield against the water. Damien's limp body lay in his arms.

"Wait!"

Balfour's eyes met hers, directing her away from the water. He lowered Damien down into the boat as the water thrashed against the wall, releasing even more of the male moths.

"Hurry, get in!" Selia said to the giant man breaking the waves as they flooded around her.

Balfour remained in place, shielding them. He directed the boat forward, using his weight to force them up onto the current before it swallowed them.

A thousand shimmering blue lights exploded around Selia, their pulse dying as the water came flooding in. Selia closed her eyes, sucked in a breath, and the boat took her and Damien away as the cavern flooded.

PART 6
REMEMBERING

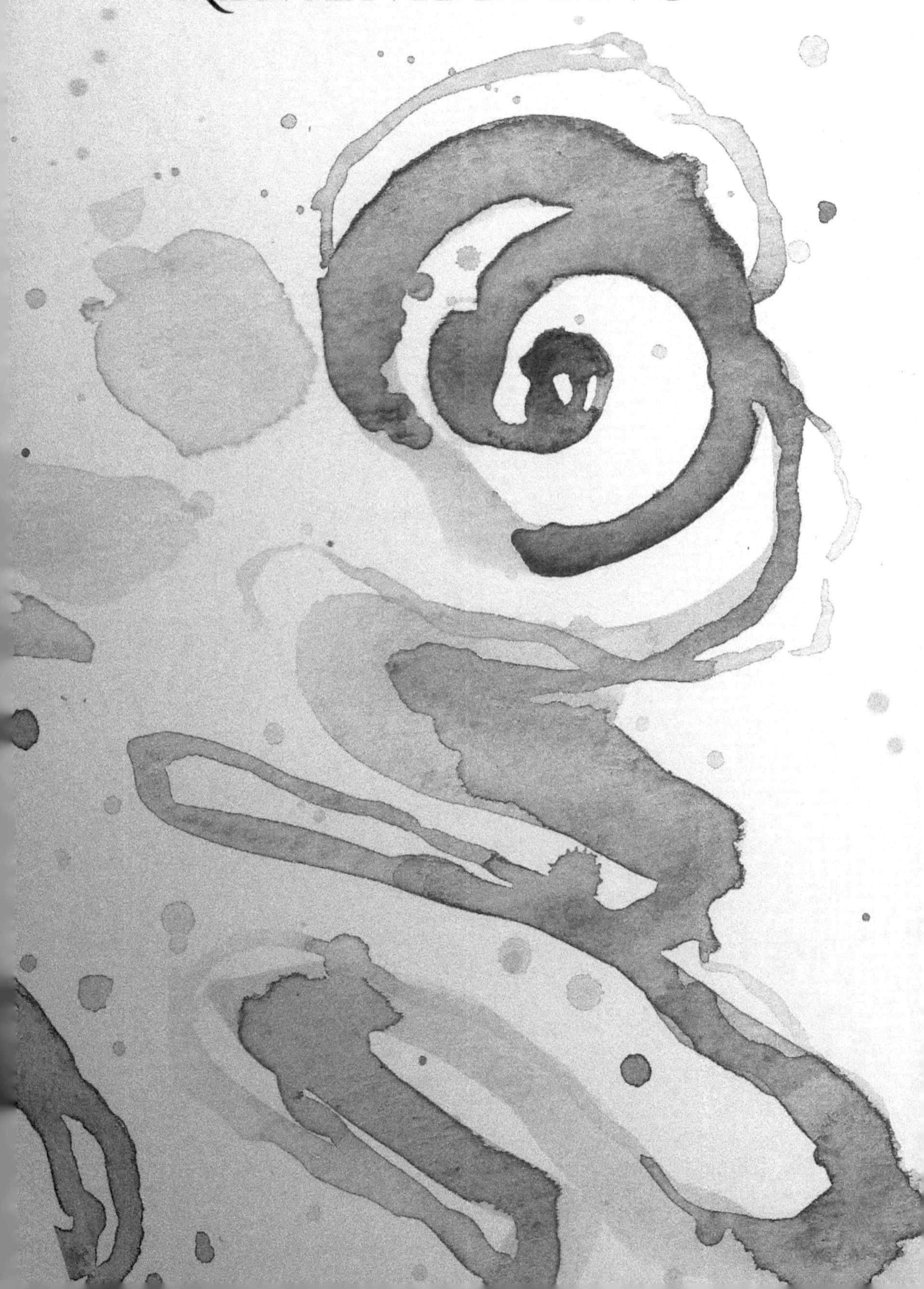

37
HEALING

Yellow rays of sunlight branched across the sky. Selia staggered to her feet, finding that her clothes were surprisingly dry.

Alex and Amy were nowhere to be seen. Henrietta was already busy scuttling from one patch of seashells to the next, sure to try them on for size. A lump of something much too large to be driftwood caught Selia's eye.

Damien's body lay in a heap not far from her.

Selia rushed over to him, her bare feet scraping against the rocks lining the beach.

She dropped to his side, tugging his shoulder over. Damien's eyes were closed, his hair in a sodden mess across his face, which had no color at all.

"Oh, Damien..." She breathed. She shook his limp body, forcing his face up toward the sky. "Please stay with me...please don't—" Her heart stopped.

What if Alex was right? What if the emerging fae queen had ended his life?

She grabbed for the bottle at her chest, remembering the light shattering into the water.

She no longer felt Damien's warmth upon her breast.

Panic ripped through her. The memory of losing his family had crystallized around his heart. Was that crystal strong enough to survive even after its light had gone out?

Selia placed her hands on his chest where his shirt had been torn. His chest wasn't moving, even though his mouth was gaping open, no breath escaped his lips.

Selia closed her eyes, forcing away the thought that he, too, was slipping away from her. She could not have come to love a man so truly, only to have his love turn into a memory.

Breath.

Memory.

Salt.

The blue memory of the talisman's journey into her hands *pulsed* through her. A blue light began pulsing in her periphery.

Two silhouettes blurred along the beach, walking toward her. One was smaller than the other.

Henrietta jostled over to the smaller of the two.

A young girl bent down, smiling at the crab as she huddled over to her bare feet. She set a small stone down on the sand.

As the exchange between Damien's daughter and the crab took place, Selia's pulse slowed, nearly stopping—her own breath syncing—crystalizing with the moment.

Maria smiled at her, giving an unspoken thank you through her dark brown eyes.

Henrietta came jostling back over, carrying on her back the newly swapped shell—a seashell fairy to a young girl—a gift for her father.

Selia took the shell and set it on Damien's chest.

She closed her eyes, focusing on the waves lapping at her feet. With an exhale of her own breath, her *pulse* returning to her now, she released that memory of Maria and Sophie back to the sea.

"*Gassspppp!*"

Damien began to cough, sending sea water out of his mouth.

"Damien!" She stammered, wiping his wet hair out of his eyes.

"Why am I out here on the beach?" He jolted, hoisting himself up on his elbow. He ran his hand through his hair, which was coated in sand and seashell fragments.

Selia glanced behind him.

Both Maria and Sophie's reflections had vanished.

Damien grabbed the seashell off his chest, bringing it to his face. "I had a dream that Sophie and I were gathering these stones on the beach."

"These stones are salt chrysalises made by the fae creature."

Damien's brows drew up. "They're *what*?"

"I found Amy in a cavern full of the fae creatures she called minca moths. She told me that when the male moth forms its wings, it leaves behind a salt chrysalis, which results in these stones." She grabbed one of them, holding it up to the light. "Over time, the stones metamorphose, transforming into salt trancing talismans. Sophie found the talisman that reminded her of your paintings. She believed it would help to get your artwork on display at the museum."

His eyes drifted past hers, returning with answers reflecting in their hazel depths. "Sophie found the talisman on the beach that morning." His eyes searched hers. "I remember now. I remember the blue lights dancing on the surface of the water, the ones Sophie believed to be fairies. Were these moths really the source of those lights?"

Silence fell between them.

Damien shifted in the sand. "Did you find the vault?"

"I did. And I was able to open it."

"Out with it now! What was this fae treasure locked inside?

"A minca moth queen was inside."

Damien's mouth dropped open. "A minca moth *queen*? That's what Amy was after? Why?"

"She locked the queen in the vault so the Order couldn't find it. I still don't know why she locked her away, other than she planned to use the creature to restore the art."

"For the vault to have opened, you would have had to guess what the fourth principle was, right?"

Selia grabbed his hand. "It was something I felt from the very beginning. When I reflected on all of the memories I've had since meeting you, there was one thing in common. Your heartbeat was there all along, beating alongside mine."

Damien's brows drew up. "Was it something to do with the heart?"

"The fourth principle was the very *heartbeat* of those memories—blue memories have their own *pulse.*"

Damien squeezed her hand. "I guess these blue memories have more power behind them than we thought." His brows furrowed. "Selia, I'm sorry. You started talking about my family, and I..." he choked up.

"You don't have to apologize."

"Yes, I do. I said some very hurtful things to you that I regret."

"I didn't understand the correlation between the talisman and your art until..." she swallowed. "Damien, your *grief* from losing your family is what the talisman preserved. When I came into contact with the talisman, your grief was reflected upon me, resulting in my memory loss. But grief wasn't the only thing the talisman preserved. The heart of salt trancing is what moonlight reflects, which in your case, was love." She glanced over her shoulder, finding the reflection of Sophie waving back at her. "I was only lucky enough to help you remember it."

Damien's skin began to ripple with gooseflesh.

Selia too, was beginning to lose feeling in her fingers.

She grabbed his arm, tugging him up. "We need to get warm or we'll both die of hypothermia."

The two made their way back to Auntie's cottage, which to Selia's gratefulness, was empty. Only Mr. Kisses was there to greet them at the door when they approached.

With a fresh pair of clothes and her hair starting to dry from the waters of the North Sea, Selia stopped by the window, where she had propped up her portrait.

Blind Moon—the sea nymph she'd never known herself to be, until a watercolor artist painted her portrait.

Damien tugged a sweater down over his head and walked over to where she stood. "Well, that's the last time I ever steal a symbol out of some folktale, that's for sure. Who knows what else that symbol is capable of." He approached her from behind. "Where do you think Alex went?"

"I have no idea. The cavern flooded and that was the last I saw of her and Amy."

Damien pressed his belly to her back, wrapping his arms around her core. "I hope the Order never comes around here again."

"I didn't tell you about my last conversation with Deidra. She did some research on the salt trancing talismans. Apparently the Order was trying to track down ones they believed were diseased."

"Diseased talismans?"

Selia nodded. "I don't know if I believe her research or not, but she mentioned something about a plague that occurred in ancient Egypt."

"Egypt? Wow. That's a long time ago." Damien gave her a squeeze. "Pulse, huh? What do you plan to do with it?"

Selia shrugged. "I guess I'll have to see what Amy has planned for the art." She ran her fingers over the paper edge of her portrait. "Someone else saw the minca moths other than Amy and I. Someone else was already well aware of their existence."

"Who?"

"Your daughter had drawn a fairy on the cardboard box that had the talisman inside. That drawing is still very prominent in my mind."

Damien's arms buckled around her. Something that could have been a sob escaped his chest.

Selia shook her head. "I'm sorry, I shouldn't have—"

"—Stop apologizing." Damien withdrew his arms from her center, walking in front of her instead. He grabbed her hands into his own, their warmth finally returning. "I'm the one who should be apologizing. I *never* should have tried to shut you out of my past. By doing that, I not only hurt myself, but I ended up hurting you." He gripped her hands tight. "You have a *gift* with this art that I want you to pursue. A gift that I was too scared to recognize."

"But..."

"I *want* you in my life. You were right about what I lost. You will never be able to replace them. But that's not your job, it's never been your job to step into that space."

Selia searched his face. "What can I do then? If I can't replace that love, what can I—"

"—Understand that you don't have to replace anything. I'm the one who needs to live up to what I promised you, to make new memories *together*. You have to promise me that they will be good enough to remember."

Selia smiled, emotion welling in her stomach. "I'll try, but no promises on that. You already know how forgetful I've been."

Damien pulled her into a hug, his body enveloping her. "I promise I will never shut you out like that again."

Selia sank into his embrace, allowing his warmth to wash over her. She pulled away looking him in the eye.

"The purpose for practicing the art—did you ever discover it?" Damien asked.

"I'm still not a hundred percent on that, however. When Amy and I talked, she did seem to remember that fertility was involved."

"Fertility, huh?"

"There's so much for me to uncover about my past, including my family. Are you willing to help me?"

"Of course, we will do anything we can to dig up your past. I'm committed to whatever it takes..."

Something darted past the window, lighting up the sky. Selia turned to find colors branching over the garden, the arch of a massive rainbow.

Damien squinted at the window, where Mr. Kisses was darting from one patch of Auntie's garden to another, digging holes and burying the garden gnomes.

"Funny bloke. What's he doing to that poor gnome? The ones with the red hats are the ones you *don't* want to mess with."

"Did you just say *red*?"

Selia grabbed one of her scarfs from the dresser and thrust it in front of him. "What color is this?"

"Purple?"

Selia smiled. "How about what's branching over the garden?"

Damien squinted out the window again. He grabbed the ends of his hair and tugged, sticking it up on end. "The color of the—great Scott—is *that* what a rainbow looks like?"

"Looks like you'll have a new color pallete to try on for size."

"Wow...I'd forgotten how beautiful..." His gaze dropped to her. "My word. Do you have *freckles*?"

Selia smiled. "Maybe, depending on the light?"

He kissed her, then grabbed her around the center and lifted her up. "Look at the colors! It's like magic!"

38
PULSE

September dawned, leaving the air cool and crisp. The days were becoming shorter. Auntie's garden was preparing for harvest. Fog lingered in the meadow, and foliage began to lose its vibrancy. With flowers becoming replaced by seed pods, the seasons were changing.

In the two short months Selia had spent with Damien at his Auntie's place, she had started to see some changes in her health.

For one, she was sleeping more than ever. Secondly, she had recovered her appetite, but she could only stomach certain dishes of Auntie's hearty food. Some scents didn't agree with her, while others were all she desired. Every once in a while, she would catch a whiff of something in Auntie's kitchen that made her a bit nauseous.

Damien started planning new series of paintings. He wanted to host an art show. He would spend most evenings staying up late, discussing ideas for the big *splash of color* he wanted to create.

Selia found herself thinking of Amy all the time. How long would it be before they met again? What were Amy's plans for restoring the art of salt trance now that she had the fae queen in her possession?

Pulse had crossed Selia's mind at least ten times that morning.

She walked outside, finding Damien had set up his easel and a new batch of paints. Brushes were lathered with greens, and a few glasses of water were stained purple and orange. He'd created a few paintings to study the quickly transforming landscape. Even though some of the flowers in Auntie's garden had nothing but brown seed pods and a few colorful stems, Damien's paintings captured the flowers as she remembered them.

Selia set her hands on his shoulders and gave him a squeeze. "Painting another masterpiece, I see?"

Damien chuckled. "I guess we won't know until it's finally dry. Reds and greens don't blend like I remember them." He wiped the rolled sleeve of his shirt past his brow. "It's been an unusually damp fall, and watercolors are very temperamental when it comes to the elements."

She laughed. "How does it feel to be panting with the full rainbow again?"

He leaned back into her. "I'll tell you one thing. Blue will still be my favorite color."

Late afternoon approached, and Selia decided today was the day she would tell him about the pulse she'd been experiencing. No, she had not been salt trancing with the fourth principle. This pulse had grown by the day, and she was certain that if she didn't act soon, the tiny rhythm wouldn't remain so quiet.

The sky was perfect. And the cool temperature wasn't going to make her break out in a sweat. For the first time in a week, she could fit into a bra without her breasts hurting.

Auntie was sitting by the thinking gnome with a cup of tea on the table. She turned to face them as Selia tried in vain to sneak past the clever woman. "Careful," Auntie called. "That selkie might put you under one of her watery spells and have her way with you."

Damien gave his aunt a wave. Teasing or not, Selia did have pressing news to share with him.

Selia hurried her boyfriend along to the edge of the garden. This was the afternoon she had awaited. She knew that Damien's memories of his family would *never* be forgotten. Their memory had helped her to make sense of her own. They would become a part of their lives now—a shared life, in which their memory would always be reflected.

She stopped. Turning to face him, she sucked in a breath and exhaled. That tiny heartbeat was about to speak for itself.

"Do you plan to keep your promise on making new memories with me moving forward?" she asked, grabbing his warm hands into hers.

"Of course I do."

"Good, because I have some news that is going to affect our future together." She squeezed his hands as tears stung the corners of her eyes. "Do you remember what I told you about the purpose of the salt trancing? That Amy said it had to do with the sea's fertility?"

Damien's brow furrowed. "Selia, love. What is this about?"

All at once, the family he lost didn't seem like a memory any longer. "Damien, I'm pregnant."

EPILOGUE

Amy had walked along the beach for the past three nights, swathing her skin in moonlight. She preferred to enjoy the moon when it was highest in the sky. Night was the time when fae creatures like the minca moth were most alive.

Sand shifted with each of her careful steps, clumping beneath her. Amy had discovered that a sea nymph found treasures buried in the sand far better with her toes. Shifting through driftwood, seaweed and other beach debris was much easier to do with her bare feet. She could turn over shells, tipping their openings up to see if a fae creature might be hiding inside.

Seashells kept the best secrets after all.

A blue fleck darted in front of Amy's face. She reached out, grabbing one of the salty wing scales of a minca moth floating on the breeze. She always found the smallest of things to hold the most magic. Fae beings thrived in places humans left alone. The smaller fae beings were often overlooked, giving them a better chance of creating a home.

This reflective blue wing scale was a good sign. The flickering blue light was the dying pulse of a male who had finished mating with his queen. His purpose in life was done. His pulse would live on in a new generation of fae beings.

Amy peered down between her breasts, finding the gentle blue glow pulsing there, syncing with her own heartbeat. The fae queen was sleeping now, but only for another moon cycle or so. She would soon awaken, preparing for her maternal flight to find a place to call home for her offspring. She would only lay her eggs in the right circumstances, ones that winter welcomed.

Amy continued sifting her toes through the sand. The soggy texture made her want to dive into the waves and salt trance like her ancestors did. When the art had first come onto land, it had changed. Restoring *pulse* was her way of restoring the art to how her ancestors would have practiced it.

A wave caught her ankle, the chilly water bringing with it a little sea treasure. Of course! The little white stones hermit crabs always obsessed over.

She bent down, grabbing one of the salt chrysalises from the male minca moth. What a beautiful, fleeting thing. She tossed the chrysalis back into the sea where it would dissolve. She continued working her fingers through the sand, shifting through the debris, until potting another treasure there. A treasure that not even the sea would reclaim.

"Oh, my!" Amy squealed, her fingers splaying in delight. Buried in the sand was a blue memory salt crystal—one that must have formed when Selia first salt tranced with Damien Malloch!

She ran her finger past the crystal's edge, moonlight reflecting on its shimmering blue body. Damien's blue memories were as smooth and fluid as his watercolor paintings. She was one step closer to restoring the art to how her ancestors would have practiced it. Remembering *pulse* was exactly the encouragement her heart needed to continue in her work.

While the art was not perfect, its major strength was also its flaw. Blue memories were a necessary burden that sea nymphs had to endure when practicing the art.

She held the crystal up to the moon, marveling as the blue edges reflected sharp, dagger-like silver. The glistening edge was *perfect*. Now, with the crystal and the fae queen in her hands, she had the tools necessary for her task ahead. But first, she would have to put the blue memory salt crystal of Damien Malloch to the test.

Amy tucked the crystal into her bosom next to the sleeping fae queen, turning her attention to the horizon of the North Sea. Before the Rusty Selkie had been there, it was a pirate tavern. And prior to that? Ancient stone circles built by Damien's Scottish ancestors, the Sgàthan clan.

Those stone circles were buried beneath layers of earth now, but Amy could still see the land as it was as though time had never passed. At the center of those stone circles were hearths that warmed her soul. The scent of burning wood filled her senses as a huntsman's hazel eyes glinted up at her from across the flames.

The scent of wood and flame burned with the cold air as Amy inhaled that memory. She remembered the herds of fae beasts who roamed the land, disappearing like spirits into Winter Forest.

Memories of that time clung to this land like salt would crust atop stone. The drums of those ancient people still sang to her, creating a pulse of their own.

Alex was wrong, so terribly wrong in how she'd mocked her teaching of the art. The Order spread many rumors about her *poisonous* ways. Poison, however, did not circulate in the bloodstream like venom did. There was a more sinister ingredient in the bottle of selkie salt skin that Amy had given Selia for practicing the art. It was something toxic to which Selia's heart was immune—something she first learned of in ancient Egypt.

Amy held her arms out at her sides, surrendering to the moonlight. Memories of her friend's dark rebellious hair blowing in the wind flooded her mind. The two sea nymphs had worked together to restore the art, before something dark and deadly had come their way. Something lurked in the deeper parts of the ocean like monster in her own memory.

Why Amy's heart had suppressed that memory for so long was due to the pain associated with it. The same pain Damien had from losing his loved ones was the treasure she needed. Dormant that memory had been, sleeping in her heart until now.

Amy inhaled a deep breath, preparing her heart for the journey that lay ahead. A long, painful memory it would be, remembering her friend who first introduced her to the powerful tides of her ancestors.

CAST OF CHARACTERS

SELIA
BLIND MOON

DAMIEN

AMPHITRITE

Henrietta

ACKNOWLEDGMENTS

Writing is not only a self journey. The written word is a work of art that pieces together thousands of little interactions, combining layers of self-doubt and dreaming. My hope is that the result is something my readers will enjoy and connect with.

I could not have created this book without the help of many others. I wanted to acknowledge a few prominent influences in my life that continue to encourage me on this writing journey.

My mom and brother who have always supported my random creative endeavors, whether it be panting, drawing, or writing.

My father who is no longer with us, but still encourages me to write in spirit.

My husband Bill, for supporting me on this journey and for making me laugh with your feedback on my first drafts.

My critique group, who has put up with my stories for the past seven years. Carly, Debbie, and Ed, you've helped me to craft my character's voices as well as find my own author voice.

My readers, because you are what brings the written word to life.

My taiko group, Sun Mountain Taiko, for drumming with me and driving the rhythm behind my stories.

My local library, where I work in the family and children's department. To my fellow library staff who provide energy and enthusiasm for reading, art, and the community. Your energy is contagious!

The park where I work, providing me with the opportunity to connect others with nature. I'm so blessed to have the Colorado outdoors in my backyard.

ALSO BY

Tidal Ancestry, book two of the Ocean Apothecary Series, will release in 2024.

Visit Amanda's website at www.amandacaseybooks.com to follow along with her writing adventures.